LLOYD RUSSELL

Escape From Little Alcatraz

Lloyd Russell

Escape From Little Alcatraz

A NOVEL

Dennis Leppanen

A Daring Prison Break

May, 1950—It started with a daring Tarzan-like escape from a London, Ohio Prison. Two desperate and dangerous convicts stole cars, robbed establishments, and headed north toward Michigan's Upper Peninsula.

THE RUSSELL BROTHERS—Lloyd and Paul, led Michigan's law enforcement on a wild ten-day chase through the Upper Peninsula's east end before being captured in a mid-peninsula swamp as a result of the younger brother, Paul, being critically wounded during a shoot out with state police. Lloyd was sentenced to Marquette's maximum security prison, and Paul was sent to Southern Michigan Prison in Jackson.

May, 1953—A Lloyd Russell led group of seven desperate inmates stage a daring escape from the walls of Marquette's maximum security facility. Thus began the largest sustained manhunt in the annals of Michigan crime.

ESCAPE FROM LITTLE ALCATRAZ—is the story of a man, keen on surviving the giant odds of survival in the swamps and deep woods of Michigan's rugged Upper Peninsula. A story of a man—fighting against all odds to save an epithet—"They ain't gonna take me alive!"

ALSO BY
Dennis Leppanen

WHOO??

COMING SOON

RUSH to GOLD

For Ansa Leppanen

What more could a kid say?

Part One

Escape From Little Alcatraz

Prologue

Sunday, May 7, 1950 London, Ohio

"OKAY, LET'S HAVE SOME LIGHTS—HIT THE SWITCH, EDDIE."

Three men rose instantly, clocking their way into an alcove as Eddie hit the switch.

"*Don't move—not a sound outta you.*"

"Okay men, you know the drill, single file now, split at the middle and exit both sides."

The Sunday night movie was rolling through its credits, the names of the film's contributors projecting on the empty screen when the three men slipped undetected into the vacant stairway.

He watched the inmates file out, some so close he could have reached out and touched them. A scratching movement from behind, irritating and insistent, seemingly magnifying itself, frustrated his quest for complete silence. He poked his brother with an elbow, listening to the three hearts beat—none in cadence with the other. *So damn loud, they're gonna hear us.*

The doorway filled with the familiar back of a trustee. *Phillips, that son of a bitch.* His balding head, large even for his broad, sloping shoulders, gave his appearance from the rear that of a primate clad in inmate gray. His long arms hung apelike at his sides as he watched the other prisoners exit the auditorium. "No lip bumping now, Grissom, Snow— move along."

A snarl formed on the lips of the man hidden in the stairway, taking all of his will-power to refrain from grabbing the ape from behind and dragging him into the stairway, wanting to choke the very life out of the scum-bag trustee.

"Phillips. Is that it? Is everybody out?"

"Yup, this side's clear."

"Douse the lights."

The plug-ugly con strode heavily to the front switch and exited without a look around.

"Ready...?"

"Hold still, Paul. Give 'em time to get outta earshot."

The wait—took forever.

"Okay, quiet now, take the lead, Lucious, I got the light." He let the beam of the flashlight shine up the stairway, leading the trio upward.

They stopped at the locked door.

"Go ahead, work the lock, Lucious. This is the first landing. Do your magic, c'mon, let's get started."

With quiet efficiency, and the steady hands of a surgeon, the door was opened in less than two minutes, sending the trio upward to the main building's attic. It took them another minute or two to pry the lock off the door that took them outside to the roof. The field ahead looked flat and even. "I'll lead the way. We gotta go all the way to the front." Russell whispered. "Stay close behind, and keep low."

"Now, what?"

They had reached the building's front, huddled behind a parapet wall, safe from the prying eyes of the searchlights. "Here, gimme a hand. We gotta snap this cable. It's long enough to reach the ground."

"What is it? What's it hooked to?" Lucious Langworthy asked, a nervous shiver passing through him. He was a tall, thin man, with high-strung mannerisms that belied his expertise in picking locks. The nervousness is what made him work fast.

"Looks like an elevator cable," Russell turned to his brother, "Paul, gimme that bar."

"What bar? Where is it?"

"That piece a heavy re-rod. Careful you don't trip on it."

"Fuck you."

"Watch yer tongue. Save the energy for the work we got to do."

They labored with a diligent purpose, working the rod in two minute intervals, then passing it to the next in line. The heavy cable was soon freed. They swung it over the side, careful not to make noise—it almost reached the ground.

"We can't shimmy down this bastard. We don't have gloves, shit, we'll tear the skin off our hands and fall half way down."

"Shut up and lissen. Let's haul it back up, I think we can use to swing down to the ground. Gimme a hand."

"Damn, Lloyd," Paul stared down, "look at that drop, a guy could get himself kilt."

"Listen, I'm going down first, if it don't work out, you boys jest go back down an' act like nuttin' happened." The con slipped to the roof's edge and looked down, he ducked back below the parapet—breathing hard. He stood back up, and reached for the cable. "Damn, it is a helluva drop. Remember, you don't know nuttin."

He wasted no time in second guessing his decision, grabbing the cable and throwing himself over the edge. He slid down the spiral cord as he swung like a pendulum in a downward spiral forcing him to grip even tighter to slow his rapid descent. The cable seared his hands, as hot coals of braided wire burned into them. The ground rushed up, meeting him with a numbing jolt. He slapped the earth with a jarring thud and his jaw snapped shut as he stifled the impulse to cry out and cuss.

Damn, I bit my tongue. He spit fresh blood and stood there willing his brother and Lucious to tackle the free-fall with more care. Hopefully, they had seen his reckless trip down.

Lucious Langworthy followed, Russell grabbed him before he hit the ground to soften the landing. He winced at the pain that shot through his burned palms. Paul handled the plunge with the deft and coordination of a trapeze artist hitting ground on the run. A sappy grin stretched his handsome features and insured Lloyd he was fine.

"Let's move," Lloyd took the lead, steering them in a direction opposite the scope of the towers, and away from their long, probing searchlights. They cleared the prison's main building and headed off into the night. Scrambling along in the darkness, they were able to pick their way by the thin beam from the moon. An hour later they found a paved road where the trio split up.

"I havta go down to Cincy, Lloyd. My gal will hide me for a few days."

"Don't be stupid, the cops will be watching her. The first thing they do."

"I'll sneak in town, careful like, Cincinnati is my home. I know all the back streets and safe alleys." He swung his head, this way and that—giving the impression he was looking in all four directions at once. He decided on a southerly direction. "Take care, boys. Look me up if you ever get to Cincy."

An irked sneer tugged at his lips. "Piss on you, Lucious. When they pick you up, you never left the joint with us."

"You know me, Lloyd. I'm not a blabber mouth. I ain't never snitched on nobody. I won't peach on my friends." He took off with long strides down the deserted highway.

The Russells watched until he was out of sight then headed north on State Road 42. "I dunno, Lloyd. I sure as hell wouldn't head home. The cops always watch your 'known' contacts after you make a break."

"Yer right, he doesn't have a prayer. He's gonna be caught in less than a week. He's a stupid ass." The prophecy would indeed, prove correct.

"It's a nice night for a stroll, Lloyd. We kin see without stumbling around like blind men."

They walked for two hours, ducking into a nearby ditch whenever a rare vehicle drove by. They entered a small village and Paul spotted a Chevrolet sitting in the first driveway they came upon.

"Dammit, if the keys ain't right there, dangling like a cheap set of earrings on a floozy," Paul declared in a voice above a desired whisper. "Damn, this just might be our lucky day."

"Hush now, let's keep it low."

Paul eased the driver-side door open, jumping behind the wheel he cranked the starter without hesitation. The Chevy's engine came to life before Lloyd could properly caution him.

"Take it easy, Paul," he growled at his brother as he slipped into the passenger seat. "For crissakes, take it easy."

"The tank is darn near full, man o' man, our luck is runnin' hot, let's find a poker game." Paul chuckled at his own feeble wit as he backed into the street. They drove two blocks to a four way stop at the intersection of

SR 40. Paul cast a questioning glance at Lloyd and drove straight through when his brother pointed ahead.

"Let's take this north to 23, then head up to Toledo. We know the area and we should be able to pick up some quick cash there."

The stolen Chevy headed northward through the Ohio night. The moon was busy parting the clouds and taking peeks through them as the brothers drove along in silence. Paul looked over at his solemn brother and wished his older sibling could enjoy the adventure a bit more.

"We're gonna need cash—before morning."

"I know, let's keep our eyes open..."

Ottawa Lake, Michigan—May 8, 4:00 a.m.

THE BROTHERS SLIPPED INTO THE NEWLY PIRATED FORD they had switched to just outside of Toledo. Once again, the keys h been left in the vehicle for the two runaways, this time on the front seat.

"I say we should a busted that safe, Lloyd. There had to be in cash in there."

"That store was a United States Post Office. Next thing you know, we got the Feds on our tail. I don't aim to be on no Wanted Poster on the wall in every post office in the country."

"Where we headed? This baby's got more pep than the Chevy." He shifted smoothly letting the clutch out and leaving a black spot of tire residue on the pavement.

"Jesus. Be careful. Slow down, we just passed a co-op, it must be for the local farmers. They gotta have a safe with a bunch a cash in it."

"Why do you say that?"

"Pull in right here, park behind the office. See that grain elevator? The farmers drop off their harvest here, and so they gotta get paid here."

The window was forced open in less than a minute and the two entered and immediately began rifling through the office. In less than fifteen minutes they were back on Michigan's State Road 23 heading north.

"You got into that safe in a heartbeat."

"A real familiar one, I've worked on them before, Paul. Besides, that's my trade. Now, keep it at the limit."

"You got it all counted?"

"Over $3600 in cash, Paul. We done real good."

"I know where we kin get us some guns, Lloyd—Caudell, he was from somewhere up north, says there's a hardware store..."

Mansfield News Journal
May 8, 1950
3 Stage Tarzan Escape

London, Ohio — 3 convicts used an electric cable to swing, Tarzan like, 70 feet from the roof of the London prison farm's main building last night and apparently made a clean getaway.

The break made at a point where there is no guard tower, was not discovered until a routine dormitory check more than an hour later.

Assistant Superintendent Victor J. Monte identified the fugitives as:

Lucious Langworthy, 32, sentenced in Hamilton County for a one to seven year term for receiving stolen property.

Lloyd Russell, 28, and his brother Paul, 25, both serving 3-37 years terms for burglary.

They were sentenced from Lucas County.

It was the second successful break from the prison in twelve years.

Monte said the trio hid in a stairway after a Sunday night movie in the prison auditorium in the main building. Their dorm is also there.

Langworthy and the Russell brothers then picked the lock on the door leading to the building's attic, tore off two locks on a door that led from the attic to the roof and made their way to the front of the building.

There, they broke an elevator cable and swung 70 feet to the ground. Monte said he had a report on an automobile that was stolen at nearby Lafayette. A 1940 maroon Chevrolet sedan, license number Z1927, but lacking assurances it was stolen by the fugitives, a routine search of the area would continue.

1

Michigan's Upper Peninsula

May 20, 1950

"GET UP NOW, OR I'LL SHOOT."

The chase had ended. Like a hound stretching in the noon day sun, Lloyd Russell rose reluctantly to his feet. He centered his gaze on the trooper who spoke and with a side-long sweep with his eyes, assured him that there were at least two guns trained on him.

Troopers Shewshuck and Collins aimed their weapons at the two fugitives. Wary and alert, they kept a prudent eye on the escapees, as attentive as if they had captured a wild animal capable of springing at them at any moment. One of the fugitives lay prone—nestled in the cool moss, not moving...

"Paul's hit bad, lost a lotta blood. Can you put your ass in gear, and get him outta here?"

"You sure he's still alive? He ain't moving."

"He's tougher than a field-corn cob, he ain't gonna die, if you get him to a doctor." Lloyd reached in his pocket for a cigarette...

"Easy boy," Shewshuck spoke as softly as his adversary had, "I wouldn't twitch if I were you. You need to move, I want to know when you do beforehand."

"I just need a smoke, that's all I'm up to."

Trooper Collins dismissed the radio just as two volunteers from the Sheriff's posse reached the clearing.

Shewshuck spoke out, "The chopper's here for the wounded prisoner. They're bringing in a stretcher to cart him out."

He's been leaking since yesterday afternoon. I tried to patch him up, best I could..."

"We figured at least one a you was hit, let's take it real slow, have your smoke, we'll see to your brother."

The chase was over, thus ended the most sensational manhunt in the annals of local crime. A multi-force manhunt that had begun in London, Ohio, extending through Michigan's Lower Peninsula, and on into parts of Canada—and for ten suspense-filled days, in a race across Michigan's Upper Peninsula.

"Where you taking me?"

"To our finest accommodations at the Marquette County Jail," Collins answered, watching as his partner accelerated up the steep incline, passing the Munising city limit sign on the west side of town.

Munising Bay glistened in the late afternoon sun, a perfect backdrop to accent the area's natural beauty. Spring was in full bloom. No one in the vehicle seemed aware of Mother Nature's resiliency in springing forward once again after another brutal U.P. winter.

They traversed the Forest Inn Supper Club and followed M-28 west towards their destination. A second cruiser followed, mimicking their every move.

The state road kept an eye on Lake Superior as they wove their way along its southern shores. The sky was a perfect blue, promising good weather for days to come. The preceding winter had been a particularly difficult one, with record snowfall and sub-zero temperatures. After an unseasonably cool start, May had treated them more than fair, the weather promising that even better days ahead.

Collins signed off the radio.

"Where's Paul? Heard anything since they choppered him off?"

"He's headed to the prison infirmary. The surgeon from St. Lukes Hospital will be there waiting. He has to dig bullet fragments out of his ass." Collins added something to his partner, Russell strained his ears but was unable to pick any of it up.

Static from the muted radio drowned out the conversation between the two state officers. They could have been talking about anything, The Job, the weather, their old ladies...

He said to himself. *I gotta know.* "I gotta know. He come to?"

"In and out, he lost a lotta blood, not to worry, your brother will make it to trial. They stopped the bleeding before he got on the helicopter."

Silence followed Collin's last remarks, as the Ohio fugitive lapsed into reverie. His navy blue shirt, darkened and stained from a week's stay in the thick swamps was open to just above the navel. A thick mat of fur, damp with his sweat, adorned his chest. It matched the hair on his head, only it was thicker. The hair on his head receded high into his forehead.

Russell needed a shave and a bath, along with a change of clothes. The twenty eight year old escapee's size belied his great strength. He stood less than five and a half feet tall and weighed less than one hundred fifty pounds. A close appraisal revealed two scars above his left eye from past scrapes with his fellow toughies. The one on his temple, smaller than the scar just above his eyebrow, grew more prominent when he raised his eyebrow.

Lloyd closed his eyes for the remainder of the trip to his incarceration.

May 22, 1950

"HEY RUSSELL, YOU HAVE A VISITOR." The guard stood in front of the cell, thinking there was finally a bit of humor in his daily routine.

"I don't know anybody up here, tell him I'm busy."

He's a newspaper writer, wants to write about you. Make you famous."

"Famous—that's the last thing I need. Naw, I got nuttin' to say."

"Okay, I'll tell him."

He shrugged his massive shoulders, changed his expression to a near grin, "Does he smoke? Cause what the hell, I got nuttin' better to do."

"I'll be back in five..."

The reporter appeared behind the deputy and smiled at the short, balding man, who was already the subject of numerous articles. "How about it? A lotta folks up here are interested in your story."

"I could use a cigarette, I run out yesterday, they're real scarce around here."

"I've got a pack of Lucky Strikes."

"Shit—my brand." The prisoner drew the smoke deep into his lungs and exhaled a stream of tobacco residue that put out the proffered light. Wearily, he settled back, allowing the nicotine to settle him, while he painted a confident sneer on his face.

The writer sat back—waiting the prisoner's every word.

"We waited till the projectionist started rolling the credits for the Sunday night movie, I signaled the boys to hit the staircase, nice and slow before the lights..."

Russell stood, paced around the tiny cell, signaling for another cigarette from the reporter.

"How did you get the money that they found on you?"

A stream of smoke billowed out of each flared nostril as he replied, "I ain't gonna tell you who we borrowed it from."

"You borrowed it, huh?"

He ignored the remark, "We borrowed us another ride on the outskirts of Toledo, I told Paul the law would be looking for us on I-94, expectin' us to go west."

"Why did you want to head west?"

"We was wanting to go to Fargo, North Dakota."

"Why, Fargo?"

"We was told that the pickings was easy there."

"What kind of picking? Robbing banks, liquor stores, what were you gonna pick?"

"Just some easy work—is all. We was gonna go straight as soon as we got a good stake."

"Then why did you head to St. Ignace?"

Again, the noncommittal shake of his shoulders. "The young one heard we could pick up some firearms there, up in the Soo."

"Any place special?"

"I'm sure it's a matter of record by now. Paul was told..." The story slowly unraveled as Lloyd Russell settled in to tell it.

2

THE AMERICAN SOO

THEY REACHED MACKINAW CITY WITHOUT INCIDENT, then took a ferry across
the Straits of Mackinac on Tuesday morning. They avoided the stolen car
on the trip across, then made sure they saw no lawmen waiting on the U.P.
side before driving the Ford off the ferry and aiming it toward the Soo.

Weaving their way along the Lake Huron coastline they arrived in Ce-
darville where they stopped for lunch. They purchased gas and cigarettes
at a filling station on the edge of town, then resumed their travel north,
following 129.

Lloyd had grabbed a newspaper off the counter paying a dime for it
while Paul had chatted it up with the attendant outside. He went through
the story headlines with rapid impatience. "Good. Nothing about us in this
rag. How much further to the Soo, Paul?"

"Less than an hour, Ace. That'd be my guess."

"Keep a sharp eye out, we don't need no screw ups. A cop comes up
behind and checks out our tags, it'll be back in the slammer."

"Check this out. I love these signs, Lloyd."

The Big Blue Tube's

"Slow down, Paul, what I just tell you?"

Just Like Louise

"What the fuck, we ain't seen another car in damn near an hour."

You Get A Thrill

"Lloyd smacked his brother, "Watch your tongue, Ma never liked cussin."

From Every Squeeze

"Aw, Ma's dead. She cussed plenty when her and Pa was fighting, which was damn often."

Burma-Shave

"Don't make no matter. Want her rollin' over in her grave? She taught us better than that, Paul," Adding, "At least when her and Pa weren't going at it."

The Russells were raised in the countryside outside of Youngstown, Ohio. Poor, dirt farmers, the brothers envisioned a better life for themselves than the one they shared with their parents. The struggle to survive on meager earnings that their parents endured was not meant for them. Easy money was their ticket out of there.

Both had been arrested before their 17th birthdays, and their assent up the criminal ladder was a rapid one.

Lloyd took over the driving before they entered the city limits deciding that it would be better for him to man the wheel instead of instructing his brother as to where to go.

They exited east going for a block before discovering the customs booth leading to the Canadian side. "Keep your eyes peeled, quit screwing with that radio—it's too loud."

"Too loud? I love this tune. It's number One. Patti Page sure can sing—"I was dancing with my darling to the Tennessee Waltz when an old friend I happened..."

"Paul, pay attention to business."

"Hell, you didn't have to go an shut if off..."

Lloyd ignored him. "Let's go direct to that hardware store. What street's it on?"

"Right off of Water Street, let's stop at a gas station and get us a map."

"Good idea. Here's a Sinclair Station, I'll pull in here.

"Hey, you get a new dinosaur, free with ten gallons of gasoline."

"Paul..."

"Yeah, yeah, I'm going."

Lloyd drummed his fingers on the wheel. "Get in, what the hell you doing now?"

"Had to rip one. Knew you'd slap me silly if I brought it in here. Damn near tore the seat out a my trousers."

"Lemme see the map."

"I got the last one in the store Lloyd. It shows the whole area. Canadian side, too."

"Okay, we take a right two blocks up. Good."

"There it is, up on the right."

"Gotcha." Lloyd pulled in behind an old Dodge pickup. "Go check it out, Paul. Let's hope your shit house partner was right."

"Damn, there's a parking spot right up front by the door. You gonna make me walk a block?"

"I don't want some nosy clerk spying these plates. This fucker is stole, don't you forget, plus, we stick out with these Ohio plates."

"You cussed, Lloyd, the exact same cuss words I used. Ma's gonna be pissed," still chuckling he slammed the Ford's door and sauntered up the street.

Paul was not only taller than his older brother, but he possessed a full head of thick, black hair that framed a mischievous face. Although he owned a hair-trigger temper and tended to carry a mean-side to his character, he projected a devil-may-care persona that riled Lloyd, who featured his parents' strict posture.

Paul wasted little time once he entered the store. He glanced around, quickly determining that he was the lone shopper. The store was devoid of customers in the mid-afternoon lull.

"Can I help you, Mister?"

"Maybe you can—heard a fella can pick up a rod aroun' here, no questions asked," Paul tested the burly, ruddy-faced cashier in a checkered, flannel shirt.

Ignoring Paul, the big clerk stepped over to the window facing the street. He looked both ways, craning his thick neck as he scanned the light daytime traffic. "What you looking for?"

"It don't matter, a couple of 38's will do. Just don't want no pussy guns. It's hard to shoot a squirrel with one a them."

"What kind of money you spending...?"

"We got cash money—more than enough. How long's it gonna take? We have an appointment out west."

"It'll take a while," the shop keeper was edgy, "come back tomorrow—say at two." He turned to greet the man who entered, the bell above his head signaling his arrival.

"Darned if we don't have a warm one for May," the newcomer greeted, "that south wind will dry things up real good. I'm getting sick of stomping through the mud." He sounded like Canada was very close. He was dressed for a summer picnic, short-sleeved shirt and pants cut off at the knees like he had been in them at the time they were being altered.

"How can I help you, Hank? How's the fishing been?"

"Not too geesly bad, Bill. Those pesky blackflies are pretty thick, and a damn nuisance. I got a couple a days off. Billy Tuscan and I are gonna try our luck above the locks. Hear the steelhead are hitting."

"That's right. Billy's got a new boat. What ya' need?

Paul slipped around the newcomer and hustled down the street to his impatient cohort who was still tapping his fingers on the steering wheel. "What the hell took so long? I could a bought the store by now."

"Tomorrow—at two," Paul jumped into the moving Ford as Lloyd cut through the adjacent alley, and out the next street.

"You could let me get in first."

"We're gonna head to Canada. Lay low there for the night. First, we gotta hide these hot wheels."

"Thanks for the apology. Sometimes, there's nobody on the planet but you."

3

THe Canadian Soo

THE STOLEN VEHICLE WAS LEFT TO hide in the parking lot of a large hotel advertising weekly and monthly rates. "I took the plates off so it shouldn't be noticed right off, as the car we took. The Ohio plates would stick right out." Lloyd stared at his brother. "What'd you find out?"

"We kin catch a bus four blocks from here and go straight into Canada. No questions asked. Won't no plates be more noticeable than Ohio plates?"

"You're right, brother. Let's boost one off that car with a flat tire. It ain't moved in months."

The bus took them across the St. Mary's to the Canadian side, to a much more lively setting than the American side. The bus driver announced. "Here's the Prescott Hotel, my friends, it's the Soo's oldest hotel, a historical landmark. It's undergoing a little renovation, but the rooms are clean and comfortable."

"Looks all right to me, Paul. I like big hotels, we don't stick out like we would in a small place." They strolled casually into the lobby.

"Well, check this out—ain't this fancy."

They fetched two different rooms, signing in under separate names. Lloyd hadn't slept alone in what seemed like ages. There was always a roommate in prison. Paul, on the other hand, had no intention of sleeping alone.

A couple of blocks down from the Prescott, the duo sat nursing after-dinner drinks. Lloyd picked at a thread of pork chop caught between his teeth. The matchbook cover was too thick to spring it out of the gap between his teeth. He summoned the bartender, "Got any toothpicks?"

Paul swirled his shot of bourbon around his molars cleaning his palette while he savored the flavor of the bitter, burnt-tasting alcohol.

"Thanks," Lloyd grabbed the toothpick from the bartender and spoke through it to his brother. "You better not do something stupid," the toothpick bobbed and weaved as he cautioned, "don't do nothing stupid, nothing you'll regret, and watch the booze."

"Hey Lloyd, this is your baby brother. Don't worry, I'll do fine. I just gotta have a little fun with the dames. I been a long time without 'em." He gave a broad smile that thinned his lips, then ran his tongue over blunt teeth that sparkled in their whiteness.

"Just, watch it. We don't need no trouble. These Canucks will lock your sorry ass up in a heartbeat. I wish you'd get a bottle and have a broad come up to visit you like I'm gonna do." Lloyd knew it was useless. "All you gotta do, is ask the bellhop."

"Man, I gotta hear some music, cut a rug. It's been too long." Paul slipped his arm around the worrier, trying to soothe him. "You're only five years older, sometimes, you act twenty."

Lloyd handed him a wad of cash and got up to leave the dimly lit bar. "Thanks, the gals are gonna love these new kickers and check out the pleats on these pants." Paul showed off his new duds by dancing a little soft shoe.

"Watch yerself."

The night was a topper for the younger Russell. His skillful dancing returned after just a couple of trips to the hardwood floor, laced with a slippery, sawdust residue. His boyish good looks and roguish appeal had the ladies laughing and waiting in turn to dance with him. Paul Russell had been incarcerated for a long enough time and was more than ready to express his resounding libido to a lady of his choice.

He picked the redhead with the big melons. She laughed the loudest at his jokes. "Here's some cab fare—for the morning." He didn't want to negotiate if she was a pro. It would ruin things,

"C'mon, let's get outta here," he coaxed her out the door and into the cool Canadian air. He pinched her rear until she squirmed.

"Say, buddy, are you being fresh?" She said it with little sincerity.

The desk clerk didn't look up from the novel he was reading as Paul pressed the Otis to the fourth floor. Once aboard, he slipped his hand under her dress...

"My, you're a bold one."

"I'm gonna show you bold..."

Lloyd told his visitor to leave. He had enough of the woman for one night. He paid her without haggling, not wanting her remembering him as a jerk. Pouring a nightcap, he finished his cigarette, stubbing it out in the ash tray—he tossed back his drink and hit the sack.

"Dammit, I can't take anymore," beads of sweat matted her dark, red hair, plastering it against her silken forehead. The red hair was surprisingly natural, as her chest heaved against the man on top. The clock on the table winked 6:00 o'clock, suggesting that the coupling had been a long one.

"Baby, we have had us a time," he rolled off and sat on the edge of the bed. He stretched for his cigarettes, lighting two. He handed the redhead one, then grabbed the empty bottle. "Damn, we're outta booze."

"It's okay. I ain't never met anybody like you, Paul. You can go all night long. It's like you been storing it up forever."

"That'd be about right. I been away."

She brushed the ash off her bosom. Deciding they were her best attractions, she pulled the sheet back down. "Where you been, in prison or something? In the big house?"

Ignoring the question, Paul leered at the bare-breasted woman, "Maybe it's my first shot at some Canadian pussy that got me so horned up."

"Sorry pal, but I'm from Deetroit." The words hung there, mingling with the insistent rapping on the door.

Paul yanked it open, his boxer shorts drooping. "Get rid a the clap nest, do it now, we got things to do before our two o'clock meet. I'll be back in twenty."

"Say, I ain't no bimbo." The slit eyes of the intruder cautioned her from adding more. Cold, stone eyes that made her shiver in the warmth of the room. She covered her goose bumps with last night's dress and was out of the room well before the allotted time.

The return trip to the states took less than an hour, prompting Paul to ask, "What was our hurry? We got till two..."

"We got things to do. We gotta be real careful, I don't want us back in the hoosegow."

4

Buying Guns

THEY EXITED THE BUS, LLOYD DIRECTING them away from the parking lot, and the stolen car. Paul was curious at first, then it dawned on him, Lloyd was being cautious.

"You really think they may look for us this far north? I don't figger they're that smart."

"What's the point of it, Paul?" He led them on a complete circle of the block. The Toledo car sat there, appearing unobtrusive and unwatched. "Let's be cautious, Paul. Let's act safe."

Lloyd went to the Ford and screwed the plates back on that he extracted from the trunk. "Put those back on the car we borrowed 'em from." Lloyd took the wheel and waited while Paul reattached the Michigan plates. Paul jumped in wondering where they were headed.

"We ain't supposed to be there till two."

"Always be early for a meet, you never know what's going down."

Lloyd's cautious action was rewarded. "Well—lookie at that."

"Don't stare at it, Paul," the police cruiser with *City Police, Sault Ste. Marie,* passed by the brothers and turned the corner at the next block without so much as a glance at the fugitives, its taillights winking as it disappeared from sight.

"Scared the shit outta me, and I ain't scared at nothing," Paul said, releasing his nerves.

"Okay, let's do this. Trade places. Quick."

"What? Lloyd, the man inside knows me. I havta go in and buy the guns."

"We are lucky if we're still buying guns. It may be set up. Make the switch—do it now. You're the wheel man." Lloyd sat up and urged Paul to scoot underneath him.

"Damn, you're being silly. The man in the store is cool, just let me go in and buy the goods." Paul's face showed his impatience with his brother.

The trade of drivers was completed just as the patrol car turned back on to the street, on the same side as the hardware store. It sat there, motor idling as it faced directly across from the Russell's stolen Ford.

"Now, whatta ya' think? The bastards are back. We been set up. That damn shop keeper."

"Okay. You might be right, they made us Lloyd."

"Ease out slow, Paul. All they know is we wanted some guns. Don't look at 'em when we pass. They might not know our ride."

Paul drove past the stationary cop car forcing it to make a u-turn. "They're right on our ass. Hit it, Paul."

The Ford's monster V-8 engine kicked into gear, jumping ahead of the orange caution light as it spit tire residue in its wake. Lloyd directed the escape through the city streets, and out to the state road that they had taken the day prior. His demeanor was as calm as moonlight.

"Turn right here. Let's go west."

"Will you lissen to this son-of-a-bitch purr? We got us a goody, it'll do a hunnerd, easy. We're already losing 'em."

"Good job, stick to it. C'mon, just keep going."

After a bit, they were unable to see or hear their pursuers. "Dammit, Paul, you are the best. You kin outrun any cop in the land."

"That, I can do. I love this baby, it has pep."

"We gotta dump it, first chance we get, Paul. There's an APB for this hunk."

"So, what we gonna do?"

Night was threatening when Lloyd ordered Paul to turn into an overgrown logging trail. "Pull in here, we gotta ditch this baby. Here's a good spot."

"Shit. We're stuck. This is as far as I kin put it."

"Leave 're here. Let's go. Hurry it up."

"What now? We can't hoof it."

"Yes, we can. We'll take to the woods."

"Jesus. You're shitting me..."

"We passed a two-track a half-mile back. Looks to be an old logging road, maybe there's an old shack in there somewhere..."

They walked a mile in the naked light of the approaching night, following the rutted trail that showed no sign of recent travel. They approached a clearing, featuring a cabin in slight disrepair. Yet, it showed recent usage. "A hunting camp?"

"I'd guess so. Let's check it out. Try not to break anything."

"Our luck is still holding, this ain't even locked." Paul pushed the door open.

They scoured the rough hewn cabin. It was typical of the northern deer hunting camps that nestled in the wooded land near the hunters' favorite deer trails. An orange crate sat next to a wood stove and served as a cupboard that held a variety of staples.

"It ain't bad, I don't see no rats."

"We're still close to the main road, let's load up on what we can use and be ready to make a run into the woods."

"I think we're safe pal, ease up."

"Paul, you simpleton fuck, we're never safe. You better lissen up." "We got two cans of soup, some pancake mix, maple syrup, a little bit of sugar, some flour, and—seven rounds of ammo for that rifle you dug out of the bedroom." Paul inventoried the cache' and packed it in a pillow case.

"That's it. Put it by the door in case we gotta scoot. We ain't gonna make a fire till its late. Who knows how long a posse will work?" Dusk was descending rapidly into the cabin's crude interior.

"I'm gonna look for an outhouse. I could take a dump."

"Hold it, Paul. What the hell was that?"

"Sounds like someone talking."

A murmur of voices, much like the mosquito buzz heard all summer in Michigan's U.P. entered the clearing. "Here's Tom Kangas's cabin. They might be in there."

"You're gonna have to shit your pants, Paul. They got us nailed. Hurry, load that rifle."

"How many out there?"

"At least six that I kin see, we can't shoot our way out with a single-shot rifle. We may be fucked, but I ain't going back in. I'm tired of the system. Plus, the food sucks."

"What you saying, Lloyd?"

The curtain didn't ripple as Lloyd checked out the men milling around in the yard. Shadows danced off them, yet it was easy to determine that there were six of them. Six men, all armed—the odds were not good.

It was obvious that the Ford had been discovered. The men stood around chatting, a couple swung flashlights about—checking the cabin for signs of a break-in. For no reason that the escapees could discern, the eerie stillness of the vacant-looking camp sent every member of the posse to the rear. *No one remained in the front.*

Lloyd eased the window open, stopping when it creaked stiffly from age and little use. Wiping off his sweaty palms, he eased it up far enough to clear their bulk. Neither man was large, in fact they were lean and could pass the narrow opening with ease. He slithered over the sash and let out a soft moan when he bumped his head. "Dammit, I cut my head, grab the rifle and the grub, hand it over, quick."

Sour sweat mingled with the cooling air as Lloyd Russell closed the window after his brother's exit.

"You're bleeding good."

"Keep moving, we're almost in the bush. Push it..." his voice was a low growl. They crossed the clearing with no time to spare.

"We made it. They're coming back."

"Move it, just keep moving..."

The muted signs from the search party signaled the end of the search. The brothers laid low after rolling into the security of the underbrush while the searchers milled around the dusky yard. Bent at the waist, the Russell brothers scurried further into the security of the woods.

"They ain't gonna find us. Let's rest till they leave."

The Marion Star (Marion, Ohio)
Posse Combs Forest For Two Ohio Escapees
Sault Ste. Marie, Michigan

May 15-(UPI)-Two convicts who swung like ape men over an Ohio prison wall led 150 police on a commando chase through Upper Michigan's dense forests today.

The jungle-wise brothers, Lloyd and Paul Russell were believed hiding out in a two mile strip of swamp along the St. Mary's river; which forms the Canadian border. Police believe they had the armed brothers trapped in a one-way out woodland between the river and a closely guarded road. An open field blocked freedom at one end and posses' of state police, local officers and veteran hunters were beating their way in from the other.

The Russells escaped three to thirty burglary sentences by swinging Tarzan-like on a 70 foot cable out of the London, Ohio, prison farm. They were thought to be heading for Canada when a storekeeper recognized Paul as he tried to buy a gun here last Thursday.

A 90 mile-an-hour chase by police forced the two to abandon their stolen auto in the Riverside swampland.

5

Life In The Swamp

They headed in a northeasterly direction, forced by the changes in the terrain to alter their direct route. They went into and out of a dense triangular-shaped swampy marshland, skirting the edge of the west channel near Neebish Island. Every change to solid hardwoods made travel much easier and was greeted with relish. The long, arduous days tromping through the muck had diminished supplies to the point of being critical, plus making the twosomes' humor testy.

"Lloyd, I shit you not, I could eat the balls off a squirrel. How long have we been in this shit? I can't live eatin' your herbs, I need a steak."

"It's nuts, Paulie, a squirrel's got no balls. It's got nuts."

Paul grimaced, "Shit. I should a knowed better." He chuckled at Lloyd's rare attempt at humor. "One thing we got going—we ain't in jail."

"Reckon we been strolling about a week, this shit's gotta get easier to walk in. Hold still, don't breathe, I just seen supper."

A rabbit, unaware that the intruders would be hunting at this time of the year, pranced in front of the starving convicts and—their stolen rifle.

The rifle's resonating reverberation echoed through the evergreen swamp, making the ensuing silence deafening in its wake.

"Good head shot, Lloyd. You didn't waste no meat."

"Didn't intend to, you said you was hungry. Besides, it was close. Could a hit it with my eyes closed."

"I'll skin 'er Lloyd, wanna make us a fire?"

"Damn, this bunny tastes good, Lloyd. It even makes this shitty swamp piss drinkable. It's a good thing we boil it in these cans, or I'd really have some trouble."

Lloyd ignored him. "We only got six shots left. We better hope to find civilization soon."

"Yeah, it would be real nice to wipe my ass with paper. I've had one awful case of the shits from that damn swamp water. Then I gotta use cedar boughs..."

"See this?" Lloyd stroked his finger of his left hand between the thumb and fore-finger of his right.

"What the hell is that?"

"I'm playing the world's smallest violin, and it's playin', "my heart bleeds for you, and your sorry ass."

"Fuck you, Lloyd. My ass hurts. It ain't no joke."

"Didn't mean to hurt your feelings. Just don't shit yer pants, those skeeters will drag you off into the swamp and have their way with you if you're running around bare-assed."

"Have you ever seen meaner bastards?" Paul waved his hands around his head trying to generate enough air to chase the annoying insects away.

Lloyd squeezed the blood out of the mosquito that was feeding on the back of his hand. "Tell you one thing right now, I ain't never gonna be caught in a swamp fulla mosquitoes again without I don't have a way to keep them off me." He swatted and scratched until he drew blood down both of his hair-filled arms. "I ain't never been this itchy—I know why those guys that escape up here turn themselves in. They can't stand these fucking bugs."

Paul stared at his brother—who was not one to talk for any length of time. This spiel amounted to a soap box lecture.

"Yeah, Lloyd. We thought they was babies when we heard they escaped, then ended up turning themselves in..."

Wednesday, May 17, 1950

"THERE'S A RADIO IN HERE, LLOYD, WANNA HEAR SOME HANK WILLIAMS?" Paul turned it on and busied himself with the tuner. "I miss this stuff, Lloyd. I'm a honkytonk man. You're too serious, I swear you are."

Ignoring his brother, Lloyd made a thorough inspection of the small one bedroom cabin. Paul kept fiddling with the dial, hoping to catch one of his favorites between the squawking and the poor reception.

"Hold it Paul, back it up. Let's hear the news." Lloyd had just reentered the living area.

Paul reversed the dial and adjusted the sound until he found the news station. Intermittent static interference interrupted the radio's reception.

The newscaster was just wrapping up the national broadcast; *Frank Sinatra was silent and didn't want to talk about screen star Ava Gardner when he arrived in Europe yesterday.*

In London, on his way home, he denounced as a 'vicious lie' the report of a romantic triangle involving him, Miss Gardner and Spanish bullfighter Mario Cabrera.

"Look at this Paul, can you believe it? We got two cans of Dinty Moore's stew. We're gonna eat like kings tonight."

"It's my favorite, Lloyd. I kin eat both cans in one sitting."

The room hushed as the brothers heard their names through the radio waves. The local announcer delivered a heavy accent loaded with a combination Finnish-Canadian brogue, not uncommon to the region.

Police reported that their search for the escaped convicts, Lloyd and Paul Russell, has shifted to Canada. The couple was reported seen in the Canadian Soo on Tuesday, and there have been no sightings on this side of the bridge. They are believed to be heading west along the Canadian side of Lake Superior.

"This is perfect Paul, now we can head back to the Soo and boost another car. They think we snuck back into Canada."

The weather has remained exceptionally warm, leaving us with a bumper crop of mosquitoes, the voice in the background droned on. "Yes, we'll grab some new wheels and head west before anybody knows where we been."

There was a new bounce in their step as they headed east, back toward the American Soo. A quick swipe of a vehicle and they'd be on their way before the local law was any the wiser.

The Marion Star in Marion, Ohio also reported that the consensus opinion of the day as it repeated the United Press story. The Russell brothers were getting credit for deeds that occurred hundreds of miles from them.

HUNT OHIO HOLDUP MEN

Beaverton, Ontario. May 17—(UP)

Police today hunted two hold up men believed to be American brothers. They robbed a motorist from flooded Winnipeg last night. Police identified them as Lloyd and Paul Russell, who broke out of a Toledo, Ohio jail.

The information spread along the wire service was often incorrect and misleading. Local authorities were more than willing to pin suspicious and illegal activity on the fugitives.

4:30 a.m.—Friday, May 19

"HEY, THERE'S KEYS IN THIS ONE," whispered Paul. "Hanging right there from the ignition. Like earrings dangling on a bimbo. We won't find easier pickings."

"Okay, shut up, get in, real quiet, I'll ease up the garage door. Make sure you back out slow and easy."

W.F. Weber was on the mail box as the car was inched out of its garage and crept away from 1900 Tweed street. The quiet residential neighborhood was still asleep as Paul maneuvered along the tree-studded streets and onto the road that would lead them to M-28 west and on the way to Fargo.

"Like taking candy from a baby, Paul chuckled, "and its got a tank almost full of Ethel, it's well-maintained and probably has just been lubed and oiled."

"Understand Paul. We been lucky. Luck don't hold. Remember that."

Paul wiped a sneeze on his sleeve. "We gotta enjoy the moment. Have some fun. Don't be so serious."

They cruised along, virtually the only vehicle on the road. *Here's a hot one, headed for number one on the top forty charts. It's Gordon Jenkins and his orchestra, known as the Weavers, with—"Good Night, Irene.*

"Keep yer eyes on the road and watch your speed." An uneasiness was gnawing at his calm demeanor. "What was that burg we just blew through? I didn't catch it."

"McMillen, I think that's what the sign said. They even got a post office."

"I ain't mailing anything. Let's keep moving..."

"Not a problem, Brother—it's a good day for a drive."

Trooper Robert Halladay tossed the dregs of his coffee out the open driver's side window and turned to his partner George Bays. "These road blocks make for a long day. Hell—it ain't even noon yet."

"Hardly any traffic at all, it's a real quiet morning," Bays said, "Now wait, here comes one from the east. I expect it's not our fugitive." He squinted into the direct sunlight.

"Good, we'll get to chat with someone, break the monotony."

"What the hell is that up ahead?"

"Damn—looks like a roadblock, Paul. How the hell did they get wind of us so fast? It don't seem possible."

"Those folks we stole this baby from must be early risers. Must be a fucking milk man. They discovered the car missing and called the cops. The state cops, I bet, who figgered it was us who boosted their ride."

"We ain't got a choice—we gotta bust through 'em."

"Here goes...I hope this Chevy is as quick as that Ford."

"It better be. I'm going try to blow out a tire on that cruiser."

"Your ass is almost in my face, what the hell you doing?"

"Lloyd's actions caused the Chevy to slow down involuntarily as Paul wondered what his brother was going to do.

Bays voice steered away from the humdrum morning. "What's that car up to, Bob?"

Tossing the rifle into the back seat, Lloyd climbed over the seat to join his weapon. Chambering a round, he hissed, "Don't slow down, dammit, hit the gas." He cranked down the rear window as far as it would go. The Coupe's rear window did not open completely—a design flaw that Lloyd cursed as he positioned his firearm.

The troopers watched the approaching vehicle slow its pace to a crawl only to hear the engine of the oncoming Chevy snarl to life and come bearing down on the shocked and surprised duo. "Watch it George, that son of a bitch ain't stopping."

With the skill and daring of the totally reckless, Paul waited until the very last second to crank the wheel to avoid slamming into the blockade vehicle.

They lurched to the side, straddling the ditch while Lloyd fed his weapon out the partially opened window and pointed it at the astonished troopers.

"Get down" Bays shouted as the rifle's retort added to the frenzied turn of events. The troopers dull, quiet morning vanishing with the sound of the bullet whizzing over their heads.

Halladay jumped into the driver's seat, starting the engine as his partner slid over and reached for the radio.

6

Tнe Cнase Is On

THE CHEVY CONTINUED WEST, HURTLING THROUGH the tiny village of Seney, passing a Plymouth that had pulled out of the local grocery. Paul banged on the horn, screaming obscenities at the driver who pulled out in front of them. They were soon roaring down the "Seney stretch" at top speeds of over 90 miles per, easily outrunning the pursuing state police. The near twenty mile stretch of curve-less road flashed by in record time as they soon arrived at the intersection with M-94 in Shingleton.

Head north, take this M-94—we kin shake 'em off on the back roads."

Detective George Strong and Trooper Stanley Gibbard, both out of the Newberry Post, sat in their patrol car. Hallady's report fresh in their thoughts. "Do you really think it could be the Russells, George? They're supposed to be in Canada."

"It sure ain't Shoeless Jackson. There was a report out of the Soo this morning of a stolen auto and the description of the car fits."

"Hello! Here comes a car now, and its hauling ass..."

The officers, with Strong behind the wheel, attempted to flag down the speeding vehicle.

The Chevy roared down on them with no intention of stopping. A dark form filled the rear window—followed by a rifle barrel. "Get down, he's gonna start shootin.' The two officers had no time to react before the Chevy was upon them.

The stolen auto raced on past. "Good driving—way to go. They're swinging around to come after us. Keep going." Lloyd watched from the backseat. He turned to see Paul's eyes, questioning from the rear view mirror.

"Keep driving, boy. I'll keep you up to snuff." Before the curve in the road could deter their view, Lloyd watched his pursuers pull over to the side of the road. "They stopped."

"What for?"

"Dunno..."

The patrol car attempted to give chase but quickly slowed down, "Shit, Stan, I'm hit. My leg is going numb. I can't drive any further."

"Pull over, George. You're bleeding pretty damn good. I'm running you to the hospital. Let's get something on that leg to slow the bleeding." The detective ran the cruiser off to the side and instructed the trooper. "Alert the others, these guys are not only armed but they're not hesitant about shooting."

"I must a hit one of 'em. That's all I kin think of. Why else would they quit the chase?"

"Maybe the road ahead is a dead end. They may be waiting for reinforcements."

"Good point, let's turn around, head back. We could get nailed, but, maybe we was lucky and I hit one."

Mister and Mrs. Lawrence Luke were driving west on M-28 returning to their home in nearby Melstrand when the state police light came on behind them indicating for them to pull over and stop.

"Were you speeding, Luke?" a concerned Mrs. Luke asked.

"No dear, I'm sure I wasn't."

Soon they were back on the road, shaken up over the incident. "He even made you open the trunk, Luke. What'd they think you were hiding?"

"They're looking for two escaped convicts that stole a Chevy just like ours. They thought we might have been forced to hide them in the trunk."

The two continued home with a story to tell to their friends about the mistaken identity.

The Russells retraced their route back to M-28, then headed back toward Shingleton. They hit the village limits, the little Chevy laboring into a slight curve. "Jesus, turn around quick, Paul," spotting the police cruiser parked at a gas station.

He shattered the station windows with a blast from the rifle as Paul swung the Chevy back to the west amid a cacophony of sounds that included; rifles firing, windows breaking, engines revving, and tires screeching. The sounds mingling to form one thought—escape. Paul straightened out the fleeing vehicle and it shot back on a return trip west.

"Give 'em hell, Lloyd. I got this baby rocking," Paul shouted over the din.

Troopers Haladay and Bays resumed the chase as they radioed ahead, reaching Troopers Beech and Scales on the State Police band. "Where are you?"

"We're south on 94. We've been monitoring the calls. George Strong has been hit, losing a lot of blood. Stan Gibbard is taking him to a hospital, over."

"Get ready. We think it's the Russell boys that just jumped us in Shingleton. They swung a u-turn and are heading back west. They just shot up the gas station we were parked at."

Robert Beach reached into the patrol car's back seat and retrieved two pump action, police-issue shotguns, tossing one to Bill Scales. Both officers were from the Manistique Post, fifteen miles to the south. Beach reached in to click on the radio, "What's your status?"

Bays, his voice pitched high in the excitement of the chase, answered, "We're doing almost ninety and losing them, that son of a bitch can drive."

Before the troopers could see the laboring vehicle, the troopers heard it approaching. Beach jacked a round into the breach, advising Scales to do likewise. "Here come those bastards, get ready, they're not afraid to shoot us."

"Lloyd, more cops on the side of the road. They got guns out."

"Go man. Go like hell." Lloyd fired off one round from the back seat before the two state officers unloaded their shotguns at the fleeing duo.

"Shit Lloyd, I been hit. Got me in the leg. I'm bleeding—it's pretty bad."

"Kin you drive? Tell me. How bad is it?"

"It's bleedin' pretty good. I kin still drive. How about I take this here road off to the side?"

Haladay and Bays roared on past the roadside officers and continued the chase south down M-94 on the heels of the fleeing cons. Beach and Scales soon joined in. "Pull in here, the Boot Lake road is kicking up dust." Bays noticed the settling particles riled by recent travel.

Just minutes ahead, the sign offering entry into **The Hiawatha National Park,** convinced the brothers it was time to ditch the Chevy and again hit the woods. "Lemme see the leg. Shit, you're bleeding like a stuck hog, let's head for that swamp. I'll have to fix you up later, right now, we gotta keep going."

Paul limped along at a painful gait as he attempted to keep up with his brother who, as was his nature, was picking the densest thicket to disappear into. After laboring for twenty minutes through thick tag-elders and muck-filled earth, he slowed, unable to keep pace. Lloyd turned around sensing his brother's stifled progress, then stared as Paul's face went blank as he pitched face first onto the dark, mossy forest floor.

7

THE BOOT LAKE RESORT

LLOYD FIXED A POULTICE OUT OF the moss to slow the bleeding, realizing he couldn't staunch it completely until they stopped for the night. He was finishing just as Paul came to.

"Whatcha doing'—playing with my ass?"

"Trying to stop the leaking, Paul. Can you walk? You lost a lotta blood."

"Sure—not a problem." He winced in pain as he was helped to his feet.

Soon the older sibling was toting the younger who was lapsing in and out of consciousness. "Lloyd, you gotta leave me. You can get away. Break me out later."

"We're gonna lie here for the night. It'll be dark soon. I don't wanna run in circles." The sun was having difficulty sending its rays into the dense swamp. The late afternoon cooled rapidly and Lloyd shivered as he foraged around for some boughs to cover Paul. Soon, he had cut out blankets of cedar boughs and first covered his comatose brother.

He stripped off his sweat-soaked shirt, ripping off pieces to use as a compress on his brother's wound. He could not completely stem the flow of blood. The black flies arrived seeking them out as Lloyd cursed them for their eagerness to penetrate his ears and eyes and even his mouth if he opened it. As the darkness overtook them, the ever present mosquitoes with their lust for blood took over.

Sergeant James Smith, commander of the Marquette Post, took charge of the manhunt. A large posse, composed of men of all ages, shapes and sizes hung about the Boot Lake Resort, awaiting instructions. They had gathered quickly from throughout the area.

Sergeant Smith had state police written all over him. He sported a thin mustache and his dark blue hat was cocked in an upraised angle as he glanced at his watch to note the time. A blue tie hung from the collar of his white shirt, showing sweat stains from the heat of the day.

He addressed the group gathered before him, "We have a plane coming in from Traverse City that is bringing us walkie-talkies. They have landed in Wetmore, and should arrive here soon. We have almost 100 volunteers, city police and sheriff's officers. We'll hunt down those bastards who shot George Strong."

Halladay said, "We hit one of 'em, there's blood in the car and a trail of it heading into the swamp."

"The troopers with the walkie-talkies are here. Who will help us pass them out?"

"I will, be glad to help out."

"Thanks, young fella. What's your name?"

"Ollie, it's Ollie Johnson."

"Good job, Ollie. Boys, line up and we'll distribute a walkie-talkie to each pair of searchers. We're gonna wait till morning, let's have a tight perimeter for the long night ahead. Let's not shoot each other, okay, let's get to work." Alger county sheriff Arthur Moote was in charge of the civilian volunteers.

First light took its time reaching the fugitives in the thick cover. It trickled slowly in and notified Lloyd that the long night vigil had ended. The drone of a plane reached his ears—he searched the sky believing it to be a search plane.

He touched the forehead of his feverish brother. Paul's sleep had been fitful, moaning in and out of consciousness. "Paul, are you awake? Can you get up? They got a plane up and the bunch on the ground will be on top of us real soon."

Paul rolled his eyes. "You go, Lloyd. Just come spring me." With a heavy sigh, Lloyd leaned against a spruce and lit a smoke, exhaling in resignation.

Russell rose briefly and paced the cell. The Journal writer offered him another cigarette which he accepted and was soon drawing in the smoke.

"Would you have gotten away if your brother hadn't been shot?"

"Hell yes—easy. Ain't nobody would a caught us in that thick shit. We would a stayed in there as long as it took. I can make it in the woods for as long as I want."

"Lieutenant Wixom said they would have tracked you down with all the men they had."

"He's fulla shit, he'd a been chasin' his tail before we was done wit him."

"Ever think of leaving Paul?"

"If it had been anybody else, I'd a left him. Somehow, I just couldn't walk away from Paul. I guess he's in a bad way right now. I was pretty sure the jig was up when he was too hurt to move. What I ain't figgered, is how they set the blocks so quick after we boosted the Chevy in the Soo. I gotta give the cops the credit there."

"Oh, didn't anybody tell you? They were looking for another escaped con, by the name of Jackson. A Negro from the Magnum farm, had run off a couple of days before."

"You gotta be shittin' me, Russell," he was visibly agitated. "We bust a roadblock meant for some nigger. Talk about luck, no wonder we're in jail."

"Fate plays a big part."

"Yeah, I guess it does. We made mistakes, but the real mistakes were made a long time ago..."

"Thank you Mister Russell, why don't you keep the rest of the pack."

"Thanks. Tell your readers one thing—there ain't no prison that can ever hold me for long."

8

The Market Basket

Friday, March 31, 1950

THEY CAME OUT OF THE PITCH BLACK PARKING LOT...

9:47 pm—Get yer ass back in there," Roscoe Lense heard the harsh command before he felt their presence. Reentering the store, he failed to deactivate the alarm. His chief checker, Allen Groh, 20, was told to lie on the floor in front of the office.

9:51 pm—A silent ADT systems alarm, sent to the Western Union Office, informed of the impending robbery. The Lansing police department was notified immediately.

Of the first five officers to arrive at the scene, only three were wounded. A fourth was hospitalized for injuries sustained during the skirmish.

The first cruiser arriving at the front of the store (north), carried Patrolmen Bob Belen, Anthony Pohl, and Berwin Lagios, who was being driven to his beat, along with Commissioner Alvin S. Potter, who was riding along as an observer.

Patrolmen Russ Detering, and Alex Hnatiw arrived within seconds and took up positions on the east side of the building.

Officer Belen, was the first to reach the front of the darkened store, unknowingly interrupting the bandits. A bolt of fire spit from somewhere in the darkness. The muzzle flashes told him there were at least two men, maybe more—before he succumbed to the salvo.

Russ Detering was a couple of steps behind. He returned the gunman's fire at he entered in a running crouch. He ducked further down as a couple of rounds zinged over his head. As his eyes became accustomed to the darkness, he soon spotted his fallen comrade.

Detering rushed to the fallen officer, lying just inside the store, unaware that four rounds had found their mark. Belen moaned, his weak cry telling Detering that he was still alive. Reaching the wounded man, he yelled, "they're heading to the back of the store."

Hnatiw and Pohl rushed to cover the back.

Shots fired, officer down. Lagios barked into the radio, *1400 E. Michigan, at the Market Basket. Send an ambulance. We need backup.*

The attempted robbery had gone horribly wrong. They had already shot one cop, maybe killed him. "It's life in prison if we get caught in here, Art. We gotta shoot our way out. Let's try a ruse, pretend we're gonna give up.

The gunfire ceased. "Don't shoot, we surrender," a voice from the back cried out. "We're dropping our guns and coming out."

"They want to surrender," Officer Detering yelled. "Toss out your weapons, easy like."

Detering approached them alone, ordering the men to disarm. Before he got close, he was greeted by a hail of gunfire that allowed for the insincerity of their surrender. The dimly lit store became alive with the burst of pistol fire as Detering exchanged rounds with the holdup men.

Before Detering could reach the shelter of the canned vegetable display, he was knocked down by the barrage of gunfire. He tried to sit up and retrieve his standard issue .38, before a wave of darkness overcame him causing him to lay back down on the cold floor.

The stickup men jumped over Detering's body and raced to the front of the store. "Hell, we can't make it out of here. We'd be cut down." The other man stood over Belen, looking down at him— ready to put another round into the prone body of Patrolman Belen. He bent over, the barrel of his pistol inches from head of the officer. Hesitating, he followed his partner toward the back of the store without firing a shot.

"Get ready, we go on the count of three," the taller one was in charge. "On three, we hit it." They ran out the back of store through the gun fire from Officer Pohl, running until the black night swallowed them. Additional officers joined Pohl at the scene, but the extreme darkness and the sporadic gunfire from the retreating bandits kept them at bay.

Pohl told the newcomers, "I didn't dare shoot before I could locate where the fire was coming from. An innocent could be passing through." Soon—another shot sent them scrambling for cover.

Confusion reigned, as more lawmen joined the scene. "Damn, it's black out there, I can't make out shit."

"We can't go after them it's like jumping into an inkwell."

Pohl said, "Where's Lagios? I ain't seen him since the shooting started." He squinted at the men around him. No one seemed to know.

Pohl looked around, a wild, desperate look in his eye, wanting someone to take charge. "He's my partner. I know three, maybe four of our men went down...And, we let 'em get away."

No one answered. The shock hung over the officers like a deathly pall.

It was apparent that the gunmen had escaped. They concentrated on aiding the emergency units evacuate the wounded to Sparrow Hospital on Michigan Avenue. It was the closest hospital to the grisly scene. The Market Basket grocery looked like a war zone.

9

A Lead

IT WAS RECORDED AS ONE OF the biggest attempted heists in the city of Lansing. Beloved policemen were down. A shell-shocked city stood vigilant. Residents had never experienced such an attack on their police.

Disbelief, was a normal thought.

Lansing, Michigan, Saturday, April 1, 1950
BOLO—Be on the lookout for two men answering these descriptions.

The police want them for the shooting of three police officers in a raging gun battle when they were surprised at the Market Basket store at 1400 Michigan Avenue.

No. 1—Between 25 and 30 years of age, wearing a hat and green plain jacket, and is believed to be approximately five feet ten inches in height. He is believed to have been hit by a bullet from a policeman's gun.

No. 2—Taller than No. 1 man, wearing a navy pea green jacket and believed to have a mustache. He spoke in a southern accent.

Lansing State Journal—Carlise Carver

Police were conducting one of the greatest manhunts in the city's history for the two bandits who shot three policemen and caused injury to a fourth in a pitched battle at the Market Basket, about 10:00 o'clock Friday night.

City, state, county and East Lansing officers were centering the search for the two gunmen, who were surprised in the robbery of the store, in a radius of 10 blocks from the supermarket. The hunt was focused there after a man resembling one of the bandits was reported seen under a porch on Clifford Street. And another one was seen running through a backyard in the neighborhood.

Using a technique developed during the war in Germany, police officers spliit into three and four men squads and started "shaking down" every house in the area under surveillance on the east side about 12:30.

A report on the was released by Edward W. Sparrow officials stating Dr. Ralph Wadley had performed surgery on Officer Belen, 23, a bullet had punctured his colon and lodged in his spine. His condition was critical, but had a good chance of a full recovery. He was also wounded in the right arm, and twice in the left leg.

Officer Detering, 27, was wounded in his right arm.

Officer Lagios, 24, was wounded in his left side, near his hip.

Officer Pohl, 27, was cut on his little finger of his right hand when he fell over a low fence in the rear of the store while in pursuit of the bandits. It required a number of stitches.

Sidney Hildebrandt, a veteran Lieutenant with the Lansing department, glanced over at his partner, Detective Earl Eddie. They strolled through the bullet-riddled store, piecing together last night's robbery attempt. "That was a helluva shootout. Look at the friggin' mess."

Eddie, acknowledging his senior partner added, "It's a wonder that everybody's still alive, though Belen is critical."

"Yeah, Hnatiw's in the hospital, too. Didn't get shot, but got hurt somehow during the festivities."

"Yeah, I heard that, too. It was a mess out there. Anything could have happened." He picked up a shell casing. "Looks like the techs missed one."

"Hear about Al Potter?"

"The commissioner? Heard he was here. Was he on a ride-along?"

Hildebrandt allowed an expansive grin, "Heard he was hiding behind a sign, must have been shitting a brick."

Eddie looked around. "It must have been behind that sign over there. On the west side of the store, that board is big enough to hide a man. I don't see another one around close enough to the front door of the store."

"Whoa, he had to have close enough seats. I can't see any holes in it from here." The detectives sifted through the store looking for anything the robbers may have left behind.

The trail was already cold, detectives worked leads, followed tips, working on nothing else but the Market Basket case over the next two days. Mayor Ralph W. Crego asked the city council at the Monday night session to post a reward for the capture of the two bandits. An amount was not mentioned.

The local radio stations and the Lansing State Journal played up the robbery at the Market Basket and constantly asked listeners and readers for any information leading to the arrest of the persons involved in the attempted robbery.

The Detroit Free Press ran front page stories with large photos of the victims as the state's largest daily reached out for information on the foiled robbery attempt.

Tuesday Morning, April 4, 1950

"LET'S GO, WE GOT A TIP, LOOKS LIKE A GOOD ONE," the phone issued orders to the still waking Earl Eddie. "I'm picking you up, taking your zilch ass to Detroit."

Eddie's partner hung up before the words kicked the half-asleep officer awake. "Who was that, Honey." She said in a sleepy voice.

She was instantly awake as the words her husband spoke reached through the early morning fog. "Sid, we gotta a big lead. It's in Detroit. I gotta go, he's on his way."

"Detroit, isn't that out of your territory? What time is it?"

"Dunno, it's early. Go back to sleep."

"I'm awake now, Earl. Let me make you coffee. This is your first week as a detective. You best be careful, these guys are bad men."

He didn't respond. He donned yesterday's clothes, avoiding a decision of what to wear. He checked the load in his .38, assuring himself that he was sufficiently armed. Allowing time for his wife to go downstairs to the kitchen, he strapped the extra snub-nosed .25 caliber to his ankle. The back-up seldom went with him, even during his patrol days. *This may not be a normal day.*

Hildebrandt idled the plain brown Oldsmobile in the drive, waiting for his new partner to open the door as the two steaming mugs of coffee were nagging at his face. Hildebrandt slid over and opened the passenger side door. "See that you woke the wife up."

"What, you think I can't make a cup a java? Scooting in, he spilled the hot coffee on his lap as he held both cups till his partner was driving smoothly down the street. "Got an automatic from the motor pool? Good, it beats all that shifting at the stop lights in Detroit."

"Thanks for the coffee. I was gonna stop somewhere before we got outta town."

"What's the tip?" Eddie grew anxious, sensing a feeling that the lead was solid.

"It may be that one of those boys in the heist was once from Lansing."

"He was from Lansing? But, he doesn't live here anymore? Tell me more. He moved to Detroit? When?"

"Yeah, he moved there, don't know when. Detroit had an informant tell 'em about two guys that have been pulling jobs around the metro area—they may have branched out further and pulled the Lansing job. Same M.O. used in all these jobs is what I was told."

"Same M.O? Now, that's interesting. And, he can name 'em?" Eddie sipped at his coffee, digesting the hot lead.

Hildebrandt was sipping and spilling. "They got one name for us. The Lansing connection. "Damn, I spilled more coffee than I drank. This damn Grand River is rougher than a riverbed."

Earl Eddie waited, knowing his partner would catch him up at his own speed. Hildbrandt was much more deliberate than was his own nature. He wanted to nudge him a little, but he knew that would only slow things down.

Eddie realized Hildebrandt was grasping for the name, not wanting to have to refer to his notes. Sidney was vain about his memory.

"Ackerman, that's the name of the Lansing shooter. He spent time in Lansing after a stint in Jackson. He joined a local church while in there, vowing to go straight and devote his life to God."

"A regular choir boy? Sounds like he wanted to ante up the collection plate."

Yes, and—and let's hope we pick him up. Appeal to his conscious, we sweat him, who knows, he might give up his partner. We might get lucky."

10
ARTHUR ACKERMAN

8:30 am—Detroit

THE LANSING DETECTIVES ARRIVED AT THE front desk of the Robbery Division. "Sergeant Wrathall? He's expecting us."

The desk sergeant pointed at the man aiming for them. The detective stood up, his mid-section showing signs of middle age. "I'm Bill Wrathall. How was the trip into the city?" His dog-sad eyes had big city cop molded into them. Eyes that said I've seen it all, tattooed in broad features set in a jowled grimace.

I'm Sidney Hildebrandt, my partner Earl Eddie."

"Two first names, huh. Gotta middle name?"

"Yeah, but it's Polock, very hard to pronounce."

Polite chuckles went around. Another detective walked up, two cops of fresh-brewed coffee in his scarred hands. "Coffee gentlemen, I'm Gordon Grant."

Hilldebrant said, "Thanks for the coffee, Gordon. First, I gotta piss, it's been a long drive."

Earl Eddie shook hands, "Say, Gordon, Bill razzed me on having two first names. It sounds like you do, too."

"Yeah. Don't let it bother you. We got a good bunch."

Once all four men were seated, Bill Wrathall shuffled around a stack of papers extracting a single sheet, typed and filled with scratched out notes. "We got a name, he pulled smoke in deep, letting the cigarette hang off his lip. "Our informant tells us that an Arthur Ackerman, age 28, recent to Detroit, has hit some local supermarkets, and a hardware store in Keego Harbor, outside of Pontiac.

"Why do you think they might be our boys?"

"Same M.O. in most of the robberies. Wait till the store closes, then forces the manager back in when he comes out. It's worked like a charm. In and out quick, no witnesses, except a terrified manager trussed up like a Christmas goose."

1:30 pm

"THIS GOTTA BE HIS PLACE. CHECK THE ADDRESS, GRANT."

"It's the right one, there's a new car in the drive, not bad for a man with no visible means of support, though I'd pick a different color..."

Wrathall took charge, keying the radio. "lissen up, I want two men in the back yard of the house. Let me know when you're in place."

"Roger—Braddock and Gates are taking Basset Street, they'll acknowledge."

"That leaves two cars to stand by. Stay outta sight, a block down, one car each way. Be ready with your riot guns," Wrathall's voice, did not display the tense current that hung in the air.

The static cling of excitement...

"We're in place."

"Remember, they shot three of us in Lansing."

"Ten-four, we're advised..."

"The four of us are going in, right up the front walk. Just like a gang of Jehovah's Witness. This warrant is the Watch Tower."

Wrathall picked up the brass knocker and rapped. There was no peep sight in the door. The other detectives stood slightly off to the side, weapons at the ready.

"Yes," Ackerman appeared, well-dressed, a successful looking salesman.

"Are you Arthur Ackerman?"

"Yes. Can I help you?" The curious look showed traces of apprehension.

"We have a warrant for your arrest. We would like you to come along quietly."

The dapper-dressed Ackerman sighed. "I'm glad it's over. I never wanted to hurt anyone. We might have killed somebody if we kept going. We had to stop." Anxious to confess, he continued, "I just got back from a Catholic Mass down on Six Mile Road. I lit a candle for the officer I shot. Yeah, I'm admitting it. I shot the first cop that came in."

Dressed in a new charcoal colored suit, Ackerman shook his head as he recalled standing over Officer Belen, contemplating shooting him again. "I pointed the gun at his head, but I just couldn't pull the trigger."

"Tell me all about the Lansing job, right from the get go." Wrathall's dog-brown eyes turned sympathetic.

"We drove down there the night before, cased the area and the store, figuring out the best place to hid the car during the job. We stayed in a flea-bag motel on South Cedar. We thought we had it all planned out. A piece a cake."

"Who's we?" Who's your partner?"

Ackerman went on, seeming not to hear the question. "After the shooting started..."

Hildebrandt stopped him. "Let's start at the beginning shall we? How about when you and your partner forced your way into the store with the manager in tow?"

"Well—my partner forced the manager back inside the door. He pushed him into the cashier's cage while I grabbed the young kid. I made him lie in front of the office and then took him to the back away from the windows."

"Had any other the officers arrived?"

"About two minutes later a policeman walked into the front of the store, and I said, "watch it." Morr—my partner started firing at the man and I ran to the rear of the store and back up front again. I found my partner and the policeman struggling.

During the struggle, Belen was thrown to the floor," Ackerman said, "I thought Belen was going to shoot me." The suspect heard his partner say, "die copper," in the shooting that followed. Officer Belen was shot in the stomach from Ackerman's automatic.

He described his partner as a "mean guy" and Ackerman claimed to "go along" rather than incur his dislike.

A search of the Ackerman residence revealed the automatic used in several shootings. Later interviews with members of the First Presbyterian Church described him as a "wobbly character."

"Name, give us a name and address."

"I, I just can't. I know he'll kill me."

The detectives looked at him in disgust. The man who had calmly helped shoot down three police officers was blubbering like a sissy. "I don't think you understand, Ackerman," Wrathall spit the words, "if you don't tell us, that's when your life will be in real danger."

"What you mean? You won't protect me in the stir? When I do my time?"

"Better than that. We'll let the word out that you talked. Squealed like a pig. We found you from word on the street. We'll set you up the same way. See, it's this way, we want justice for our own, we can't find your partner, we'll find justice on the street."

"You'd do that, after I cooperated?"

"You haven't cooperated until we get a name and address. We call that cooperation."

"Alright. It's Charles—Charles Morrison."

"Where's Morrison now?"

"Where's Morrison now?"

"Probably in Royal Oak, at his parent's house. That is, if he isn't shacked up with a broad somewhere."

"Got an address? We'd like to pay him a visit."

"Yeah, but don't tell Charles I squealed—please." Arthur Ackerman had new regrets.

"Okay." Wrathall opened the door from his office and shouted across the squad room. "I want four squad cars for backup." He turned to the detectives, "Plus us four, let's go get the bastard."

Charles Morrison's afternoon nap was disturbed in the rudest of manner.

11

CHARLES MORRISON

WHILE THE COMBINED FORCES OF DETROIT and Lansing were arresting and interrogating his partner, a weary Charles Morrison was climbing the stairs of his parent's home in nearby Royal Oak. He headed up to his old bedroom that he used on an irregular basis. He sighed, planning on getting in a long afternoon nap.

Removing his shoes, he lay down on top of the bedspread. His thoughts drifted to the great night on the town he had just experienced. What was it? Liz, yeah, that was her name. He grinned as she tried to play it coy. Play hard to get. He liked that, he liked the challenge.

After dropping a bundle at Hazel Park, he went to a joint a few blocks away to rinse away the bitter taste of the stupid luck. He sat, stirring a whiskey with a splash, looking her over while she yakked with her girl friend. She sat, twirling dark strands of hair while pretending not to notice his attention.

She wore her hair in the style of the day, soft and curly, and cut short on the sides. It involved an arduous process of pin curling and rolling. The invention of the hair blower was yet to arrive, so it required long hours of drying hair naturally to capture the required softness, but this one had the time to do it.

Charles owned a brooding, thoughtful look, that he knew the dames found handsome. He nodded his head, signaling that she join him.

He watched her cross her legs, a cigarette dangling from pouting lips. He noticed the bright lipstick stain on the filter as she held her hand up while she sipped her drink and chatted idly.

He winked, saluting her with his drink. She noticed.

She faked ignorance of his attention until a man who was obviously close with her friend, joined their table. With a 'three's a crowd' expression on her pretty face, she turned and looked directly at him. "Sit down," he gestured at the chair next to him.

She knew his type, this one was not going to get up and seat her. The tough guy had always appealed to her. And—they didn't come much sexier than this one.

"Lemme buy you a drink, then we'll ditch this joint," both knew the outcome was no longer in doubt.

They ended up in the early morning hours at her place, somewhere off Fenkel on the west side. They went to a *Blind Pig*, gambling a little—steadily drinking after closing the legitimate bar at two—they partied there until five.

"Will I see you again, Charley? I had a great time." The sheet partially covered her nudity, as she looked at the good-looking dark-haired hoodlum.

"It's Charles," liking the large, full-breasted image that the mirror provided. But he had to straighten her out from the quick. Show her who's in charge here. "I need respect, you better respect me if we're going to get along."

"I'm sorry—Charles. I didn't mean anything by it." Instinct told her this handsome stranger possessed a mean streak. The gun in his coat pocket told her he played rough. Tough talking guys who packed, she held to the highest respect.

He finished fussing with his tie, liking the image, his and hers, as she approached timidly.

"I'm really sorry."

"It's alright, baby," he squeezed her nipple, watching her face to see if she would reject his harsh hand. He squeezed it again, with more pressure, a calloused smirk marring his handsome features. "I'll be back, but I don't take kind to my babes seeing other men. You know what I mean?"

The temperature in the room dropped noticeably as the smiling lips spoke the words but the cold, dark eyes conveyed the deeper message.

A shiver coursed through her, "I'm a one-man woman, Charles. I'll be here for you."

Lying there, dozing off and on, Morrison relaxed. "It's been a rough week, maybe I'll take Liz and get out of the state for a while—go to Windsor, in Canada. Wait till the heat dies down. I can stand some more of her loving..."

Charles Morrison slept, not realizing how long it would be before his next date with a beautiful woman.

"Name, give us a name and address."

"I, I just can't. I know he'll kill me."

The detectives looked at him in disgust. The man who had calmly helped shoot down three police officers was blubbering like a sissy. "I don't think you understand, Ackerman," Wrathall spit the words, "if you don't tell us, that's when your life will be in real danger."

"What you mean? You won't protect me in the stir? When I do my time?"

"Better than that. We'll let the word out that you talked. Squealed like a pig. We found you from word on the street. We'll set you up the same way. See, it's this way, we want justice for our own, we can't find your partner, we'll find justice on the street."

"You'd do that, after I cooperated?"

"You haven't cooperated until we get a name and address. We call that cooperation."

"All right, It's Charles—Charles Morrison."

"Where's Morrison now?"

"Probably in Royal Oak, at his parent's house. That is, if he isn't shacked up with a broad somewhere."

"Got an address? We'd like to pay him a visit."

"Yeah, but don't tell Charles I squealed—please. He's a bad number." Arthur Ackerman had new regrets.

"Okay." Wrathall opened the door from his office and shouted across the squad room. "I want four squad cars for backup." He turned to the detectives, "Plus us four, let's go get the bastard."

Charles Morrison's afternoon nap was disturbed in the rudest of manner.

12

"Shoeless Willie

May 18, 1950

WHILE AUTHORITIES SCOURED THE EASTERN U.P. looking for the Russell brothers, a 35 year old Negro trustee, walked away from the Magnum farm of the Marquette prison. Not only would he play a role in the Russell's capture, but his absence would play havoc with the farm's upcoming baseball team.

"Shoeless" was their star pitcher. He pitched barefoot and when asked why he explained, "I get more English on the ball." He also was a fan of Satchel Paige, the greatest pitcher of the old Negro Leagues. In making his escape, he would subscribe to Paige's philosophy, *Don't look back. Somebody might be gaining on you.*

"Shoeless" had one more trait in common with ol' Satch. No one in the prison system knew his exact age. *Age is a question of mind over matter. If you don't mind, it don't matter.*

May 20, 1950

Bolo—Be On The Lookout—For a Negro male, approximately 35 years old, he may be driving a stolen gray 1948 Ford Club Coupe with Wisconsin license number 16357, or a 1940 Dodge Panel truck bearing the Michigan license 4055-CX. Both vehicles were stolen in the Marquette vicinity. Two fingers on his left hand are crippled.

Road blockades were set up in key spots throughout the U.P. The black man should be easy to recognize in this rugged, desolate country. Negroes were in fact, a curiosity. The Russells' luck was about to run out, thanks to Jackson, who was in the throes of leading law enforcement on a merry chase.

10:15 am

"MICHIGAN STATE POLICE, NEGAUNEE POST," the dispatcher answered. "Hello, this is Mrs. Somola at the Standard Oil station, I just saw him," excitement filled her voice. "I'm pretty sure, it had to be him. I mean, how many are here...?"

"Excuse me, Ma'am, who did you see?"

"The missing Negro, he just walked up and bought a gallon of gasoline. Paid for it in pennies, acting real nervous. He was fumbling so much. It made me nervous, to tell you the truth, I was scared silly."

"Pennies? Say, wait a minute, lemme look at this morning's sheet—this is curious. A gumball machine was broken into in Marquette, right downtown. You're out on the highway at the new station on 41?"

"Yes, he had a glove on his left hand, and like I said, he was nervous. I watched him head west on the highway, always looking over his shoulder. He kept looking around, then he broke in to a run and disappeared on to a side road. I called you right away."

Chief of Police for the city of Marquette, Rudolph Swanson, headed up the investigation by city police, as the state police, were by this time, in the middle of a gun battle with the boys from Ohio.

Using guards from the prison, along with city police, Swanson set up road blocks on the highway west of Sagola, and on U.S. 41 and M-28 west of Michigamme. A filling station on West Washington street in Marquette had been burglarized and about $2.00 worth of pennies had been stolen.

L'Anse, May 22

"WE'RE AFTER THE STOLEN CAR, IT JUST BROKE THROUGH." Trooper Tom Tobin of the Wakefield Post announced. "Guzin fired one shot at the vehicle, after a warning to stop. We don't know if he hit anything."

The troopers spotted the abandoned Ford less than three miles short of L'Anse. The Wisconsin tag assured the officers that it was the stolen auto. A quick search confirmed their suspicions. "Here's the loot from this morning's break-in," Bruno Guzin discovered. "There's a small radio, candy bars and cigarettes. He left in a hurry."

"He didn't have time to take 'em," Tobin added. "He must have hit the woods on foot." He looked around—suddenly aware of his surroundings.

By Sunday afternoon, the force tracking Jackson was mobilized and in full swing. State Police from Baraga and L'Anse, along with sheriff's officers from three counties combed the rough, swampy, heavily wooded terrain. Three planes from Muzzy airport south of L'Anse made several flights hoping to fetter out the elusive escapee.

Today's strategy called for a tight blockade of the area. All local citizens were alerted and warned not to leave their keys in their cars.

"There is not much chance of him getting out," Sergeant Forest H. White, in charge of the L'Anse post said. "The capture most likely will come during the night since Jackson's been operating after dark and laying low during the daytime."

Correspondence and assorted papers found in the car positively identified the escaped convict. Run Willie, run. So Willie ran.

L'Anse, May 25

A TIP LEADS OFFICERS FROM THE L'ANSE post to check out Mass City, in Ontanagon County.

Crews on the Copper Range railroad company reported seeing "a Negro" in between two "gondolas" on the train at McKeever Junction.

Frustration began to show on the law-enforcement troops on the ground. How was he eluding them?

Again, the elusive Jackson is believed surrounded. A posse, determined to capture him, searched the heavily-wooded area outside of Mass. Since escaping a week earlier, he was believed to have stolen two cars and broken into two filling stations.

On Monday, the 26th, the Russells were issued warrants from the Chippewa County Prosecutor James A. Henderson, charging them with breaking and entering in the nighttime for the alleged entry into the house of Pat Donnelly at Barbeau. They were also charged with breaking and entering in the nighttime at the home of Captain Lewis R. Mitchell in Soo Township on May 17th and the garage of W, Weber, at 1900 Tweed Street on May 19. The maximum sentence on each charge is 15 years.

May 31, The Mining Journal—Robbery Confessed By Russells

LIEUTENANT WILLARD W. WIXOM, UPPER Peninsula state police commander, announced today that Paul and Lloyd Russell, Ohio desperadoes captured in Alger County May 20th have confessed to two burglaries in Ottawa Lake, Michigan.

They have not signed a statement, but they have admitted orally to taking $3600 from the Ottawa Lake Co-Operative Elevator Company. They also told police they broke into the Ottawa Lake Post office, but took no money.

When captured, police found $3,308.22 in their possession, Lieutenant Wixom said.

Preliminary examination of the pair on a charge of attempted murder is scheduled for June 2 in Justice T.J. Walter's court in Munising.

Escaped Convict Steals Two More Vehicles; Still At Large In Ontonagon County

WILLIE JACKSON WAS STILL AT LARGE, believed to be between Bergland and White Pine, in Ontonagon County.

A busy Willie, stole two vehicles during the night, then abandoned them both when they ran out of gas, and was seen by a Bergland resident about 12:30 am on M-64.

Apparently, sometime during the night, Jackson stole a car in Painsdale, in Houghton County, and abandoned it in Ontonagon. There, undaunted, he stole a pickup truck, and abandoned that south of White Pine.

Again civilians were cautioned about leaving their keys in their cars, as the escaped convict was last seen heading north on M-64, toward the Porcupine Mountains.

A Marenisco general store was broken into, although nothing was taken, Jackson was believed to be the culprit. Officials suspected that he had been scared off. The Wakefield Post was alerted to a sighting at a lumber camp in Gaylord, about two miles from the Wisconsin state line. The caretaker told police, "Yup, the fella said he was lost and walked through a swamp from Marenisco. He looked it, too. He was pretty chewed up by bugs, you know, we got lots of mosquitoes and blackflies out now."

It wasn't until later in the afternoon that a trucker informed the hermit-like custodian that the black man he had fed earlier was an escaped fugitive.

A blockade was established on both sides of the state line today with Wisconsin highway patrol from Tomahawk and sheriff's officers from both states.

Convict Still Free; Steals Another Car

JUNE 6, 1950—ESCAPED CONVICT WILLIE JACKSON was still at large this morning on Route 64, near the state line, and is believed to have stolen another truck, this one in Wisconsin.

A 1949 half-ton truck was stolen yesterday in Winegar, Wisconsin, two miles south of Gogebic. An intensive search is being conducted by Michigan and Wisconsin law enforcement agencies. Authorities believe he has been able to elude the police blockades by tramping through the dense swamps and forests of the U.P.

June 12, 1950—Hazelhurst, Wisconsin

ONEIDA COUNTY SHERIFF MELFORD KROUSE RECEIVED a call saying the fugitive was just spotted climbing on the outside of a passenger train as it was going through Hazelhurst. Krouse assembled his men and waited for the train at Tomahawk.

"Here comes the train boys, get ready," Krouse set his jaw in a grim manner. "We can't let this slippery bastard slip by again."

"There he is. Stop—Or I'll shoot."

Willie jumped off the barely moving train, racing across an open space heading for the wooded sanctuary beyond. He was running like the fox, he had become.

Tomahawk Patrolman Howard Rose, raised his .351 Winchester rifle to his shoulder, drew a bead at the fleeing man, and fired a single round.

Jackson, clutching his left leg, went down like a November 15th whitetail deer. He was immediately surrounded by armed men.

"He's bleeding bad, you must a hit an artery, Howie." Jackson was showing signs of rapid shock.

The rifle blast had severed the femoral artery. He was taken to Riverview Hospital in Tomahawk and given blood plasma. His condition improved some during the night.

"Is he gonna make it?" Under-sheriff Fred Bruno asked the attending physician.

"He's lost a lot of blood, but yes, I think he's out of the woods."

Bruno watched the prisoner, then shook his head. "You sure led us on a merry chase."

When captured, Jackson had a loaded revolver in his pocket, but he did not attempt to use it. He also carried a tobacco pouch filled with cartridges for the revolver.

Jackson's adventure had lasted 25 days, and although he was apprehended only 150 miles from Marquette, he had traveled over 500 miles during his run to freedom.

In that time, he stole five automobiles and broke into two filling stations and a couple of stores. Sentenced from Wayne county recorder's court, Shoeless was serving a 7 and ½ to 15 year sentence for a burglary conviction in 1946 when he escaped.

Paul Russell, who had been in the Marquette prison hospital while being treated for a shotgun wound in his hip, had been removed to join his brother in the Marquette county jail.

13

Meet The Gang

THE TWO MEN MERGED LEISURELY INTO THE OPEN YARD. Neither man paid attention to the other, one sniffed the morning air, cool for July, cigarette in hand, he was searching for a light. To the casual observer, each appeared unaware of the others presence.

The voice was low—guarded, "Got a light, Joe?"

"Sure, Red. Got another fag?" They edged closer to each other. He accepted the cigarette and fired up a match.

They discharged the smoke simultaneously into the air, strolling along at an unhurried gait. A closer look would reveal, two hardened, desperate men doing time in the state's toughest, maximum security prison.

"Friggin' weather, it's after the Fourth of July. When we gonna see summer? I sure would give anything to get outta this dump." John 'Red' McDowell drew the smoke deep into his lungs, then exhaled a perfect 'O' directly at the overhead watch tower. He uttered through pursed lips, "Hear about that new con?"

"Russell? The one that shot it out wit the cops this spring?"

"Yeah, him and his brother."

"Why, what'd ya hear?" Prison gossip was the primary means of communication.

"Hear? Shit. I talked to the man himself—last night."

"He's already in the general pop?" Joseph McMackin was a habitual criminal from Detroit. He was serving a ten-thirty year term for armed robbery.

McMackin was slightly taller than his prison mate. He was slim-waisted and wore his brown hair cut short with a curl down his forehead. He had a wide-set nose hidden within his high cheekbones.

"Yeah, he says there ain't a prison made that kin hold him."

"Shit, wait'll he's been here a while, he'll find out different. He'll hope for a transfer, they don't call this pen Little Alcatraz, for nothing."

McDowell leaned in closer, "Lissen to this shit. He said it would take him a while, study the joint over real careful. Work out a detailed plan. He said he's gonna need help, he's gonna   keep his eyes peeled out for a few good men he kin trust." McDowell looked closely at McMackin. "This shit comes down—you game?"

"Hey, John, you ain't thinking of going with him? Even if you make it out, you'll get busted again and end up doing more time. That is, if you don't get your ass shot."

"Hell yes, Joe. I'm gonna go wit him—if he lets me. If this bird comes up with a fool-proof scheme, and I can fly outta here with him, I'm gonna do it. Hell, as it is, I'm an old man before I ever get out of the system."

"How old are you?"

"I'm already 36. I need my freedom, I'll kill for it."

"When I finish up here, they're gonna send me down to Missouri, I got some federal time I have to do. I'll bide my time till I get there."

"Joe—you better think about taggin' along too, if we get the chance."

"I dunno, I gotta get going..."

The confab abruptly ended, and they parted ways, drifting off in opposite directions. The stir was alive and buzzing with the news of the new prisoner, the one that wasn't planning to stay.

May 3, 1951

"YOU BUSTED OUT BEFORE?" The voice, in hushed tones, knew the answer to the question.

"Yeah, I broke out from downstate, that's why they put me here."

"I also heard you're in for life."

John Podolski, turned to his inquisitor, "I was sentenced to life, don't plan on serving it."

"You're the kind of man I'm looking for. Cause I ain't planning on it, either."

"Whatcha' plan on doing? Flying over the wall?"

Podolski, wearing thick lenses, generated the appearance that one would associate with a bookkeeper. He certainly did not a jewel thief who shot a killed a Detroit cop during a heist gone wrong. The looks of an accountant, not that of a man who would shoot his way out of a foiled robbery attempt.

"No, I ain't gonna fly outta here. But, I gonna find a way out. I'm working on it. It's gonna take a few good men. Keep your eyes peeled for the right guys. They gotta be cool, steady, and can keep their mouths shut."

"Lemme know what kind a talent you need. I got some connections..."

Late August

JOSEPH MCMACKIN WAS GOOD LOOKING, in a tough guy mold, his nose slightly crooked, having only been broken once. As yet, he hadn't thrown in with the conspirators, having heard too many tales of the failed attempts to leave Little Alcatraz.

The terrain around the prison was not conducive for escape, with barriers such as Lake Superior on the east, and a steep mountain to the west. To the north was the city of Marquette, all three directions produced limited opportunities, leaving the south, the only realistic avenue of escape.

A thick woods, full of man-eating mosquitoes and other biting insects patrolled the area from spring till late fall, when the odds for escape were the best. Many a potential escapee had succumbed to these pests and returned to the prison on their own, unable to deal with the conditions. Winters, with their harsh cold and unrelenting winds, would kill quickly in the sub-zero temperatures and waist high snow drifts.

Road blockades could easily be set up on all the major escape routes along this barren, God-forsaken land. Heisting a car and running off to freedom was something that required a bold, reckless manner, and a tank full of luck. And that's after an inmate figured out a way over the wall. *Hell, I must be nuts to even be thinking about it.* Joe McMakin mused. He tossed his cigarette into a handy butt can and went back to work.

"Ain't nobody busted outta here in thirteen years. And that time, they only made it to the Wisconsin border," McMackin explained. He was playing the Devil's Advocate to the mounting plan, wanting a reason to back out, knowing the odds were truly against them.

"You don't hafta go along," Russell reminded him. "You gotta keep your mouth shut. We ain't begging people to catch this ride."

"It don't hurt to be careful..."

"How'd they do it? Red McDowell tried to change the subject back to the topic at hand.

"There was four of them, they took the warden hostage, along with some parole board member. I bet they shit their drawers."

"There was four of 'em, back in 39,' it was a spur of the moment deal. They didn't have a plan." Russell spoke in hushed tones. "I've been studying boys, day and night. We ain't going out till everything is just so, when all the bases are covered."

"I studied, too. Back in 22,' fifteen boys went out." McMackin said.

"Right, that was thirty years ago, and they got caught after a couple a days out, 'cause they didn't have a plan. We're gonna hole up, in a safe place. Wait 'em out. Hell, I kin live in the woods forever."

Russell steered the talk away from foiled escape attempts. He didn't want to dwell on the killing of Doctor A.W. Hornbogen in August of 1931 where the three convicts who barricaded themselves in ending up killing themselves after two hours when realizing escape was futile.

From 1921 through the decade, numerous attempts to escape had been thwarted by prison officials. These incidents too—Russell chose to ignore and avoid debate.

McDowell said, "How we going out, Lloyd?"

"I got some ideas, it still too early to say."

"We go at night, whatcha think is best...?"

"I ain't figgered it all out yet, Joe. If your in, that's four of us. I need three,maybe four more guys. We're gonna need a diversion."

"Have anybody in mind?"

"Yeah, I got one. A new guy, he just come in. He's got a rep, a cool one when the shit goes down, a real brass set swinging. The only trouble, he's supposed to be a hot-head.

"Oops," said McDowell, "we gotta bust up, here comes a screw."

14

A Troubled Past

THE PLOTTING INMATES HAD ONLY TOUCHED on a couple of the escape attempts that had occurred throughout the colorful history of Marquette Prison.

The Marquette Branch Prison was built between 1895 and 1899 near the banks of the Carp River and the shore of Lake Superior in south Marquette. The structure cost $150, and materials included sandstone from quarries in south Marquette and Portage Entry, (walls and trim), slate from Huron Bay (roof) and copper from the Keweenaw Peninsula (decoration).

Additional buildings were added over the years, and the prison was designated a maximum-security institution (the most violent and hardened criminals in the state were incarcerated there). The sunken gardens were constructed in 1922.

In 1921, the sixth warden of MBP, Theodore Burr Catlin, was appointed. Soon after his appointment a grand jury began investigating the prison. The chief clerk was found guilty of embezzling funds.

September brought the escape of three prisoners. First was Arthur "Gypsy Bob" Harper who escaped by hopping the fence. This was the first escape in seventeen years. Ten days later, two other convicts escaped over the same fence by using a ladder they had made from scrap lumber found in the prison yard. It was being used during the construction of additional cell blocks. All three convicts were caught and returned to prison.

This was not the end of "Gypsy Bob's" trouble-making. On December 11, 1921, along with two other convicts (Jasper Perry and Charles Roberts), Gypsy Bob attacked Warden Catlin, Deputy Fred Menhennett, the deputy's son Arthur, and prison guard Charles Anderson in the prison movie theatre. The three convicts were armed with knives. They stabbed their unsuspecting victims numerous times. The movie theatre was in total chaos, surprisingly, no other inmates got involved in the attacks.

The main target of the attackers was Warden Catlin who managed to close himself in a room until other prison guards were able to restore order and subdue the three attackers. All four of the victims eventually died from complications caused by their knife wounds.

The assailants were flogged on three different occasions. On Monday, December 12, 1921 Harper and Perry received thirty lashes each and Roberts received twenty five lashes. Perry and Roberts received twenty five lashes each on Tuesday and Wednesday. Harper was not flogged because he was acting insane (smashing his head on the floor) and eventually put in a straight jacket to avoid other personal harm.

The punishment of flogging was approved by the governor in certain cases such as this. The murder case was eventually dismissed because the flogging had served as the punishment.

They could not be legally punished again because that would be considered "double jeopardy" so the State of Michigan no longer had a case against Harper, Perry, and Roberts. The three remained at MBP to serve their life sentences with no further punishment.

In March 1922, five inmates attempted to escape through the roof of the west wing. They were successful, but were recaptured by prison officials soon after their escape.

In May, "Slippery Jim" Cushway and two other inmates escaped while at work. The three escaped in a car that Leo Carney stole from a place near where he worked and picked up the other two on the way to Milwaukee. Cushway had escaped numerous times from prison. Many other escapes were successful in the 1920's.

In April, 1923, two fugitives, Steve Madaja and Russell Smith, escaped through the roof of the west wing and were never retrieved.

On June 21, two inmates working in the prison lumber yard were found missing. George Bloochas and George Natchoff had escaped; Natchoff had stolen a .45 caliber automatic and about 40 rounds of ammunition.

The hunt began for these two fugitives. Bloochas was captured first and he warned the police of the danger of Natchoff because of the weapon he possessed. During days of battle in a swamp, Natchoff fired many rounds, killing one deputy, Frank Curran, and injuring another. Eventually they killed Natchoff, who had a total of fourteen bullet holes in his body.

On August 27, 1931, three convicts (Andrew Germano, Charles Rosbury, Martin Duver) from Detroit opened fire in the hospital. The three first shot Doctor A.W. Hornbogan and then proceeded to the second level of an old factory and barricaded themselves in.

Gunfire was exchanged for two hours. At one point a white flag was waived and a bottle with a note attached was thrown at the warden. The note read, "We have a bottle of explosives that will wreck this place, unless you give us a car and open the gates."

The warden responded with "Start shooting again, boys!" Tear gas bombs were eventually used and the three mobsters killed themselves as they realized their capture was inevitable.

The mobsters' motive for the assault seemed to be revenge on Doctor Hornbogen for the death of their friend, Fred Begeman. He had died of heart disease and kidney failure under the doctor's watch.

The three intended to escape but their plan failed and the fatality list consisted of Dr. Hornbogen, Fran Oligschlager (trustee shot trying to help the doctor), Andrew Germano (convict), Charles Rosbury (convict), Martin Duver (convict), Frank Hofer (convict who was armed but never engaged in the shoot-out and killed killed himself after his other three confederates killed themselves). This attempt caught national headlines, including the New York Times.

15

Working The Plan

Two Weeks Later

THE NEW GUY, CHARLES MORRISON, WAS now 30 years old. So dark, his hair was almost black, he stood stood a bit over six foot one and weighed a solid one hundred and seventy pounds. His looks could have landed him a job in Hollywood, even if he couldn't act. A mean brooding look, a vicious streak, and a penchant for the easy buck, had landed him in Little Alcatraz, doing life in Michigan's maximum facility.

When the short, swarthy inmate with the quiet, forceful leadership asked him if he was interested in a break-out," Charles had a ready answer, "I'll start looking for some weapons, and, I'll get some."

Here's something else you could keep yer eyes out for..."

"Gotcha, Lloyd. You been busy."

Throughout the summer of 1952, the Lloyd Russell gang formed within the walls of the penitentiary known as Little Alcatraz. Russell knew he had but one chance for escape, it had to be done perfectly, without a hitch. Morrison would keep his end of the bargain, the others may not be so reliable, but they were, expendable.

"Heard you been turned down, Burgdurf," Russell greeted the aging prisoner.

"Yeah, I reckon I'll spend my remaining days behind these bars. Being told when to go to bed, when to eat, even when I take a crap."

Me, and a few of the boys are thinkin' of making a move. We could use another man." He was casual, like he was discussing the weather, which, on this warm autumn day, was perfect.

Standing in the yard, they watched the leaves, most still hanging from the trees, forming a melange of bright red with orange and green sprinkled among the beautiful landscape that was Mount Marquette.

Lloyd Burgdurf gazed at the dazzling scene that Mother Nature had painted, noting that his days were numbered. In a voice just above a whisper, he said, "It's gonna get cold soon, I'm too old to go snowshoeing."

"How old are you."

"I'm going on 59, a four time loser. I got nothing to lose by making a run."

"We're going to wait till spring. The idea is to find a place to hole out, lay low till we can make a break out of the state. Sooner or later, the law will ease up, we gotta be patient, then we make our way south when the heat's off."

"Where do we hide?"

"First, we figger out a plan to bust out. We got all winter to do it. Then, we leave, but only when the time is right."

Christmas Day, 1952

"HERE'S HOPING THIS IS OUR LAST CHRISTMAS IN THIS HELL-HOLE," McDowell rubbed his hands, exhaling steam into the frigid air.

"It's colder than a well-driller's ass in the Klondike," Morrison chuckled, "and a merry friggin' Christmas to you."

"What's up?"

"Russell said the screws are relaxed today, we're gonna meet at the Christmas dinner."

"News?" John McDowell was eager...

"He has a plan, the man figgers out the smallest thing." Morrison shook his head in awe, "He wants things broke down to the exact minute. He ain't leaving nothing to chance. Yup, Lloyd's got a plan worked out, and you're gonna like it."

5:30 PM

THE PRISON INTERCOM SYSTEM WAS SWITCHED TO WDMJ, and the local Marquette radio station was sending Christmas music out to their listening audience on this cold, blustery holiday. The unfortunate DJ who caught the holiday shift was introducing the next tune. *By special request, here is Jimmy Boyd's number one hit, "I Saw Mommy Kissing Santa Claus."*

"Me and McDowell are gonna be working together on the engineer-maintenance crew come the first of the year," Russell announced.

"How the hell did you pull that off?" A genuinely pleased John McDowell beamed. "It'll be great working with you. And it'll give us a chance to steal the tools we'll need."

"I told you I been planning," Russell's attitude was smug, "We'll be moving around, give us a chance to scout, make a plan for the run."

"What will me and Morrison be doing? How do we fit in?" McMackin said.

"You guys are gonna be in the steward's division, so I want you staying put." Russell hinted of the burgeoning plot. "We're going out in Cell Block C."

Morrison jumped up. "Lloyd, you ain't told us everything."

"That's right, I'm still working on our 'get outta jail free card,' the less you know right now, the better. We don't need no leaks. Keep mum. I mean it."

This time Charles Morrison displayed a glimpse of his famous temper. Glaring at Russell, he snarled, "My mouth stays shut, my eyes stay open. This caper is mine too, I better know what's going down."

Tension caused the air to become static, the inmate power clash was between two powerful, desperate men. Christmas and its music was lost in the exchange. "I'm in charge," hissed the balding convict, "I'm going out, with—or without you."

Morrison shrugged, the confrontation over. "Hell, Lloyd, you're the boss. It's your plan, we'll do it your way."

Russell nodded his approval and waved the other two men off, then said to Morrison. "John Podolski, from the tailor's department is going with us."

"He's in Cell Block C?"

"Right, he is."

The seeds of Lloyd Russell's escape plan were planted.

He walked off, knowing Charles Morrison was a loose cannon. Someone he'd have to keep a close rein on.

16

Cell Block C

Spring, 1953

THE WEATHER WAS WARMING RAPIDLY, A hard, difficult winter had left the residents of the Upper Peninsula greeting the warm south winds with affection. Endless storms had brought mountains of snow to the Lake Superior watershed, causing the inhabitants to rejoice the departure of 'cabin fever' and embrace the return of spring.

Inside the walls, Marquette Prison was bustling with anticipation, and an on going current of latent activity. Prison officials easily attributed the hum and excitement among the inmate population to the seductive harbingers of spring that were showing up daily.

The Mining Journal reported the successful smelt runs that provided residents with an abundant supply of the fresh, tasty little bait fish. Rolled in flour, salted and peppered, these treats were devoured, as they ate them, bones and all. Even the crisp, fried tails were munched by many.

A war was being waged in a far off land called Korea. Hank Williams died on the first of January, age, twenty eight. The radio played hits like Perry Como's, "Don't Let The Stars Get In Your Eyes." That gang that sang "Heart of my Heart," was retold daily by The Four Aces.

The tree-covered hills and granite bluffs to the north of Marquette, were again visited by enthusiastic fishermen anxious to tackle the

Dead River, and the small lakes that formed from the sections that were dammed up for electrical purposes. The unpaved roads were muddy and slick from the spring rains and the melting snow.

The runoff first produced the delicate blue Hepatica and the Blood-root, whose large, lobed leaf protected it from the cold winds of spring and opened only after the plant was pollinated. Later in the spring, the large white-flowered Trillium and the yellow-flowered Trout Lily would bloom. There was a bounty of wild flowers close to the river banks and along the roadside for passing motorists to enjoy. Stands of plants caught the eye, tall and beautiful, with delicate feathery leaves and umbels of fading white flowers. Wild greens, mushrooms, and fiddlehead ferns were foraged and eaten by the native population.

Soon the large, powerful rainbow trout would follow the smelt into the river mouths. Furtive, spear carrying fishermen, with one eye out for the game warden, would sneak to the streams attempting to pierce the brilliantly colored, spawning trout. The deep red flesh was every bit as tasty as the Pacific Salmon that was served in the fancy restaurants.

These delightful game fish were also caught legitimately with hook and line, using its own spawn was a favorite choice of bait. The first one to catch a female found himself with many 'fishing buddies.' The meat was often smoked or canned for future use.

A favorite of the Finnish community was to 'salt' the fish, eat it 'raw' with potatoes boiled and slabs of thickly buttered home-made bread. The skein (spawn), from the female was passed on from one fisherman to another and wrapped in cheesecloth, weighted, and tossed out as bait during the spring ritual.

In the prison library, a determined, meticulous inmate studied the edible plants of the Midwest. Lloyd Russell was learning from past experiences. The hungry days endured while he and his brother Paul traipsed through the northern Michigan swamps would not be repeated. This time Mother Nature's bounty would be used to his advantage.

Burdock root—Collect the root in the spring...

Chicory—A perennial plant that is commonly cultivated...

He studied the *allium porrum*, a wild leek, he learned about the dandelion, stinging nettle, burdock root, yellow dock, and an enormous variety of roots and berries that he would utilize to survive the Michigan wilderness. He noted the medicinal herbs to be found, acquainted himself with their properties and poured over pictures so that he could readily identify them.

He learned how to protect himself from the major nemesis of his and brother Paul's. Avoiding hunger and providing protection from all biting insects, were the keys to survival in the rugged north. He ordered the gang to bring Vaseline with them, a petroleum jelly easily obtained within the prison.

He studied the speckled brook trout found in little streams throughout the U.P. This time he planned on surviving indefinitely. Worms, grubs, grasshoppers, a variety of insects could be used for bait.

There were even bigger fish to fry within the walls of confinement. The pieces, ever so painstakingly slow, were falling into place. McDowell and Russell made their daily rounds within their realm as workers on the prison's maintenance crew.

"I've been talking to Burgdurf. You know him?" Russell asked his redheaded partner. "The one working on the radiator crew?"

"I think so—he's an old man?"

"Yeah, that's the one. Wears peepers and looks like a retired professor."

"He wants to go?" McDowell muttered, "He'll slow us down. I don't like it."

"You miss my point. We need him. We need his partner. A lifer name a Saunders."

"Another old fart, what do we need them to tag along for?"

"Cause—we're gonna use them. It's that simple."

"I don't see how..."

"Think about this, John. Burgdurf and Saunders are working together, repairing radiators. Think a minute. They're using acetylene torches."

"The torches, they're gonna cut us out? Jesus, why didn't I think a that."

The next day Russell found Burgdurf. "Have you talked with your partner?"

"Yeah, I have. He's waverin' a bit. I keep telling him he ain't got nothing to lose."

"How old is he?"

"Just turned 55. I said, what you wanna die in here for?"

"Tell him—I wanna have a chat wit him."

Morrison stopped by the tailor. "Lloyd says, keep on yer toes, it could be any day now."

Podolski, his gray speckled eyes gazed up at the much taller man. "I been getting spring fever awful bad lately." His left eye wandered off in an outward cast, like he was looking over Morrison's shoulder.

"Nice as it's been, I'm gonna enjoy the outdoors even though I'm a city dude. Screw the camp out, I'll get a hotel. I know, it ain't gonna start out that way." Morrison chuckled as he walked away.

John Podolski, alias Martin Majewski, convicted cop killer, stared at the back of the exiting Morrison, knowing that they were both cut from the same cloth. The tailor returned to his work, wondering if he would ever be outside the walls again without wearing shackles.

May 20, 1953

THE RADIATOR DETAIL WAS PROGRESSING, the weather, bright and sunny. Robins were chirping outside the prison walls. Inside, the final plans were being implemented. Russell and McDowell had freedom of movement that left them able to coordinate with the other conspirators. The day of reckoning was fast approaching.

"We got three knives, Morrison snatched one out of the kitchen at supper last night. Tonight, he's gonna put an edge on it." McDowell said. "That guy is a little wacko but I think he's got our back."

Russell ignored the comment about Morrison's character and shrugged his powerful shoulders. "That should be enough. We should only be dealing with a couple of guards. I doubt they'll put up a fight."

"What about Saunders? Is he aboard?"

"Burgdurf assured me that we get a torch whether Saunders goes out with us or not. He won't try to stop us from takin' 'em. The torch and the tank, I mean."

"How we all gonna congregate in C Block? Won't the screws raise hell when we go in together?"

"Here's what we're gonna do, Red. We wait till two, that's the changing of the guards. McMack, Morrison, and Podolski are already in there. We tell the new screws that we havta help Burgdurf and Saunders wit the plumbing on the radiators."

"Do we know who the screws are?"

"It don't matter. We're going out, one way or the other."

"You're right, Lloyd. I can feel it. This is gonna work. God damn it. It's gonna work."

"I toll you, there ain't a stir that kin hold me for long."

"When we going? I got ants in my pants, Lloyd."

Russell paused, looking around before he answered. "I'm thinking Friday, Mac. I still got a couple of things to work out."

"Friday, huh? I've got nuttin' else planned."

The two conspirators moved on, performing the day's mundane tasks, prison life's boring day to day routine in the state's maximum security facility, was interrupted by the music of John McDowell's cheerful whistling.

Thursday, the Last Supper

THE DIN OF CONVERSATION DIMMED TO a murmured buzz when Lloyd Russell entered the mess. He casually glanced around, without seeming to. He noted the gang was present. The familiar odors from the kitchen were blending in with the sounds of supper in the big house. A blind man could make his way around, just by the sound and smell, do it without a cane.

He strolled toward the tables, with hawk-like eyes that saw everything. There was an empty seat next to Morrison. Charles would ensure no one sat there. McDowell and McMackin looked up as he passed by. The old men were there, too. Podolski was sitting by himself. Ever the loner. There was Burgdurf, his slight nod sealing the deal, for next to him sat, John Saunders, the final—missing piece.

Russell sat down, a smug look on his face. "The pieces fit, it goes down tomorrow." After three years of meticulous planning, it was finally coming down. His eyes were restless as he spoke, always moving, looking around the room, never settling on anything.

He cut his meat loaf with the same care he did for everything worthwhile. Using his fork, he fed the marbled meat into his mouth, hissing the final word. "Tomorrow. You better be ready to do your part, we won't get a rehearsal."

Russell's final words of advice were, eat a big breakfast and lunch. Food may become scarce. It always is for men on the run.

Morrison grinned, a leer that showed how close to the edge he was. "Gotcha."

Evening, the dark of night can keep a secret.

HE LIE ON THE COT, GOING over the details over and over in his mind. This was his chance. The key was over-powering the guards. Once they were locked in cells, they would use the torches to cut the bars out of the window in Cell Block C. He knew which window. It faced the west, away from the guard towers. There would be a hasty sprint to the pump house.

Once outside, they would enter the pump house and cut the phone wires. The old trustee, Lloyd forgot his name, wouldn't dare to interfere.

There was a part of the caper that Russell kept to himself, it was the key to making this break work. He had to divert the law, slow them down. How? Create a diversion. And, that distraction would come from the escapees themselves.

Yes, the smile went undetected in the dark, gloomy cell. *The old timers will be the diversion.*

17

A Torch To Freedom

Friday, May 22, 1953

The Iron Mountain News
Missing Girl Found Alive After Two Days, Two Nights In Woods
MENOMINEE—LITTLE TWO AND A HALF YEAR-OLD Beverly Kay Bradly, missing for two days and two nights in the Upper Michigan bush country, was found alive and in good condition about noon today. Officers in the posse reported by radio that a Coast Guard helicopter which joined the search at 10:00 am spotted the little girl in the woods about one mile from the grandparents' cottage.

FEARED BEAR KILLED HER

The two day search took a grim turn today when officers ordered that any bears that are sighted be killed and their stomachs examined. The Milwaukee tot strayed from the yard of her grandparents' cottage Wednesday at noon.

A large female black bear with two cubs was flushed from the brush within two miles of the cottage yesterday. Sheriff Edward Reindl issued the shoot-to-kill today.

Meanwhile, Beverly Kay's father, Paul A. Bradley of Greenville, Ohio, joined in the hunt after a harrowing dash from his home in which his car left the road and over-turned at Plymouth, Wisconsin. Not seriously injured he was brought the rest of the way to Menominee by relay of sheriffs' cars.

The aircraft picked her up and returned her to St. Joseph's Hospital here. Ground searchers reported that the tot was in good condition.

At 2:30 pm, all seven members of the Russell gang were gathered in Cell Block C. A simple nod from Lloyd Russell put the plan into action as he and John McDowell grabbed a surprised guard, Officer Joe Butula, and with a makeshift knife to his back forced him into a cell by himself, using the manual switch at the entrance.

"Just behave, Joe, we ain't gonna hurt you if you behave yourself."

Meanwhile, Officer John Osterburg was attacked by inmates led by Morrison and McMackin. "You son of a bitch," Morrison slashed at an inmate who came to the guards aid. He was prone to animal-like fits when enraged, his hair stood up like a rabid coon as he spit at the men in his way. "Get in that cell, you bastard, all you assholes get in before I carve you all up."

"You cut me," an inmate gasped.

"He got me, too."

This set Morrison off once more. In a rage, he snorted through his thick nose hairs and lunged at the men being herded into the cell. McMackin, nearly missed being stabbed, as he moved in to block Morrison's actions. "Let's go, Charles, we got work to do. Keep your head, dammit."

Morrison shook his head, as though surprised at where he was. He gathered himself quickly, "You're right, Joe. I'm cool."

"C'mon, let's keep moving, we ain't got much time."

The cell door slammed shut and further violence was diverted. The inmates owed a debt of gratitude to Joe McMackin. The trigger-tempered Morrison's adrenaline was overflowing and that made him a very dangerous man.

Russell had already directed Burgdurf and Saunders to the west window and within minutes they cut into the bars with the acetylene torch. They tossed the severed bars out the window opening, making it large enough for a quick escape. "Careful, they're still hot," Saunders said. "Pour the water on 'em, Lloyd." An anxious John McDowell led the way, and one by one, the prisoners dropped through the opening.

A sixty yard sprint brought them to an embankment—stumbling downward, they raced toward the pump house that was a football field away. Burgdurf fell to his knees—Russell snatched him to his feet before he could pitch forward all the way.

An unsuspecting airplane flew over low, causing McDowell to stop and look up at the circling aircraft. Unaware of the escape attempt, a photographer snapped pictures of the scene below, oblivious to the proceedings. So unaware—he didn't develop his film for several days.

"Keep going John," Russell yelled. "We gotta make the pump house, let's hustle. Get the lead outta yer ass, boys. Run like your pants are on fire."

Breathlessly, they burst in on Clare Townsend, a short term trustee. "Cut the phone lines," Russell ordered. "Towny, you're gonna keep your mouth shut till we're long gone. I hear you squealed early, and I get caught, you might as well shoot yourself now."

Clare Townsend shivered in the sudden draft caused by the warning. Unable to find his voice, he nodded his assent.

The seven men hit the icy water of the Carp River, the stream only knee deep at this juncture. They crossed the fourteen foot width swiftly, then rushed over a hill to the safety of the woods west of the prison.

"Follow me," Russell took the lead and set a rapid pace into the dense forest, ducking through the underbrush as he turned southward on his trail to freedom.

Townsend waited until they were well out of sight before heading to the Warden's office. He arrived to report the escape and discovered that Norman (Red) Reynard had already beat him to it.

"Michigan State Police," the bored voice answered the call to action.

"This is Warden Jacques, we've had a major escape, maybe as many as seven convicts..."

The state police were immediately joined by the Marquette County Sheriff's department, Marquette City Police and the prison guards. Thus began the biggest manhunt in the history of the state of Michigan...

Their famous roadblock in a perimeter went into effect and encircled the prison area. The Warden asked radio stations WDMJ and WJPD to inform the local citizens and to caution people living near the prison, alerting them to guard their weapons and car keys.

Morrison caught up with Russell, who was sitting on a maple stump, taking a breather. He had led them on some sharp uphill climbs, using the jagged rocks to heave themselves up. "Who's still with us, Charles?"

"There's a couple still close." He gasped, catching his breath. "One's gotta be McDowell, you kin hear him bitchin' from the left field bleachers. I would think Joe is with him."

"I hear 'em, John would be the mouthy one."

"It's his nature to complain, plus, none of us are mountain climbers."

"Here they come now. McDowell does look agitated." Russell waited till they pulled up next to them, gasping for air. "Anybody else close behind?"

"No, not that I could hear," McMackin heaved a sigh, "It was all I could do to keep up. These are some steep hills. Them old farts gotta be far behind."

"Exactly," McDowell chimed in. He bent over, resting his hands on his knees, sucking wind. "Ain't no way they could climb up here."

"Good. The plan is working. We need the diversion. Let's get going. We go due south now. We don't need them to catch us now." He was referring to the older escapees.

Charles Morrison grinned like a skunk eating cabbage. "I toll you Lloyd had it all figgered." He bowed, "I gotta hand it to you, Lloyd. It went smooth."

"Let's get moving, I take the lead. We go single file, John, take rear, we do a fast walk. Stay off the roads..."

18

Freedom Can Be Fleeting

6:00 pm

JACK MESSENGER, 48, BECAME AWARE OF his dog's prolonged barking. Jack lived on Pioneer Road and the incessant yelping by his springer spaniel, who had just delivered puppies, warned him that a stranger was on his property.

He put the dog and two of her pups into his jeep, and began driving up and down Pioneer Road between the city dump and County Road 553. "There he goes girl," Messenger braked to a halt. "I betcha that's one of those escaped convicts."

He eyed the spot where the furtive suspect crossed the highway and waited until a patrol car arrived. Michigan State Police Sergeant Anthony F. Spratto stepped out. The veteran detective walked over to Messenger, his hand resting on his sidearm. "What are you doing, Jack? You shouldn't be out here, we've had a major prison break."

"I seen a man run into the bushes right over there," he pointed to the spot of entry. "Maybe ten, fifteen minutes ago. He was looking suspicious, I heard about the jail break..."

"Good job, Jack. Let's take a look."

Trooper Ray Rudman joined the two men who had by that time, walked to the point where the fugitive had entered. It was almost funny,

83

the suspect wore prison issued clothing, yet was easily seen by the three-some when they entered the thicket. He was facing in the wrong direction, his ability to hide deeply impaired by his sense of direction. He offered no resistance to the arresting officers. Lloyd Burgdurf, age 59, enjoyed less than six hours of freedom.

A contingent of prison guards was on hand to greet the returning prisoner. He was delivered to Warden Jacques office to undergo extensive questioning. The Warden was set to grill Burgdurf of the escape plans for the remaining fugitives.

He blamed his quick capture on his age and told the Warden that he was unable to keep up with the rest. "I had nothing to lose, I just decided last night to make the break."

Jacques told him that the 1952 parole board had not "closed the door" in his case, to which he merely shrugged and added, "the other fellas plotted the deal, I just decided to go along for the ride."

Lloyd Burgdurf was placed in segregation, Block F—disciplinary.

Law enforcement officers combed the city throughout the night, closely inspecting sporting goods shops and hardware stores, where guns would be available, and keeping close tabs on parking lots for anyone attempting to steal a car.

"Fucking mosquitoes," Charles Morrison cursed the voracious insects. "I ain't never seen 'em this bad."

"Here, rub some of this on your face and arms." Russell was busy crushing the leaves and bulbs of the leeks. He mixed it with the petroleum jelly that he had ordered all of them to bring. He found mallow and began crushing the leaves and flowers. "This will help the itch, and keep the swelling down." The purplish-pink, trumpet-shaped flowers had just begun to bloom.

May, with its bloom of wildflowers, was the main reason Russell had waited so long to make the break. He would have a lot of new growth to wild-craft. McMackin was covered with the stinking, onion-shaped herb. "This shit really works, they're still buzzing around me, but they're feeding on Chuck."

"It's Charles, asshole, not Chuck, not Charley."

"Cut it," Russell stepped in, "we're gonna be holed up together, damn it, we better get along or you'll find yerselves going off on your own."

"The moon is coming out," McDowell said. It's pretty damn full."

"Good, we'll take it slow and easy till we figger everybody's asleep, then we haul ass south till we see first light." His cigarette flared in contrast to the thickness of the dark woods as he added, "Travel slow by night and hole up during the day. That's how we do it. 'Cept for tonight, cause tonight we gotta see of we can outrun the first road blocks."

The plan was altered as they covered much more ground than they had anticipated. The moon led the way as they wove their way through the shafts of light that led the way on the main north-south deer trail. They easily outran the initial Saturday morning road blockades.

Three years and two days after being captured with brother Paul in a Seney swamp, Lloyd Russell was free once more. The vow that no prison could hold him was again a reality. He led the foursome in a southerly direction, vowing solemnly to himself. *This time, I'm not going back...Not ever.*

Saturday, May 23—The Mining Journal

CUT BARS ON WINDOW IN DARING Escape—Bob Biolo's front page alarm shared the details. Seven desperate and dangerous criminals escaped from the Marquette Prison at 2:55 Friday afternoon and six were still at large and being sought today in the biggest police manhunt in Upper Michigan's history.

The fugitives, all long-term convicts and renowned escape artists, broke out from within the prison walls by locking two prison custodial officers in a pair of cells with several other inmates at knife point, the biggest wholesale break since 1922, when fifteen convicts tunneled their way out of the prison.

One of the convicts, Lloyd Burgdurf, 59, who was serving a life sentence for fourth-offense burglary, and who was considered the least dangerous of the group, enjoyed less than six hours of freedom. Burgdurf was captured...

Jack Messenger, 48, a Marquette school bus driver, will receive a $50 reward for information leading to the apprehension of an escaped convict.

A large number of other state police posts in both Upper and Lower Michigan arrived last night and this morning to join in the search.

With them arrived Captain Earl Hathaway, 7th District Commander from Traverse City, who aided aided in the capture of the notorious Russell brothers in Alger County.

Captain Hathaway will aid Captain Thor Person, the local district commander. State patrol trooper Chester Nottinge, Traverse City, flew the state police plane, a piper cub, up from Traverse City yesterday afternoon, and this morning began air-patrolling the area west of the prison with state police Corporal Raymond Zeni of the Marquette Post.

Two United States Coast Guard helicopters also were to be flown up here from Traverse City this afternoon, to be deployed in the manhunt. Use of helicopters for escaped convicts is believed to be the first in Upper Peninsula history. Negaunee, Ishpeming and Munising city police and Alger County sheriff's officers joined in the search today.

Officers this morning were checking a series of tips, one report concerned a fire seen last night several miles west of the prison, another was of two men seen at gravel pit near the Athens Mine in Negaunee, and a third concerned a report of two strange men two miles east of Munising.

Officers believe, however, that the convicts will remain "holed up" in the woods, where it is easy to hide less than 50 feet from a searcher, and wait for an opening at nightfall.

"We are checking and investigating every possible tip or lead," Captain Person said this morning.

"Every effort is being made to apprehend the convicts."

The Mining Journal was read with much interest in households all over the area. Lloyd Russell had made good on his famous boast. "There ain't no prison can hold me." He was on his way to becoming the most infamous outlaw in the annals of UP crime lore.

19

THe HunT InTensiFies

THE RESIDENTS IN AND NEAR THE CITY were fearful, for both themselves and their loved-ones. They alerted the police to everything that seemed the least bit suspicious, or just a bit out of place. They tuned in their radios and kept their children close to home. These men had killed before and were not to be taken lightly. These were not your run-of-the-mill walk-aways that summers often brought.

Captain Person sat in the operation center at state police headquarters basking in the warmth of the afternoon, which was a sharp contrast from the sharp of the morning cool. Reports had been coming in at a steady stream. His office had received almost sixty tips.

The morning's hunt had been concentrated in a triangular area south of the prison between County Road 553 and U.S. Highway 41. An intensive sweep was also made in South Marquette, where a convict had reportedly been seen in two different places within the space of an hour.

"At 6:55 am, a cab driver told one of the city boys he saw one of the convicts at the corner of Champion and Genessee streets. The call was relayed to us and we dispatched seven patrol cars and fourteen officers," Person said. "The area was totally canvassed and no one was found."

Sightings occurred in the Park Cemetery area but the general consensus was that the remaining convicts were not believed to be in the city proper. The room was buzzing loudly and he would regularly wave a hand to silence the attending officers and newsmen. "We're gonna get a lot of false alarms, but we have to treat each call as the real McCoy. Don't be lax out there."

He went on to state that additional manpower was provided by twenty five National Guardsmen from Marquette Company B and Ishpeming Headquarters and Service Company. "Governor Williams has authorized 100 guardsmen from the 107th Engineer Battalion to be ready to jump in."

"Who's in charge of them?" Hathaway asked.

"Let's see. Lt. Col. Leonard C. Ward, that's what Warden Jacques said. The warden stated that the governor said it was his call to make. Up to Jacques, I mean."

"How's the cottage-to-cottage and camp-to-camp search going?"

"It's slow going. Finding the places on the plat map. We have three conservation officers leading our men." Person found a sheet and read off their names. "Alger Lahti, Arthur Saviluoto, and Frank Marshall. I'm told they know the area. That's a plus."

"Has there been any recent break-ins? As cold as the nights have been, I'd seek shelter." A reporter from Escanaba said.

"None reported. Sooner or later they've got to make a break for it." Hathaway said. "They are just not made up to stay put too long."

Up until noon, no cars had been reported stolen. No crimes attributed to the escaped felons had occurred. Most of the tips merely resulted in the rousting of harmless drunks, vagrants, hobos, hitchhikers and fishermen.

Captain Person emphasized that people should not hesitate to phone in anything they regarded as suspicious. "We're asking for the cooperation of everyone, especially those living in the outlying areas on cottages, farms, etc.—to be on the alert."

He further noted that Earl Hathaway's expertise as a blockade specialist had helped them seal off the immediate area as well as key points elsewhere in the U.P. "I believe Earl has them contained for he reacted without hesitation and got his men in place."

Again they misjudged Lloyd R. Russell.

The men in the operation center started to move about, indicating that the briefing was over. The search commander added a footnote, "We'll stick to the local search pattern until we have conclusive proof that the fugitives are no longer in the area."

As evening approached, the first report of any consequence from the north part of the city came in when the night watchman at the Gannon Lumber Company's mill, off County Road 550 said he saw two men sneaking around the mill. He shouted to them to stop, but they ran away.

Michigan State Police," the duty officer answered. Catching what seemed like his 100th call of the day.

"Officer, this is Edward Gauthier, I own the little grocery on the corner of Seventh and Spring Street. You know where it is?"

"Yes sir, how can we help you?"

"Well, after thinking about it, I think it was him. I mean, it was one a those bad guys, and he was here, right in my store. You know one a them boys broke out of the prison."

"Tell me sir. What did he look like? What made you think it was him? What was he wearing? It couldn't have been in prison duds. How long ago he leave?"

"He had a tattered coat and his pants were ripped in the seat. I'm sure it was him, from his picture, I mean. The ones in the Mining Journal. She thinks it was him, too."

"Who would that be?" The officer busied himself, putting out the call.

"A lady here in the store with me. She met him coming in. Told me right off, he looks like one a them convicts." He added in a whisper, "I sold him some milk and crackers."

Sounding more than ever like a routine tip, the tattered coat and ripped trousers indicating a passing hobo. "I don't think those escapees took cash with them, so how is he buying milk and crackers? Don't you worry, I'm sending cars out now."

They soon converged on the vicinity of the store, moving cautiously as they arrived. City Patrolmen Tom Christunas and Warner Wieland began closing in from the west side of Spring Street while Sheriff Al Jacobson and Under-sheriff Adrian Pequet along with police clerk Joe McDonald began driving in from the east.

They spotted movement up the tracks—human movement....

"Over there, by the tracks," Christunas spotted a figure skirt around an iron ore car on the South Shore Railroad tracks. He and Wieland exited their cruiser and started pursuit on foot. At the end of Spring Street, the furtive man slipped back to the other side of the iron car. The pursuing officers directed their flashlights at him as Christunas fired a warning shot in the air.

"We're police officers, stop or we'll shoot."

They listened to the shuffling on the opposite end of the car, the warning shot had not flushed the suspect out, which indicated he may have something to hide.

The sheriff and his crew held their positions as they witnessed the two city cops close in. Christunas took the right side of the car, Wieland—the left. They converged on the suspect and Wieland immediately snapped the cuffs on the over-matched hobo.

"All clear, we got him." Christunas shouted.

"Let's go," Wieland said, "It's back to the joint for you."

"Well, who do we have here?" The arresting officers admired their catch. Joseph Saunders, alias; Frank Pizchowiak shook his head and sighed. His taste of freedom had lasted less than two days.

This time the state police escorted their new captive to the operation headquarters, where he was soon undergoing an interrogation.

10:30 pm—Captains Person and Hathaway were joined by Sergeant James A. Smith, for the questioning of Saunders.

Saunders denied knowing where the other fugitives were. "I became aware I was separated from the rest ten minutes after the break. The ran too fast for me."

"Where'd you get the money for the milk and crackers?" Smith asked.

"Someone threw it over the wall to me when we got out," was the seasoned reply. Hardened criminals were not an easy interview. And this one had spent most of his adult life going through this type of questioning. "I got a lot a friends inside, one a them must have thought I could use a buck or two on the outside."

Saunders allowed that he spent Friday night near the Cliff's Power & Light Company's dam, on the Carp River. He would not say anything about the others. Like Burgdurf, Saunders was brought back and placed in a disciplinary cell. The 55 year-old, convicted of armed robbery in Genessee County, was back in 'Little Alcatraz,' to finish serving out his 'life sentence.'

Sunday, May 24—Warden Jacques held an afternoon briefing with the principal law officers that included the media. He would be the last political appointee to hold the warden position in the state of Michigan.

He disclosed that two inmates were wounded by the escapees during Friday's breakaway. Jacques said that the inmates, whose names were not given, were cut with knives when they apparently objected or interfered in some other way with the convicts making their escape. They would not say who stabbed them in fear of retribution. Prison rules demanded it.

One inmate was cut in the abdomen and the other was cut in the arms and neck. Both were hospitalized and later released.

Warden Jacques said it was first believed that the two inmates had a scuffle between themselves. Due to the escape and search activities, the matter was not given much attention. Prison officials later discovered that it was not a routine matter.

One of the other inmates told the warden that they had given the escapees "a little lip," and had "popped off," and we were "put in our places," by the escaping convicts.

The injured inmates did not want retaliation when or if the fugitives were returned. The prison code of silence was being honored, and was coupled with the prevailing wisdom, the chance of escape from Little Alcatraz was slim and none.

20

THE TRACKS AT CHERRY CREEK

THE TWO COAST GUARD HELICOPTERS FROM the USCG's Air-Land-Sea Rescue Base at Traverse City, the only base of its kind in the country, were used in the search over the weekend. They were sent back on Monday morning in the event of an emergency arising elsewhere.

The tips received were sometimes odd in their nature. An investigation of a campfire turned out to be a local resident, Fred Keel of Marquette, who was training his beagle hounds in the dark. Duke Delayre, standing atop the Fisher Street hill saw two men run from the hill north toward the South Shore Railroad tracks.

Friday night's march south had proved to be a stroke of luck. The four men found the traveling much easier than anticipated. The bright moonlight provided a beam of light that guided them through the rugged terrain. The occasional light blinking in the distance was a rare north bound auto weaving along what Russell suspected was U.S. Highway 41.

He had poured over maps in the prison library, managing to filch a copy for the escape. Thus far, it was working according to plan.

The winding highway, full of sharp twists and turns drew them close to it at times, then would disappear for stretches, and would reappear off in the distance. The terrain was hilly and at times rocky, but the going was made easier by the early season growth. Later into the season the woods and fields would thicken and make travel difficult at best.

"How much further we going? My feet are killing me," John McDowell complained. "I ain't used to this shit."

"Hold it, I hear water running up ahead." Russell ignored the man's plight. "Soak 'em in there for a minute. But, I don't give a shit about your feet. You just gotta keep movin' or stay with the vultures. I don't give a damn."

The earth grew damp, a promise of the spring run-off rushing toward a stream that would ultimately flush itself into the Lake Superior watershed.

Minutes, later, Russell called a halt. "Charles, you and McDowell take the lead. We're gonna do what we discussed earlier." Russell's preparation was thorough. "C'mon John, try to stay in Charles' footprints." They wanted it to appear as though only two sets of footprints crossed. They navigated the creek and the muddy ground surrounding it and quickly crossed the highway. "Head across that farm yard, keep low."

"Shit, that fuckin' mutt is gonna give us away." A neighboring dog yelped a greeting.

The four men froze—like deer in the headlights...

"Keep movin." Russell prodded the men forward—the moment of panic ebbing. "We're in the open, let's get across the yard. Hurry up."

The foursome gained the safety of a large building and slipped into the large bay of a hay barn. The large opening allowing for the hay to be unloaded to the lofts above on both sides. Large forks attached to pulleys dangled above their heads looking ominous in the dim light. They were used to draw the loose hay into the barn.

Morning light was fast approaching, the night shades of black, thinning to gray. "Let's climb up into that mow right now." Russell grabbed a pitchfork for a weapon, then just as quickly threw it down. "Just our luck somebody'll need it and come looking."

"This ain't the fanciest joint I ever slept in, but I'll take it, Morrison yawned. "This is where that saying comes from; Let's hit the hay."

The men scrambled up the ladder built into the barn wall. The roomy loft was missing most of its winter load. "Most likely they fed the cattle after evening milking so we should be safe for a while. Damn, that daylight snuck up quick."

McMackin stretched out on the loose hay, "Hell, I kin use a nap, I've had a busy night."

That got a chuckle out of the whole gang, who realized just how tired they were. The adrenaline used in the breakout had kept them going all night. "I'll keep watch first," the balding con said, "we don't want anyone visiting us in the middle of a snoring session."

Roy Conant's dog's continuous barking had failed to alarm Roy or his wife. Even the fact that she was running back and forth between the house and Cherry Creek did little to roust him from his bed. The dog had done that many times before.

It wasn't until a neighbor informed Roy Saturday afternoon about the massive escape did he consider calling the sheriff. That afternoon he finally made the call about the dog's antics.

After Conant's call, officers rushed to the scene to investigate, near the creek they found a sandwich wrapper, then spied two sets of tracks in the muddy earth. The tracks led across Conant's neighbor's farm yard, and in each case a big track was made first, then a shorter print followed directly in the steps of the bigger one. It became apparent that it was a ploy to give the impression that there were only two men crossing. Could it be the Russell bunch?

They checked all the residents in the area, and no one reported seeing any strangers in the area since the break. They decided that this was at least six and one half, maybe seven miles from the prison. The escapees would have had to have made superb time to have come this far. As rugged as the going had to have been, it would have been a significant feat. One that was highly unlikely considering the convicts lack of knowledge of the area.

The excitement continued Sunday night which stirred up a large contingent of townspeople. Between 6:00 and 9:00 pm it was reported that four men had crossed U.S. 41, near Coles Hill. An abandoned campfire was also sighted south of the Brewery Location.

Monday's Mining Journal—Large Crowd On Coles Hill

WITHIN MINUTES, SEVERAL THOUSAND TOWNSPEOPLE LINED up along the highway and viewed the proceedings from the hill overlooking the South Shore Railroad tracks. Between 300 and 400 hundred private automobiles were parked along the highway, slowing traffic considerably, and almost snarling it at times.

The investigation disclosed that the four men were actually three boys and a dog who had been seen crossing the highway. The campfire was found to be an innocent adventure.

The newspaper went on to report that every camp and cottage in the area was being checked for possible ransacking, and every road and trail in the district was under close watch.

All trains were slowed down and inspected before they left the area.

"We believe the convicts are still within the immediate area of the prison," Captain Person said. "We are following up on every lead in hopes of catching them when they finally make their break through the blockade."

The radio stations repeated their public announcements urging people to keep an eye on their personal weapons, especially those living in the outlying districts.

Word spread that Mrs. Robert Wallenstein, home alone in her cottage at Lakewood while her husband was at work, plunked herself down in her living room with a double barrel shotgun across her lap, vowing to shoot anyone who tried to enter unannounced.

Saturday morning in the hayloft provided little sleep. The barn's owner bustled about below them, entering the barn just an hour after they had settled in. He was a small dairy farmer who went about milking his small herd of cows and tending to his other barnyard chores. At the moment he was moving what sounded like heavy cans about.

The foursome lay in the dappled sunlight unable to sleep. If one dozed off and began to snore, he was immediately and rudely shook awake. The loft hideaway had not been the perfect place to roost.

The fact that it was Saturday, unsettled Lloyd Russell immensely. His meticulous planning had not considered a Saturday morning holed up in a farmer's loft. He forced the others to stay put and keep quiet while he tracked the farmer's movements.

On a day like this, anything could come into play. Kids were out of school, a hayloft was a popular place to roust about. Play tag, hide and seek, take the neighbor girl up here to learn a little about the birds and the bees—Lloyd knew the possibilities, he was raised in a farming community.

The farmer could get company—yes, anything could happen. Minutes later, he listened as a vehicle entered the farmyard and approached the barn. The scraping of hydraulic brakes and the pull of a diesel engine indicated that it was a truck. The driver positioned the truck, backing it into the designated spot as the farmer shouted out instructions.

Lloyd worked his way to a crack in the barn siding and looked down into the yard below.

Almost directly below him, a curly-haired man who appeared to be in his early twenties jumped out of the truck and greeted the farmer. They began loading heavy milk cans into the back of the truck with **Northern Dairy** in large letters on the side.

Straining intently, he could make out the voices floating up to him. He was quite sure he had heard the farmer tell the driver that 'he was taking the missus into town' as soon as the chores were done. The driver handed him a receipt for the milk and climbed into the truck.

"See you Monday, Cliff. Have a good weekend. Are you pitching yet?"

"We start practice next week, but we don't have a game until after Memorial Day."

"Okie dokey, see you then."

The wait was less than an hour before they heard the front door of the farmhouse open and close as the farmer and his wife climbed into a Chevrolet pickup and drove out of the yard, heading for their Saturday afternoon shopping trip.

Lloyd felt the relief flowing in. *Good. I didn't want to kill them.*

The foursome made their way down the loft and slipped into the nearby woods undetected—long before Roy Conant made his call.

21

THE TAILOR

High Society Struts At Kennedy Wedding
By Agnes McClosky

NEW YORK, MAY 23—IN A WEDDING sparkling with pomp, orchids, and champagne, a radiant Eunice Mary Kennedy became the bride today of Robert Sargent Shriver, Jr. It was one of high society's fanciest flings since the heyday of the four hundred.

Intimates of Financier-Philanthropist Joseph P. Kennedy, the bride's father, who was once U.S Ambassador to Great Britain, would neither confirm nor deny published estimates that the opulent affair cost in excess of $100,000.

The 1,700 hundred guests joined the bridal couple in the white-flowered starlight roof of the Waldorf-Astoria Hotel where a luncheon reception was followed by dancing that continued for hours.

Sunday, the weatherman decided that it was time for a change. A cold, driving-rain made life miserable for all who had to venture into it. The mercury had dropped to thirty eight degrees and was the coldest late May temperature in many years. It was only six degrees above the record low for this date, that having been recorded in 1931.

A check with local assistant meteorologist Emil Ellington confirmed that last night's winds had reached upwards of 40 miles per hour and that today's high would max out at fifty degrees. The long range projection was for slightly below average temperatures. The searching officers needed accurate weather forecasts to aid in their search plans.

The capture of Saunders led the locals to believe that more of the escapees could be lurking in the area. Possibly they were attempting to board an outgoing freight or passenger train. Many went to their respective homes and dug out their weapons, loading their shotguns and deer rifles to protect themselves amidst the almost hourly sightings, especially around the Ridge Street cemetery.

The Mining Journal

OFFICERS DIRECTING THE CONVICT MANHUNT, THE first in the history of Michigan in which helicopters were used, speculate that Morrison, who shot (wounded) three police in a supermarket stickup in Lansing and Russell, the Ohio desperado, who wounded a state policeman, may be competing for the leadership of the group. Convicts generally thrive on leadership.

Podolski, who killed a policeman in Detroit during a jewel robbery, also is regarded as being one of the most dangerous of the group, and officers in the search are warned that ("they'll stop at nothing to avoid capture.")

I've been duped. John Podolski, the tailor, was having a bout of deep frustration. *I'm one fuckin' dummy.* His annoyance was reaching new heights.

He didn't like traveling at night. He was leery of the bright moonlight. He had been separated soon after they took flight from the prison. Had they shaken free of him on purpose? Was that the plan? The younger ones had disappeared right quick, within ten minutes of the break. The Tailor stopped to clean his glasses; his left eye casting outward, wandering on its own as realization set in. *Yup. I've been duped. I was the patsy all along.*

He rose from the boulder that he had been sitting on, enjoying the last of his smokes. He used them sparingly, savoring them by smoking just half of one at a time. He spit a glob of greenish phlegm onto the ground. *Piss on it—I'm on my own.*

"I'm screwed, it just a matter of time before they pinch me, then it's back to the joint for me."

He didn't like traveling during the daylight hours. He kept seeing cars, people, and airplanes. He'd duck into the thick brush and woods every time anyone was near. *There must be seven, eight planes up there always circling, and at least a couple of them whirlybirds.* "I'm an idiot," he said aloud. "Can anyone be this dumb?"

To add further to his vexation was he kept getting lost. He couldn't seem to get away from that damn big lake. He couldn't escape Lake Superior. Every time he had a clear view of the countryside, there was that damn water. He could not seem to steer clear of her. She taunted him with a wave of her clear blue water, beckoning with a frothy white splash from her magnificent hand.

May 25, 1:55 pm

PODOLSKI FOLLOWED THE RAILROAD TRACKS, MOVING along slow, casual, like he hadn't a care in the world. He was on the edge of a town, its name he wasn't sure. Had the look of a mining town, he saw a sign, **Negaunee,** printed in block letters. What the hell kind of name is that?

Chicago & North Western Railroad was emblazoned on the side of a car when he spotted two men. "Freeze," the bigger of the two spoke from behind the pistol aimed at him.

"Don't shoot, I'm not armed," Joseph Podolski, alias Martin Majewski, was heading back to serve his life sentence.

While prison guard William Williams trained his weapon on the prisoner, his fellow Marquette guard Reino Sippola used the state police walkie-talkie to radio in their capture. "We got Podolski here at Buffalo Location by the LS&I junction over by the Athens Mine," the heavily loaded Finnish accent informed.

"What street do we come in on, over?"

"Ann Street." Williams nodded the affirmative. "Yup, come in on Ann Street."

State Police Sergeant George Strong, wounded by the Russell brothers back in '50 came for the prisoner. The bullet fired from the stolen rifle by the fleeing Lloyd Russell had pierced the radiator of his police car, then ricocheted from the steering column and came up through the dashboard. Strong had been in serious condition from the four fragment wounds below the knee and the shrapnel wound in his arm. Luckily, no bones had been fractured and all that remained were the scars as a daily reminder.

Lloyd Russell—again. Sergeant Strong was anxious to see the man and his gang back behind bars.

His prisoner seemed resigned to his fate and said little on the short trip back to Marquette.

Strong welcomed the silence...

Captains Person and Hathaway greeted Strong and his prisoner upon the return to the prison. The interrogation commenced shortly thereafter, Once again it was in Jacques' office. Like the other captured convicts, Podolski didn't know where the other four were.

"These stories are beginning to sound all alike," Person summed it up after the intense grilling of the latest returnee was completed.

Hathaway agreed, adding, "It sure as hell looks like the older ones were used as decoys by the four younger ones. They lost Podolski 10-15 minutes after they broke out."

"They might have sacrificed them by sending them west while they headed southeast to Alger County," Person's suspicion was right on the money.

That was just a few of the suppositions the officers tossed about as they voiced their opinions of the actions of the remaining four men and their desperate bid for freedom. They guessed that the older three were sent west to get plucked off individually, one by one, at the same time luring the search party to concentrate on the area of the latest arrest, while the foursome sought safe haven in the opposite direction.

Sergeant Smith recalled how Lloyd Russell, most likely the group's leader, "laid low" in the Sault Ste. Marie area for ten days, then stole a car when most everyone thought that they had moved on to Canada. They had been captured by sheer coincidence, when they ran smack dab into a blockade set up in Seney to stop Willie Jackson.

The consensus among the officers was that the rest were still holed up in the heavily-wooded area within 12 miles or so of the prison. The feeling was based on the fact that Russell, who had trouble with blockades in the past, would argue with Morrison, who had successfully run a blockade in his sordid past. The thinking was, sooner or later he would convince his cronies to steal a car and ram it through a road block.

"What did you think of Podolski having that cash on him?" Hathaway chuckled.

During the usual "shakedown" of the convict, the officers asked him if he had any money.

"Money," Podolski mused, as he unbuttoned his shirt, as if to say he was yearning for some cash.

"In other words, you're flat broke."

"I'm so broke, I can't pay attention."

Just before the shakedown was concluded, Prison Inspector Charley Aho calmly unfolded the prisoner's left hand, and found $21.00 (two tens and a single), which had been carefully folded up and hidden under his thumb.

The cash had apparently been in Podolski's possession since before the break, because it was worn and showed evidence of being folded for a very long time.

Tuesday, May 26—The Mining Journal

CAPTAINS PERSON AND HATHAWAY ISSUED JOINT statements today in the wake of the third escaped fugitive captured yesterday in Negaunee.

Captain Hathaway is principally on the blockade job in the search for the remaining four. The 7th District Commander is an 'old hand' at blockades and the belief prevails if they try to 'run' them, they will have a tough job getting through.

Russell is believed wearing a Marquette Prison guard cap and officers have not ruled out the possibility that they may try to grab a hostage to enable them to go through a blockade.

They also sense there will be a gun battle with the convicts before they are apprehended. The thought being that they will arm themselves before they make a run.

Last evening state police asked radio stations WDMJ and WJPD to broadcast calls to the effect that they would pick up the guns which had been left in cabins since the deer season.

Within a short time, the state post police post was literally swamped with calls, and officers had to cancel the request, as calls were clogging up the phone lines.

Officers continued making a cottage-to-cottage and camp-to-camp canvass for possible break-ins, all patrol cars on free-lance detail (not on a specific assignment) were sent to investigate all side roads, cottages and any abandoned farms they may run across.

Up to this morning, no cars had been reported stolen and an average of 20 tips or more were coming in daily. Each tip was investigated thoroughly.

None of the convicts captured so far had any weapons, that meant the four at large still possessed the knives. Although, most believed the convicts were still in close proximity, they extended blockade points out further to Iron Mountain and Menominee due in part, to some of the tips. The state police blotter noted:

1. - Tip in early afternoon of the two men on Highway M-48, at Trout Lake (Chippewa County) who had made no special effort to hide their faces.
2. - Tip at 4:36 pm from South Shore railroad foreman, who saw two men walking hurriedly on the tracks from Sands.
3. - Tip at 6:45 pm at Crystal Falls, motorists see two hitchhikers go into the woods, and of seeing them swerve into a side road and disappearing.
4. - Jack Patton, owner of the Tioga Tavern on M-28, near Deerton, along with another man chased two men into the woods in the rear of the tavern. Police are watching the area closely.
5. - A man, teaching his daughter how to drive, saw two men near National Mine jump into the woods when he drove within 100 yards of them. He drove further along the road but did not see the men come out of the woods.

The police blotter further noted that a man was jailed on a charge of tipsy driving after he was stopped at a roadblock in Negaunee Township.

The residents of the city of Marquette relaxed a little after a tension packed weekend. With Podolski's capture in Negaunee, the general belief was that the remaining ones still on the loose, were hiding in the woods.

The conditions of the Upper Peninsula's swamps and forests would claim their victory. Coupled with nature's icy blasts and unyielding insect population, it was just a matter of time.

22

This Town Is Too Hot

THE COLD RAIN HAD FINALLY SUBSIDED and did much to improve the spirits of the four men. Sunday had been a particularly troublesome day. It had been a divided camp as Morrison advocated a break from their less than ideal conditions. He argued vehemently with Russell, with clenched fists, he was about to commit a mutinous act, "I'm takin' that car, and I'm outta here. Fuck them road blocks..."

"Over my dead ass, Charles. That car stays where it is—until I say different."

"I kin go through you Lloyd, you ain't my keeper. I decide to take that ride, you'll have to go over my dead body to stop me."

"Have it yer way, I kin arrange that in a heart-beat. Sometimes you act as crazy as a goose flying backwards."

"Yer a shrimp, I got you by twenty pounds. And, I'm fast and I'm tough."

"Don't be so sure a that, I've taken down bigger men than you—much bigger..." The soft-spoken reply carried a malice that was flung like a hammer.

Joseph McMackin rubbed his tired hazel eyes and emitted a sigh of relief when he heard Morrison begin to joke around with Russell. Not that Russell ever joked with anybody, yet the tension eased like the hammer being slowly released on a twelve-gauge shotgun.

"Jesus, you guys, we're in this together."

At five foot ten, Joe actually was the second tallest of the remaining four. He carried a medium frame that housed 153 pounds, he was wiry and he was scrappy. An old fracture set his nose slightly crooked to its left, and gave the armed robber a sort of ruggedness to his almost handsome face. As the cold, driving rain forced its way into their makeshift camp, tempers had shortened with each blast of the freezing air. John McDowell, Joe's best friend in the stir, had sided with Morrison in voicing a desire to steal a car and make a dash out of the area.

In the early hours of Sunday, they had discovered a car housed in a barn near their hideout. Morrison and McDowell opted to run for it, blast through whatever blockades they had to run, and head hell-bent for Wisconsin. Russell insisted on waiting, said he would kill any man who tried to steal the car before the time was ripe. Something the other three fugitives did not doubt that he could do. It would be through him if anyone was to remove the car.

"Lemme tell youse two something right now, and you better lissen up—I ain't going back to the joint. Not tonight, not never. I brung you guys along so we all would be free. You wanna fuck this up, you get outta my sight right now. And, you're going without the car."

The seething voice was a deadly rattle, "You fuckers try to screw this up by trying to take that car, yer dead. Real dead."

"Easy, Lloyd," McMackin soothed, "you're the boss. Nobody has a problem with that."

Morrison still shook, and it wasn't from the cold. His violent nature had taken hold of him. He struggled now to control himself.

Russell slacked off, giving the other man room, giving him a chance to save face.

Finally..."Yeah, that's right, Lloyd. It's this fuckin' weather. I lost my cool, is all."

Joe McMackin broke the impasse. "We're all cool. You got us this far, we'll follow you the rest of the way out. You're the boss. Right, boys?"

The murmured reply was in agreement.

The crisis passed. Russell pointed out the safety of their hideout, the neighboring farms that they could raid furnishing them with fresh milk, poultry, and meat. "I'll show you how to live off the land. There's lotsa grub here, we kin wait out the law."

McMackin had pleaded with the volatile men, and had at least temporarily convinced McDowell that waiting was the best thing to do. Morrison's quick temper ebbed, and they struggled through the damp, bone chilling night enjoying a repast of chicken courtesy of the farmer who owned the automobile.

Russell had grabbed a pail from the first barn where they had spent their first night, and had boiled the chicken in it, first plucking the feathers. He gathered leeks and used the onion-like bulbs to season the chicken. He had it boiling in a bucket.

He ordered his 'city slicker' cohorts to dig up burdock root with a shovel they found behind the barn. They were stuck with burrs from their socks to the hair on their heads, as the tall plants hugged them all over while they worked. Muttering as they worked, they smoothed the ground and returned the shovel where they found it. They agreed, returning the 'borrowed' items would keep their new neighbors from becoming suspicious.

Last night's dinner was a surprising delight. The chicken was moist and delicious, well-seasoned and tender, the boiled burdock gave them a potato-like flavor that was passable but needed butter. Fresh greens, dandelion and purslane, a bit bitter and could have used a dressing, were consumed entirely as Russell pointed out their nutritional value. "There's lotsa vitamins in those greens. These are a little bitter, they taste better when they first pop up."

The tea, he made out of leaves he called herbs, was delicious, a real treat after the meal was finished, it pleased them with a fine mint flavor. It cleaned their breath, leaving their mouth with a fresh taste, since the brushing of their teeth had been sorely neglected. Russell insisted that they boil the water that came from the nearby creek before drinking it. Lloyd Russell would keep them alive and fed with the knowledge he had absorbed while timing their breakout.

The following morning which McMackin decided was Tuesday was their fifth day out. He and Russell had gone back to the barn and had gathered enough eggs to boil for breakfast. "Leave some, we don't want the old man getting suspicious. Tomorrow," Russell whispered, "I'm gonna teach you how to milk a cow. But, today, I'm gonna go fishing."

"Your kidding, I ain't seen a lake. You gonna fish in a mud hole?"

"The crick has got them little speckled trout in it. They're tasty little buggers."

Soon he was busy fastening a makeshift hook on to a string that was attached to a fairly straight stick he had discovered on one of his foraging trips. He had caught a glimpse of a speckled fish darting in and out of the rocky shoals before settling in a deeper pool of the nearby creek. He knew that the rocks and debris housed worms and grubs, all the bait he would need to entice the tasty brookies. Lloyd Russell had promised his men a fish supper.

The boy scrambled among the rocks looking for more crayfish. The 'cheese-whiz' jar that he squeezed in his left hand, held two of the crab-like crustaceans. "There's one"—he leaped to a rock ready to pounce on it when a whirring sound grew near and shattered the still air.

The seven year-old lad spun out of his crouch and looked up at the helicopter circling down on him. "Holy s—t," he yelled as he splashed across the creek and up its bank. He dropped the jar as he scampered up the steep embankment on to the gravel road.

"It's only a youngster playing in the creek," the passenger told the pilot. "Let's follow this east to the Slap Neck."

"Roger."

The boy darted up North Ferguson Road, his short legs churning up the gravel as fast as they could take him. He looked back over his shoulder at the retreating helicopter.

"Mom, Mom." He burst into the front porch where his mother was wringing out clothes through the Kelvinator washing machine. "I just saw the Highway Patrol in a chopper."

"That's nice dear, I have to get these clothes on the line, then I'll fix you lunch. How about a nice grilled cheese sandwich on homemade bread?"

"Sounds good. But honest, Ma. It was Broderick Crawford and the cops. The f—rs swooped right down on me, they were practically in the creek."

"Watch your tongue, young man. I should wash your mouth out with soap." She picked up the clothes basket and pushed it through the screen door. "Ever since the Salo boys came back from Korea, you've been talking just awful."

"Aw, Ma—I'm sorry. What were they looking for?" He followed her to the clothesline.

"Oh my, I bet it's that Lloyd Russell. They're looking for him. Until they catch him, you are to stay in the yard."

"Aw—Ma..."

The two storms subsided, the one furnished compliments of Mother Nature, and the other, more violent and lethal was man-made, both had been endured or diverted.

"Dammit, be quiet, he could be up in another hour or so. We gotta work fast, save some milk so the farmer don't notice."

"I don't think I kin milk no fuckin' cow."

"Shush, I'll do it this time, Joe. Just pay attention. All you gotta do, is hold 'em like this, then squeeze them teets, aim it into the bucket."

"The tits? Man alive, those tits are ugly. The farmer gotta put 'em in a brassiere."

"Yeah, sure Joe. Act yer age..."

23

THE WAITING GAME

The Mining Journal – Wednesday, May 27

LAW ENFORCEMENT OFFICERS CONDUCTING THE SEARCH for the four ruth-
less criminals who fled Marquette Prison on Friday, intensified their search
within the immediate area of the prison today in the belief that the fugitives were "lying low" and waiting for an opportunity to get through the
blockade.

Lloyd Russell, Charles Morrison, Joseph McMackin, and John Mcdowell were described by officers as "dangerous convicts who will stop at nothing to elude capture.

In disciplinary cells within the prison are the three older convicts—
caught one by one, who claim that the other four planned the escape
and invited them along the night before. Late this morning, a group of 30
state police and prison guards, under the supervision of Sergeant Anthony
Spratto, began sweep of the Carp River, from the original point from where
the felons left the prison on Friday.

Dozens of tips have been received since the sensational break, and
practically all have proven unfounded, following their investigation by
officers.

Events during the night and early today have illustrated two things:

The speed with which leads are probed and the long distance to which the search has spread were cited. Several examples of the officers' efficiency and the swiftness of the "cleanup" of suspicious reports are as follows:

1 – At 5:00 this morning, a motorist reported a suspicious man trying to flag him down on M-95 between Witch Lake and Republic – A state police spokesman said a motorist had a dead battery.
2 – 4:35 pm. Yesterday—The report of three strangers riding a gondola on the RR tracks south of Seney was checked and the men were not fugitives.
3 – State police from the Cheboygan post ran down the report of three unshaven men who purchased wine and cigarettes but there was no connection with the fugitives.

Causing the most excitement last night were two reports (received within ten minutes of each other) from two motorists, one of whom had his wife along, of a man crossing highway M-28, beyond the Marquette-Alger county line. He was seen heading into the woods, in the vicinity where the convicts could be hiding. Both motorists and the wife of one identified the man as being Joseph McMackin.

Checked immediately by its six officers in three patrol cars, it was discovered that the man was a tourist employee, looking for water from a creek, as the radiator of his old model car, which had been further down the highway, had run dry.

Some of the calls police must spend time and effort on are quite obviously useless, but this is not discovered until the report has been probed. One of these incidents is shown by the "bread incident" of yesterday afternoon.

A woman on a farm near Rock summoned officers, saying she had seen a man near a swamp, and that it was possible, "a barn had been ransacked."

Sent to the scene was State Police Sergeant Edward Goldsworthy, of Gladstone, Raymond

Rudman and Richard LaCosse, of Marquette, Trooper Bruno Guzin, Wakefield, and Trooper

Hershal Barton, Rockford, and Deputy Sheriffs Cully Johnson and Elmer Lepisto, Gladstone.

Officers found a part of a sandwich (one slice of bread, folded over), in the barn, and this could be important, since the bread could be checked with the type baked in the Marquette area. However, the search disclosed, the bread came from the kitchen of the woman who called in the report.

"This case shows how we sometimes have to put a lot of effort on a tip," Captain Person, directing the manhunt pointed out. "We are investigating every report regardless of how vague."

Rain and cold weather may have been hampering the movements of the convicts, but with clear and warmer weather today, this situation could change.

The story went on to say that the law found it impossible to search the entire wooded area. They cited the vast expanse alone, plus the heavily-wooded and hilly area caused many logistical problems. The U.P. forests that in the past had spit out those who had used them to avoid detection was now hiding the Russell gang.

Answering a direct inquiry from a reporter, Captains Person and Hathaway, admit that blood-hounds would "definitely be an asset in a break such as this." (There is no provision for the use of bloodhounds by law officers).

The captains agreed that, since the trails of the convicts were discovered near the prison within twenty minutes after the break, the blood-hounds could have proven of immeasurable value. They noted, that the hounds must be well-trained and are costly to maintain, but that the manhunt, likewise, is at a premium.

However, because of a strong loyalty and great devotion between Lloyd Russell, probable leader of the convicts, and his brother Paul, now imprisoned in Southern Michigan, at Jackson, officers say it is "not beyond the realm of possibility" that Russell, if he succeeds in getting away, will eventually go to Jackson to wait for his brother to make a break.

Two state police planes were still being used in the search today and the posses includes the same contingent of law officers.

Tension and terrorism has eased among Marquette area residents, with continued reassurances by Captain Person that all state police will remain in the area.

Officers do not anticipate that the fugitives will get away—without getting into gun battles with police.

On the humorous side, the chase is creating quite a hardship for the lumberjacks and hobos, used to sleeping anywhere on the streets or off the railroad tracks.

One bum, after being picked up by the police a second time, exclaimed with surprise, "Wow, this town is hot. Every time you wake up you find someone staring at you with a gun in your face."

Several harmless "floaters" have been warned to "straighten out" and avoid unnecessary investigations, or face vagrancy charges.

24

Pelissier Lake

Thursday, May 28—Headline—The Mining Journal

FUGITIVES SPLIT UP IN PAIRS— Belief among law enforcement officers this morning led them to concentrating their search for four escaped convicts in two major points:

(1) Near Pelissier Lake, eight miles south of Marquette Prison, and (2) near the Cusino Conservation Prison Camp.

The area near Pelissier Lake, northwest of the intersection of County Roads 480 and 553, in Sands Township, is where a logger last night reported seeing two men answering the description of Lloyd Russell and Charles Morrison, who are thought to be the leaders in the sensational break from Marquette Prison.

Alger County Sheriff Arthur Moote, who, with Munising Police Chief Urban Trombley and other Munising officers, has been working diligently on the convict search, saw two suspicious men this morning near Cusino, eight miles east of Munising.

State police this morning (at 12:45) received the first report of a stolen car in this area since the break, occurred. It was a pickup truck, owned by Joseph Hamel, of Champion, which was taken from his home in the village.

The truck was found by officers several hours later, abandoned on the new (unopened) Highway US 41, about ten miles east of Champion. Its left front was damaged, Officers, who checked the area thoroughly, said the keys had been left in the truck before the theft.

Police this morning checked the area near a spring, a half mile north of the Cooper Lake Road, in Ishpeming, where city police at 10:44 last night discovered fresh foot prints.

Such leads can never be discounted, officers point out, in as much as the fugitives must obtain their drinking water in this manner.

"The call came in at 7:35, Earl," Thor Person informed his counterpart as he entered the war room. "They tell us it looks like a solid lead." The six foot commander removed his police issue hat and tossed it on his desk. He combed his dark hair with his fingers, trying to shake out the matted snarls. "Damn, this is one tough job. Sometimes I feel like we're chasing our own tails, I need a week's sleep to catch up."

Earl Hathaway grabbed a chair from the corner and brought it to the desk. "Bring me up to snuff. I caught a little of it on the radio getting my ass over here."

Hathaway was a tall, slender man, towering almost six and a half feet. He kept his hat over his thinning gray hair as he sat down.

Sergeants Smith and Spratto were already seated for the briefing, anxious to get out into the field and chase down the new lead.

"A logger over in Sands Township cuttin' pulpwood said he saw a couple of guys acting suspicious. He saw them twice, the second time he got close enough to talk to them."

"He must have got a good look."

"Listen to this," the 8th District Commander's voice displayed its raised excitement level, "he described one as short and squatty, which could be Russell, the other one was taller, and resembled Morrison."

"Damn, he must have been crapping his pants when he recognized them."

"Especially, once he thought that's who they were. He said the first time he saw them, they had a box of food. The second time the box was gone."

"What kind of box?" Spratto said. "That could be important in determining where they're hiding."

"Darn right," Smith echoed, "We'll have to see if those suspects left it behind."

"Good point, let's make sure we follow up on that."

"What's the latest word from the scene? I had to put my headlights on while I was driving over here," Hathaway noted. "It'll be dark soon."

"I sent every available car as soon as the farmer called it in. Now, it looks like we'll have to drive the woods in the morning."

" The logger must have went to the nearest phone soon as he could get away."

"Yes. I would imagine he just couldn't excuse himself and race right out of there." Person nodded to the two sergeants. "Go ahead, check things out, and set things up for the morning."

Earl Hathaway leaned back, struck a match to his pipe, then puffed deliberately on the stem until the tobacco glowed, then sent a cherry flavored odor throughout the room. "Shows we're thinking along the right track, Thor."

The tobacco residue wafted over the captain's head as he replied, "Do you mean about them splitting up. Taking off in pairs?"

"You bet, if that logger is right, it looks like the four split up. That would give them a better chance for at least one, maybe two, getting away."

"The only thing that doesn't click here, Earl, is the pairing. We always figured Russell would take either McDowell or McMackin, and Morrison would go off with the other. The only thing that might make this sighting work, is, that the two Macs would insist on being together. Warden Jacques said that they were pretty close inside."

"Yeah, you would think that Russell would plan a long deliberate getaway, and—Morrison loves to move fast."

"One thing is for certain, you never know for sure what they will do. A man on the run is, unpredictable at best."

"Amen to that, Thor."

"Well, let's hope tomorrow, brings a few answers."

The cold, rainy weather had the officers believing that the fugitives wouldn't be out, moving about. The full moon was approaching, that could promote movement.

All U.P. Alerted

OFFICERS WERE ALSO CHECKING ON WHAT they suspect may be an important clue in a 1937 sedan which they found last night abandoned in the prison restricted area.

The car was found a mile south of the prison, on highway 41, near the rock cut. It had no license plates attached, but underneath the front seat were 1953 Illinois license plates, which earlier this year, had been stolen.

There were two sandwiches in the glove compartment and two socks near the Carp River, and further up the river they discovered an abandoned campfire.

The socks, found when they and other officers combed the area along the Carp, were positively identified as being prison issue socks.

At 1:42 pm yesterday afternoon, police probed a report of a man seen in the woods near Chatham Corners. This and other reports received from distant points prove that residents are on the alert throughout the Upper Peninsula.

Two unidentified men were seen in an abandoned coach on the railroad tracks east of Republic at 4:45 yesterday afternoon. They were eating lunch when an official of Lake Superior and Ishpeming Railroad Company came along, and the men dashed off into the woods. The men could have been hobos, but police aren't taking any chances, and are canvassing the area.

Baril Promoted By State Police, Gets Post In Marquette

PROMOTION OF SERGEANT LAWRENCE J. BARIL, COMMANDER of the East Lansing Post, to the rank of Lieutenant and his assignment as assistant commander of the eighth district with headquarters in Marquette was announced by Commissioner Joseph Childs.

Baril succeeds Lieutenant Willard Wixom, who recently retired. He is a native of the Upper Peninsula and was born in Lake Linden.

Had the four convicts, hunkered down in their lean-to, knew how much havoc and commotion they were causing, they would have busted a gut with laughter.

25

Meanwhile, Back At The Hideout

The Mining Journal—Sunday, May 30

Full Search On-Despite Pouring Rain

A DRENCHING RAIN WAS MAKING IT miserable in the woods for law enforcement officers and their quarry. Every available lawman was ordered to join the search in the area near Pelesier Lake, where at least two of the fugitives are believed to be hiding out.

Many of the officers have worked 14 to 16 hours in a stretch on the chase, but, were in the belief that "at least two convicts are there."

Alger County Sheriff Arthur Moote, Munising Chief Urban Trombly, and other local officers are working closely in the hunt near Shingleton.

"A man could hide in broad daylight only 10 or 15 feet away from a searching officer."

Located Thursday afternoon on the bank of the Chocolay River, southeast of the prison, was some fishing equipment. Included in the knapsack were a pair of socks (not prison issue) and bait. Officers said that would be insignificant, but for the fact that there was also a pouch of prison issue tobacco in the knapsack.

Police do not believe that the convicts would have abandoned the fishing equipment, which would have been of much value in the woods with their many trout streams.

Since all the fugitives are "escape artists" they would have expected to be in the woods for a long stay, and would be looking for all food sources.

John McDowell shivered in the damp lean-to that had been home for over a week. He ran a moist hand through his red hair and peered at the beads of rain drops trickling off the hideout's roof. He watched as Morrison played with the hatchet they had taken from a neighboring barn.

Red sat and reflected. He had already visited the real Alcatraz and had been transferred to Marquette from the federal pen at Leavenworth, Kansas. He finally broke the silence that had lasted for the past hour. "Charles, do you think he'll make a move tonight?"

"We gotta do it soon. Folks will put two and two together after we hit them cars last night. If we screw around here, we'll be getting heat around here real quick." He added, "Hell, I know when they took me down in Detroit, there was so many coppers I could a been Dillinger."

Joe McMackin slipped into the lean-to, shaking his drenched head like a mongrel pup, then gave an affirmative nod to his red-headed pal. "We wait a half-hour or so, till it gets good and dark. Lloyd's as tight as I've ever seen him."

"Where is he?" Morrison said, firing the hatchet into the soft earth.

"He's watching the bar, the ol' lady that owns it left in her car a while ago. Lloyd figgers this'll be a good time to go in."

"Man, I need a cigarette," Morrison moaned, "along with a nice tall drink served by a sexy blond with no clothes on."

McDowell, the oldest of the four at 39, grinned at the picture painted by Morrison's idea of life's creature comforts. "Naw, right now I'd settle for a Hershey bar, fed to me by a naked lady with really big hooters."

"Hooters? Do they hoot when you squeeze 'em?"

"No, they just make you hoot when you look at 'em, like you was an owl in heat."

"An owl in heat? John you been in the woods too long. We heard that owl barking behind us the other night, in the tree right there, wish I'd a knowed it was in heat."

"What would you have done? There ain't no branches near the ground. Fly up there?"

"I would a done something—hooters and all..."

"You believe it? It's Sunday already, we been on the lamb for nine days already."

"Yeah Joe, time flies when yer having fun."

Even through Russell's vast knowledge in gathering their meals, the foursome still lacked the everyday pleasures that most take for granted. The escapees had a keen insight into what it felt to be without these little necessities so their appreciation of them were ten-fold. The accumulative time spent in the penitentiaries around the country had not dampened their taste for life's finer pleasures.

"Okay Joe, it's been a half an hour, lead the way."

26

The Idle Time

THE RAIN HAD SUBSIDED WHEN THE the three men made their way through the thick, water-soaked underbrush to join Russell, who was crouched beneath a large maple tree, the leaves forming a protective canopy. They stared at the sign that bore the name, **The Idle Time Tavern,** then followed their leader as he approached the vacant bar.

"Let's try these windows in the back first. We can stay hid back here." Russell directed Morrison and McDowell, who possessed the pry tools. They attempted to open the rear windows, first one, then the other, under the stern warning of their leader. "Don't break any glass, the neighbors will hear it."

Morrison moved on to the the front, impatient to get in. He worked the front entry, which faced the south. He quickly smashed the cheap lock and entered the bar before the others could get around to join him.

"Inside, quick. Take what you want, but move it. We gotta be out in a heart beat."

The four men went about gathering the rewards the break-in offered. Russell constantly prodded them to move with haste and remain quiet. "Take just what we need. We gotta move. That's it, let's go."

"Here's a Hershey's—but its got nuts. No hooters."

"What the hell you talking about, Morrison?"

"It's a long story, Lloyd."

"We ain't got no time to hear it. Cut the bull shit. Grab those jackets off that rack, there by the door—they're gonna come in handy." He herded the men out while Morrison swiped the coat rack clean.

They made their way back to their woodland retreat with Russell admonishing the jubilant crew to keep it quiet. No one noticed the damp conditions as they hustled back.

"Dammit boys, you're acting like kids out for some 'trick or treats." The trek from the Idle Time to the hide-away seemed an eternity to the thirsty, sober foursome.

Back in the safe confines of the crude living quarters, the gang inventoried their night's work. Morrison lit a cigar as he took a pull from a bottle of beer. "Jesus, does that ever taste good, gimme a shot from that bottle, Red."

"Fuckin A, Chief. Here ya' go."

"Take it easy, we can't get rowdy. These woods got ears."

"You got it, boss, but the McDowells do love their whiskey."

"We split the money, in case we get separated," Russell announced after a quick count of the tavern's proceeds. "Over three hunnerd here, we'll get almost eighty bucks a piece. I always split fair, straight up the middle."

"We're rich, I'll drink to that."

"Once we're outta this state, I'll show you boys rich. I'm heading west, it's up to you if you wanna tag along."

Sitting there in their "new" shirts, the convicts were clean shaved, thanks to the meticulous planning of their leader. They hit the booze as though they were thirsty old sailors, reaching port after months at sea. The shirts, courtesy of the patrons of the Idle Time, were loose-fitting but passable.

None of the foursome was carrying any extra baggage, and they were all in above average shape, thanks to Russell's constant cajoling throughout the winter months. He had coaxed and prodded the men to walk and exercise. Finally— it had paid off.

Lloyd Russell knew that he couldn't hold the men back, and now that they were drinking, he also knew one other important truth. There would be no stopping these men from stealing the car from the barn, and making a run for the Wisconsin border. The only real question he had to answer is; *do I go with them?*

Officers thought they had a good lead on Sunday, when a resident in the Cornell area, south of Rock, said he saw a man in the woods. Officers combed the area, but found only footprints and one lone trout in the woods. Radio stations broadcast a report from police, asking all fishermen, who had been in the area to notify police.

Among those who did were three anglers who said they had been fishing in the area, and caught only one trout, the fishing was so bad that they had even lost the one trout they caught.

Since the state police had not told the fishermen about finding the trout, they knew, after checking time and location that the report was without merit.

The escapees continued drinking a heavy mixture of whiskey, wine, and beer. They were indulging in the spirits that had been off-limits to them for years. Sobriety, or lack of it—was about to become an important issue in their thought processes.

27

It's Party Time

"WHAT THE HELL WAS THAT? IS THERE SOMETHING OUT THERE?"

"I'll check 'er out, Lloyd." McMackin grabbed a stick and crept slowly toward the thrashing sound in the brush. "Dammit, I forgot all about you." His sheepish grin was wall to wall.

"What is it, Joe?" Lloyd's tone was losing its patience.

"It's the chicken we took this afternoon from that farm on the other side of the bar. You was there, Lloyd. It's just fussin,' doesn't like being tied up, is my guess."

"You didn't kill it?"

"Naw, we was gonna have her lay us some eggs first. We're city boys, we wanted to see how they did it. We always bought our eggs at the grocery."

"Did it lay a dozen eggs?" McDowell wanted to know.

"Hell no. They don't lay no dozen eggs a day. Go on, put some water to boil. We ain't eaten all afternoon. I'll show you what happens after that there chicken leaves the grocery store."

"All dat's missing now, is a few broads," Morrison took a deep pull from a beer bottle, then belched the gasses into the dense air. He was feeling surly, but was able to control most of his feelings. Russell didn't run him, not now, not ever, they were all free men.

"Why don't ya' give the chicken, oops, the chick, a good stiff drink. Loosen her up a bit, then she's likely to dance wit you."

"That's a good idea, c'mon here honey. Charles is buying. I tell you guys, three years ago it wasn't this much trouble. I just gave 'em a look."

"A look? What kind a look?" McDowell was interested. I ain't never lived on a farm, but I can't believe you can simply look at a chicken and make it lay eggs."

"You're a hoot John. I'm just saying, maybe I'm a little rusty wit the women—after three years. Wait, here she comes."

"He ain't shittin'—look at that, she went right up to him. She's slurping that beer like I ain't never seen."

"You ain't never seen? John ain't seen a live chicken before. It's that, or he ain't ever seen a woman. She's like other wimmen, only with feathers. Just get 'er drunk first."

"Wait a second," John chimed in. "That reminds me of a time I was down in Texas, down by the Mexican border, they served me drunken chicken there, come to think of it. Course, I was the drunk one, the chicken was just burnt."

"Pollo Borracho, John."

"What's that Joe?"

"Drunken chicken, or loco pollo, crazy chicken."

"Then, let's give 'er another one, we'll have us some drunken chicken."

"Look at her, she drinks like a damn fish."

McDowell stood up and clapped his hands together. Remember this one? I'm a getting' too old, too old..."

"There you go," Charles. John McDowell jumped right in, "I'm too old to cut the mustard anymore. Just toooo old..."

"The water's boilin'—anybody wanna skin the chicken?" The question was a real mood buster.

"Hell no, Lloyd. We was just gonna dance with her. Look at her go, just a flapping and staggering around. We're just having fun."

It appeared true, the chicken was loaded, not stuffed—simply inebriated. She was thoroughly enjoying herself. Feathers flew as she joined in with the revelers and put on a show of her own.

The voices grew louder and more boisterous within the lean-to as the drinking progressed. Lloyd finally pulled Joe McMackin aside as the talk turned to stealing the car in the barn and making a run for it. His mouth was set in grim determination as he struggled to maintain control of his temper and the men he led.

"How sober are you, Joe? Can you get that car running? I checked—the old man didn't leave the keys in it."

"Not a problem, I got a little buzz going—nothing I can't handle." He tossed his empty beer bottle on the ground, "I've hot-wired many an auto. I'll be fine." He took a last pull off his cigarette, tossed it in the fire, and stared back at Russell confidently.

Russell regarded him briefly, before nodding his approval. "Okay, let's go get it. Let me get these yahoos organized first." Russell turned away and approached the two revelers. "I want you to lissen up."

Morrison suspected that Russell had made the decision. "Hell—what we waitin' for? Red and I got a couple of hot dates."

"I don't give a shit about that. I won't put up wit no foolish shit. We got us a tough road outta here. We kin make it if everybody does what their told." He stared at the two men who had been drinking fast and furious. "Youse got anything to say...?"

"You're the boss, Lloyd. Just show us the way out." Morrison gave a mock salute.

The Ford Coupe was housed in the barn where Russell and his cohorts had stolen most of their eggs and chickens. They had milked the farmer's cows. The remains of the chicken soaked in the bucket, uneaten, as excitement and alcohol made them overlook their hunger. The time was near, the ten cramped days in this bug pit just about over.

"Get everything together and put it in the ditch by the road, Joe and I are going for the car." The soft-spoken voice filled the air with authority and set the hideout in the Yalmer woods into a flurry of activity with these simple words, "Let's move it."

Everybody sobered a noticeable degree once the call to action was made. Morrison and McDowell had the booty gathered and waiting at the road's edge when Morrison hissed, "Listen, I hear someone coming. Damn, it better be them..."

28
OFF—RUNNING

Monday, June 1

THE FORD COUPE PULLED TO THE gravel road's edge, McMackin had expertly crossed the ignition wires, he waited behind the steering wheel while the others loaded up the possessions and climbed inside. Prison issue clothes as well as new civilian clothing were tossed in the trunk and back seat.

Russell joined him in the front seat and pointed ahead, "That's east Joe, the cops are gonna be watching U.S. 41. We could avoid a blockade by heading this way."

The sign at the first intersection displayed that they were traveling on Yalmer Road. Russell's map indicated a trail that led toward M-28. Peering intently into the blackness that was pierced only by the car's headlights.

McMackin said, "If this gauge works, we ain't going real far."

"What's it say?"

"It's almost on empty, the old man could a kept it filled it for us. We ain't gonna get far with no gas."

"Keep 'er going, let's take it as far as she goes. Some times them gauges don't work. Course—he don't drive it much. Mostly it just sat in the barn."

"This damn road is one son of a bitch," McMackin complained, "Look at those ruts, we're bound to get stuck."

"Just keep 'er in low, and try to avoid them deep ruts, ride on top. It can't be much farther. Once we cut outta these thick woods, the road should be dry."

The 1949 Ford Club Coupe dug through the mud-strewn two-track road. It was no more than a logging trail cut into the thick maple woods. Suddenly, the front end dipped sharply causing the rear wheels to spin helplessly in the black muck.

"We gotta get out and push. We're lucky we don't have a big old Buick. We kin lift this little ol' coupe right outta here."

The foursome piled out to assess the situation. "I say we push 'er backward, Morrison said. "Looks like our best bet. Then we kin throw some brush in the hole, get traction, and drive across it." He stood in the beam of a headlight while Russell surveyed the dilemma.

"Yer right. Put 'er in reverse Joe. Ride the clutch. C'mon Red, quit playing with yourself and give us a hand."

"I'm a coming boss, just had to drain the monster."

"You mean the minnow," McMackin grinned through his open window.

"Let's go, get some brush in that hole." Morrison was tearing branches off the bottom of a blue spruce. He was joined by McDowell and they quickly had the deep mud hole filled.

"Take it easy now Joe. Take up the clutch real slow. Them back tires should be able to grab while we push."

The Ford eased out with their second effort. "Way to go, Charles got the right idea. Now, let's throw some more brush in that hole."

"We're ready to go, Joe. On three, just gun 'er, we'll do the rest. Keep it in low."

The little Ford spun its tires and scurried through the bough-filled muck sliding sideways before catching solid ground and straightening itself out. The trio of pushers ran to the vehicle wiping mud splatters off their pants. The vehicle sat idling, resting from its muddy bath.

Russell returned to his spot in the shotgun seat and again studied his map. "Just a little further Joe, we'll make it to highway M-28. Keep yer eyes peeled for another ride. We'll trade this one in."

"Yeah, this ain't good on the engine. We're working it hard, running it through this shit in low gear."

"Run 'er till she drops dead. We got no other choice."

"That's a fact. She got us through the thick stuff. I can't believe she's still running. It's gotta be just fumes, unless the gauge is a liar..."

"What's the time?" Morrison broke the silence after twenty minutes. The booze he had drunk had made him drowsy, and he had just woke up from his short nap.

"I dunno, it could be three, four, I'm just guessing. Looks like we got some time before first light. Look up ahead, that's the highway. Take a right, that should be east."

The Ford coughed, sputtered, then finally quit. As if thoroughly insulted by its riders' ambition to ditch her. McMackin looked at Russell. "Let's just push it in the ditch. Then grab our stuff and head for those lights up ahead. They ain't that far."

The sign ahead read; **Lakeside Tavern,** a dark Buick of 1950 vintage sat alone in the graveled parking lot. "It's locked," Morrison said, absently kicking the rear tire. He tested both doors of the blue, General Motors product. "Yup, the driver's door is locked, too."

McMackin and McDowell had made a quick check of the auto's exterior and had not found a hidden key. "Break the lock on the passenger side door," Russell ordered. "Quick, Joe. Do your magic. Open the trunk Red. Let's load up."

"Which way?" McMackin asked, as he backed out of the tavern's parking lot.

"Keep heading east, and hand me that damn map." He had taken a reverse trip on this highway three years earlier in the backseat of a state police cruiser, but as he now remembered, he had slept most of the way.

"This is a peppy little bastard, the Ford was kind a sluggish. Course we was going through a ton of mud." McMackin steered them along M-28 into the graying dawn after his comments had been ignored by everyone. The beauty of the Lake Superior shoreline escaped the eyes of the early morning travelers. It hid its magnificent colors of contrasting rocks and trees in the cover of darkness that failed to reveal the splendor of the deep blue water as it crashed into the shore.

The Buick rumbled over the bridge at the Rock River, past the little hydro plant furnishing local power that was nestled above the smooth rocks formed by a small set of rapids, that sat cozy and quiet in the early morning hours.

Russell, as usual, cautioned, "Watch yer speed, how's the gas tank look?"

"A little better, shows just under a half a tank." McMackin squinted at the gauges and then happily announced, "This baby's got a radio."

"I'll look for a local station, see if they're wise to our move." Russell reached over and fiddled with the tuner. Static reverberated through the radio speakers as he twisted the dial. "Shit, it don't work."

"Sometimes you gotta give 'em a rap," McMackin slammed the dash and a clear voice penetrated the car's interior. The men listened in silence as the early morning weather report ended with a singing radio commercial.

"Yes, when you have to brush in a rush, use Brisk Toothpaste. It's florinated. Before we break for the news, here's Patti Paige with the number one song in the land. "How much is that doggie in the window?"

It wasn't long before they were singing along and howling at the tune's zany lyrics. "Roof, roof, and arf, arf bounced off the stolen vehicle's interior.

"Hold it boys. We'll drive through Munising before we look for gas. We should have plenty to get through there. No sense screwing wit the city cops." A check with the two in the rear sends him off into an angry snarl. "Dammit Red, put that damn jug a wine down. We gotta be sharp, I want youse to stay down and outta sight. Make it look like there is only two of us."

Dawn was peeking at them as they maneuvered through the city of Munising. They followed M-28 as it became Munsing Avenue, moving slowly through the sleeping town.

McMackin down shifted to meet the steep rise of Wetmore Hill. They chugged along in second gear, passing a cemetery before reaching the top.

A few scattered houses indicated they were in the village of Wetmore. "Take a right here at this junction at M-28. See, there's a station right there." The road sign indicated Federal Forest Highway 13, a road that cut through to the U.P.'s southern border.

"Wasn't you and your brother caught near here in '50, Lloyd?" Morrison asked. "This must be close, huh?"

"Yuh, it was close," making it clear the conversation was over. He wasn't about to discuss that it was another seven-eight miles to the east.

"The station is closed. Let's fill up." Joe pulled up to the fuel pumps. "Don't look like much to them locks. Quick, let's bust 'em and start pumping."

Working as swiftly as an Indianapolis pit crew, they soon had the Buick's tank filled. Morrison found an empty five gallon can from the side of the station door, and they quickly filled it and stuck it into the trunk. McMackin jumped back behind the wheel and the foursome was back on the road—heading south to freedom.

The radio refused to work again, no matter how they banged on it. It vexed the convicts' leader, "Dammit, I wanted to keep track of what the law was up to. They must be wise to us by now—they gotta know we're on the run."

29

Heading South

HIGHWAY 13 CUT A STRAIGHT PATH through the Hiawatha National Forest, built by the Civilian Conservation Corps, it was a picturesque ride south to the shores of Lake Michigan. Tall, statuesque pines, and clear, blue-tipped inland lakes, offered a vivid and color-filled drive that once more was ignored by the men on the lam.

"Do me a favor, when you find a spot— pull over, I gotta take a shit." McDowell requested. "Hey, that looks like a rest area up ahead."

"It's a camp site, John."

"Same damn thing Joe. There's gotta be a place to take a dump."

They entered the campground at the Wide Waters of the Indian river. An outside privy was easily located and McDowell hurried from the vehicle, unbuckling his trousers as he waddled to the outhouse door.

The other three men exited after him to relieve their bladders into the early morning dew. No campers were present on this Monday morning as the facility had just opened for the summer season. The river's width at this juncture made it appear to look more like a small lake. Immediately after the duty call, the Buick was back on the road.

They met but a handful of oncoming vehicles, the highway almost devoid of traffic. There were but a few homes or cabins—several signs and billboards announced lakes and resorts spurring off in both directions from Highway 13. The ride south was taken in near silence. The alcohol and adrenaline rush had left them depleted.

"Now it's my turn. Damn, I'm thirsty," Morrison said. "I'm drier than a popcorn fart. I sure need something cold and wet. Stop if you see a river, anything will do."

"It's all that booze you sucked down last night. It dries you right up." Russell shrugged at McMackin's questioning look. "Stop when you see something. Hell, we could all use a drink."

"There's another campground up ahead, this one's on the left." McMackin slowed and cautiously signaled a left turn by thrusting his arm out the window even though there was not another vehicle in sight. **Flowing Wells Campground** was a scenic stop where the Sturgeon River rushed head-long through the the slick rocks and large boulders that attempted to slow it down. White, sudsy liquid produced the foam that the river used to bathe itself on its journey to Lake Michigan.

The thirsty crew slurped the cold, refreshing water as they took turns using the long handled pitcher pump to quench their thirst. They were quickly back on the road—and in less than a half an hour, McMackin was braking for a major crossroad.

Nahma Junction, said the sign. "Turn right, we'll be headin' back west again, then we'll head south and west to the Wisconsin border. I don't see it any other way."

"We're making one damn big u-turn."

"We got no choice, Charles. We can't cross on the fuckin' ferry at the Straights and head down state. Same with the Canadian border. We'd be pinched in a minute."

"That's true Lloyd." McDowell agreed. "I'm the only one that don't stick out."

"That's funny Red. Only like a sore thumb. Red on the head—like a dick on a dog. That's what my brother Paul used to say. You guys would like him—I wish we could swing down to Jackson and bust his ass out."

"Maybe some day, you kin."

"Yeah—maybe. Right now we gotta drive. Get the hell outta this fuckin' U.P. It's been nuttin' but trouble for me."

They traveled west and caught glimpses of Lake Michigan as they cruised along. Cottages sprinkled the shoreline and an occasional boat dotted the horizon. They crept through Rapid River, a small village, crossed the Days Creek, a smelt-dipping hot spot, on their route to Gladstone. They were unaware of the danger lurking there.

They traversed Little Bay De Noc, and the little fishing village of Kipling, making good time on their southerly gesture around the lake. The day warmed considerably—though not near as warm as the reception facing them just a short mile down the road. Something told them, they were not as safe as they felt. The law had to be wise.

They became uneasy, the cons knew that everyone suspected they were on the run. The tavern break-in, the two stolen cars. Yes, the Upper Peninsula was on the look out for— four escaped convicts in a stolen Buick...

"Keep it slow, keep it easy, dammit, you almost run that light."

"It would a been more suspicious to slam the brakes—I just nicked the yellow—we'll be fine." The stoplight was the only signal in the town. "Think we can stop soon? I'm tired, and I need something to eat."

"Naw, that's way too risky. We gotta play it safe—extra safe. Shit, that's the bastard law right down there. Dammit. They got the road pinched off."

"I knew we should a hit that hardware store in Munising—got us some guns. We can't shoot it out with our thumbs," Morrison was instantly agitated and spoiling for a fight.

"Do I make a run at 'em, Lloyd? Bust through?"

"We ain't shootin' it out wit them, even if we get some guns. See those cabins, Joe? Just pull in there—nice and easy."

The dark blue Buick crept casually into the **Kozy Kabins** rentals and inched its way along the tree-lined drive. Lloyd directed them to continue until they reached a dead end. Fishermen and their families were busy unloading their gear and setting up their cabin for an excursion out on the Bays' De Noc. No one paid attention to the men who exited the stolen car.

"Take everything with you—let's just move out—easy as can be." The men had to combat the maddening urge to run, waiting to hear the yell that they'd been spotted.

McDowell led the pack. The red-head was always fit to be tied when it came to caution. Lloyd struggled with his self-control.

"I said, easy now, John. Let's just take a stroll in the park."

Indeed, under the encouragement from their leader, they moved along amiably, leaving the Buick behind them as they wandered toward the Escanaba River. "Ouch."

"Shut up, we're almost there. You fuckers better be able to swim."

Lloyd spotted the river—as the dense brush swallowed them up.

30

In Hot Pursuit

Monday, June 1

The Mining Journal-At 12:30 this afternoon state police located the car stolen from Edwin Peura, Deerton, by convicts earlier today. The automobile was found abandoned along the Escanaba River, near the power dam, between Gladstone and Escanaba. Police are surrounding the area.

Law enforcement officers this morning were concentrating their pursuit of the four escaped convicts in Alger County, where the fugitives are believed to have fled after breaking into a tavern and stealing two automobiles in Marquette County.

This morning a police searching party also located the "hideout" where the convicts apparently "laid low" for the past few days. All four are believed to still be together.

The hideout-a crudely built lean-to, under brush and thick woods was located two miles east of the Idle Time Tavern, 13 miles south of Marquette, on Highway US-41, which was broken in to last night.

After stealing between $400 and $500 cash, plus liquor and clothing, the convicts apparently returned to their hideaway and had a party, then got up enough nerve to steal a car and make a break.

When Theodore McMaster, a farmer who lives a half mile north of the tavern, discovered his 1949 Ford club coupe missing at 6:00 am this morning, he immediately phoned the state police.

He had not left the keys in the car, so it was concluded that the convicts 'crossed the wires' on the motor to start the automobile. They apparently drove east on the Yalmer Road, then cut over on to Highway M-28, and abandoned that auto in the ditch, about 12 miles southeast of Marquette.

At the Lakeside Tavern, on M-28 near Deerton, a 1950 Buick, two-door coach (colored blue, license number LP-6494), belonging to Edwin Peura, Route 1, Deerton, was stolen early this morning, and officers believe the convicts took the auto after ditching the other one.

The convicts apparently headed east on M-28. A motorist this morning reported seeing a car answering the description of Peura's being driven east, and that it had two men in the front seat. Two others, the motorist said, were huddled up in the rear.

Early this morning the lock on the Federal Forest Service Station, on M-28, near Munising was broken in to and about 22 or 24 gallons of gasoline were stolen.

Two state police planes, one from Lansing piloted by Corporal Barney Froberg, and the other, by Trooper Charles Nottage, Traverse City, were aiding in the hunt.

Mrs Elma Erkkila, proprietor of the Idle Time, said her establishment was broken into between 8:30 and 10:00 pm Sunday night, when she drove into town. In addition to the cash, five quarts of wine, some bottles of beer and liquor, cigarettes, cigars, candy and gum and three jackets, one yellow, one navy blue, and a tan one were stolen.

Mrs Erkkila also stated that several cars parked at the tavern had been entered Saturday night, but, it was thought to be "some local people" and she did not report the incident to the state police.

Stolen from the cars Saturday night were three white shirts, a pink dress, a bar apron and a patchwork quilt—all articles which had been cleaned and included in a laundry package.

Law officers found the convicts' hideout in a swampy area to the rear of the tavern early this morning. And they know it was definitely the fugitives hiding place—because some of the Marquette Prison clothes and a crude filing knife from the prison were left in the lean-to.

Apparently the four convicts—were all together and made the break after disposing of some liquor last night, officers believe.

At the hideout near Yalmer, the officers found crude tools and equipment which the convicts had been using to cook for themselves. A pail filled with a half-boiled chicken, the feathers plucked, and a jug partly filled with milk, were among the articles found.

The convicts evidently had been milking some cows owned by McMaster, the same farmer whose car they stole.

This morning, on learning that the fugitives had been stealing milk, he commented, "I began to wonder why the cows weren't giving as much milk lately as they usually have."

Since one of the knives used in the break was left at the hideout, officers believe the fugitives have guns—possibly obtained through breaking into some cabin. A hand hatchet and other tools that were stolen from the Norman Nelson farm also were found at the hideout.

Used razor blades also were found at the hideout, indicating that the felons had a chance to "shave and cleanup" before making their break in the stolen cars. Russell would see that they kept themselves groomed so that they wouldn't 'stick out.'

State Police Commissioner Joseph Childs arrived on Saturday and he spent the weekend being briefed by Captains Person and Hathaway.

By the time word had gotten out that the convicts had made a run for it, Childs had headed back to Lansing, unaware of the gang's latest shenanigans. It appeared that the Russell gang had luck on their side and were blessed with an uncanny ability to choose the right time to make their break.

Local journalists and writers from as far away as Detroit and parts of Ohio sat in on the warden's press report. "Would it help to raise the reward money being offered? Maybe even double the amount?" A writer from the Free Press asked.

Warden Emery Jacques sat back and shook his head at the question. "No, I don't think doubling the reward money will expedite the apprehension of the escapees. I think we already have the full public cooperation in our search."

Deputy Warden Ben Luoma slipped into the office long enough to drop off the new guard assignments and point to the report he placed on top. He lingered momentarily to assure himself that the warden had made note of the report before he withdrew from the office. His bespectacled boss nodded an acknowledgment before reaching for the telephone.

The reporters waited and listened while Jacques spoke to an unidentified official within the prison system.

The reward being offered by the Michigan Department of Corrections now stood at one hundred dollars. He hung up the phone and reached for the latest report that Luoma had just laid down. It stated that the stolen Buick had been found after an unidentified woman had spotted it before noon today. Warden Jacques picked the phone a second time and dialed the state police war room.

The headquarters for the state police search had taken on an identity of its own. For two weeks, information and reports had been assessed and maintained, assignments constantly meted out, the room had been a constant hub of activity.

Today was even busier than usual. The convicts were now on the move. The large map on the wall would have made a combat general proud as officers stood around it citing blockade points and noting possible escape routes.

Captain Person hung up his phone after bringing Warden Jacques up to date on the latest convict sightings and trooper deployment. "Earl, excuse me a minute, could you come over here?"

Hathaway left Sergeant Smith to work the road blockade placement and joined Person at his desk. He stuffed his unlit pipe into his mouth and waited for the captain to begin.

"Our men are back after going through the hideout with a fine-tooth comb. They got all the shit bagged and have dropped it off here. Corporal Ottie Buelow and Trooper William Teddy assured me that they sifted through the site thoroughly. George Strong was supervising, he's a damn sharp detective."

"Learn anything new, Thor?" Hathaway scratched at a stick-match with his thumb, sending up a burst of blue flame that turned to red as he sucked the glow into his pipe.

"Just the wine bottles left behind and an empty toothpaste tube. The rest you know about.

But listen up, this'll frost your nuts." Person waited until the pipe was lit before moving on with the report.

"The two group of kids who told their teacher about seeing four men going toward that hideout, saw them just yesterday. The teacher didn't think anything of it, didn't think it important enough to report, so it was late in the day before she called us. Had she reported to us right away, we might have taken them right there at the lean-to."

"That was down in Skandia? You gotta give them credit, they sure as hell waited us out. And—they must have made it in there before the blockades were set."

"Right it's hard to second guess. It's hard to say if they would have still been there, but dammit Earl, we sure would have been close..."

"How about the fact that our blockade being so close to those cabins? Not one of our boys saw that blue Buick—or anything suspicious."

"Nope. Our guys saw cars come and go from there all morning. There was nothing suspicious or out of place about that at all. The fishing is hot in Big Bay De Noc right now."

"The Ford Coupe of McMaster's was muddied up pretty darn good. They must have gotten it stuck in the back roads. Find anything in the Buick?"

"There were two empty cartridge shell boxes underneath the seat, but we think they were Peura's—he's the owner of the Buick. Also, there were two empty five-gallon gas cans in the trunk. They must have emptied them in the Buick before they reached the cabins."

"How soon are we deploying?"

"Immediately, Earl. The 'war room' is moving to Gladstone. We'll conduct the search from there. It appears they're headed for the Wisconsin border."

"I can be packed and ready to go in a half hour. I'll ride out with a couple of the detectives."

"Good. I've notified everybody to alert the residents in the Gladstone-Esky area to be on the alert and sure they remove their car keys."

"The gang's run for the Wisconsin border had everyone's adrenaline pumping, a sense of an impending showdown with the desperadoes loomed on the horizon.

31

THE LLOYD RUSSELL STORY

June 1, 1953

THE MARQUETTE MINING JOURNAL REPORTED ON a story about an intense interview taken at the time of Lloyd Russell's capture with his brother in May of 1950.

Tape Recording of Russell

A bit of history preserved for the ages exactly three years ago has become of considerably timely importance today.

It's an hour and a half recording of an interview by Sheriff Albert Jacobson with Lloyd Russell, then 28, believed to be the leader of the four convicts still at large from Marquette Prison. The tape recording was made while Russell was lodged in the Marquette County jail, pending his appearance in circuit court, after his capture in a chase across the Upper Peninsula, a pursuit that made headlines throughout the mid-west.

Importance Noted

Jacobson, a member of the Board of Directors of the National Sheriff's Association, was quick to sense to sense the importance of Russell's capture, after a bit of diplomacy, he persuaded Russell to describe his criminal record.

147

Jacobson told him the recording could be used for juvenile crime prevention work. During the slack period in the manhunt on Memorial Day eve, officers heading up the chase had an opportunity to take time out and listen to the recording handled by Under-sheriff Adrian Pequet during Jacobson's interview.

Officers in charge of the convict search, after hearing the recording, praised Jacobson for his work in obtaining it, and declared the knowledge they gained from the recording such as the habits and customs of Russell, etc. will aid them in the search.

Russell was a farm boy in Ohio when he got on the road to crime. Regarded as a "hick from the country" by the "city slickers" he got kicked around by quite a bit in his youth.

At Home In the Woods

THE CONSTANT ARGUING BETWEEN HIS FOLKS didn't help either, he said. One thing led to another, and he finally got a thirty three month stretch in the reformatory.

"I had always gotten along in a small town," he said. "I liked to do things with my hands—woodwork and shop—and I think such courses would help a lot of boys from going wrong, as not all are adapted to book-learning."

He also told how he spent a lot of time in the woods—hunting, fishing and trapping. Those later experiences, officers believe are unquestionably helping the convicts elude capture today.

Bad Associations Hurt

HIS BAD ASSOCIATIONS IN THE REFORMATORY didn't help his cause Russell states in the recording. "I was regarded as a bad boy," he said. "And I wanted to be a bad boy and I was a bad boy."

After getting out, he went to Toledo, where he "went wrong." The bad example set by his parents was always just words flying around and didn't help him get straight.

Absence of Money Hurts

HE FOUND IT DIFFICULT TO GET a job outside. Finally he found one, and worked seven days a week, making good money. Everything went right until one night his car broke down. Then, he lost his job. This was followed by a heat wave, during which his services weren't required. The lastcheck he cashed was for $27.00 was a far cry from the $90.00 plus he had been averaging. "That did it, I began working time and a half after that—full time for the company and a half a day on the side for myself."

Past Catches Up

HE GOT MARRIED AND QUIT THIEVING, he didn't say he quit safe cracking (his specialty). One day, his brother Paul got arrested. "I don't know what for," he said. "But I went down to the police station and I guess my past caught up with me. They arrested me, and found all my burglary tools at home, and a pail of cash. I got three to thirty seven years in the Columbus penitentiary."

Russell said that in prison, he missed his freedom. He enjoyed walking in the woods alone. He hated forced to associate with men of all types and beliefs. He was basically a loner, his instincts made it difficult for him to trust other people.

It's Aggravating

"I SPENT 24 MONTHS IN ONE LITTLE CELL, ONE LITTLE CUBICLE, AND IT WAS MIGHTY AGGRAVATING." Discouraged when rejected for parole, he would trade two years off re-sentence for one year of freedom. "It's a rejuvenating feeling to get out."

Although getting along good, and transferred to a prison farm, he said, "Come May and the grass starts getting green, I start getting itchy feet. (He probably got itchy feet this May, too, officers point out).

Leaps Out Of Window

HE THEN TELLS HOW HE GOT out of prison again. "The first time was an over-the-wall break from the pen" He and brother Paul picked up cash in Toledo and headed up the road through Michigan.

Russell relates about his well-known stay in the Sault Ste. Marie area, how the police spotted them as they went in to purchase guns. The police took up chase and they sped down a gravel road ("sometimes doing a hundred miles an hour") until they finally abandoned the car and headed for the woods.

Though closely chased, they managed to lay low for ten days. Once, when a cabin in which they were in was about to be searched, Russell dove out the window, and suffered cuts above his left eye, the scars from which he bears today.

After stealing a car and running a blockade set up for Willie Jackson, an escaped Negro trustee, at Shingleton, Paul was hit in a gun battle with state police (in which Detective George Strong, Marquette, Marquette, was also wounded), and they were captured in a swamp.

"I was glad it was over," Russell said. "There is no telling what might have happened to Paul," (who stayed in a prison hospital for a week.)

"I'm just a country boy at heart," is the manner in which Russell winds up the interview, but which officers add, "an extremely dangerous one."

Of course, many of the more wicked incidents are not included in the recording—but it gives a remarkable picture of the type of man officers are in pursuit of today.

32

Give 'Em The Slip

Wednesday, June 3

Dulles Warns, Near East, South Asia Imperiled By Communism

WASHINGTON (AP)—SECRETARY OF STATE DULLES returned from his survey trip to the Near East and South Asia declaring that this strategic area, like China, could fall victim to Communist domination.

Carroll's Corners and Chandler Crossing were turned into an armed camp Sunday afternoon as five law enforcement agencies and many farmers and other civilian volunteers responded to the report that the four convicts were in the area, Sheriff William Miron reported.

Sheriff Miron estimated that one hundred people were present, most of them armed. He said the whole area was surrounded. "We had the area sewed up."

The tense search went on all afternoon, ending only at 7:00 pm when it was discovered that three innocent fisherman had been the cause of the alarm.

After escaping one police dragnet, the four escapees fell into another one at Flat Rock, northwest of Escanaba in Delta County. State and city police and sheriff's deputies had a wooded section south and west of the county roads under close surveillance and forty officers were coursing through the brush after an alarm was sent out by two Escanaba city policemen.

Working along the north side of the Soo Hill section where the last clues had been found last night, the policemen came upon fresh tracks. After following them for several minutes, they heard trampling in the brush, and ultimately heard someone beating a hasty retreat .

Raising an alarm, the cops took chase, guided by the tracks and the noisy retreat, they gradually gained ground. They were soon joined by car loads of state police and deputy sheriff's.

They again made a thorough search of the area, painstakingly back-tracking, searching every inch. It was slow work, as the thick brush was contrary to their every movement.

From the Gladstone headquarters, Thor Person paced the office. "We think they'll be sticking close to roads. They really have to, this country is strange territory for them." He glanced up, looking for commentary from the men in the room.

The men in the room murmured their assent, like hounds on a wounded boar. Sergeant Spratto broke the spell, "What about the evidence found this morning? Was that Mining Journal bill from the theft at the Idle Time?"

"Damn right, I think it was taken from there. They might have been div-vying up the money there and just threw the bill away."

"It makes sense," Hathaway agreed.

"Let's get this clear gentlemen, we thought we had 'em in the paper mill area, yet some how they gave us the slip. They're a wily bunch, and they will do just about anything to avoid capture. Think about it—they'll do anything..."

Captain Person rose and went over to the large map of the local area, finding County Road 414. He pointed to a specific spot. "Here is where the youngsters saw them. They were near a large brush pile, and the kids from the Soo Hill Grade School spotted them during recess."

"That's what—two miles west of the paper mill?"

"About that, I would estimate."

Spratto voiced a thought, "Do you think they would chance swimming the river?"

"That's very possible," Person said, "these are desperate men."

The room grew noisy, the men expressing their opinions on the con-victs' options. Person silenced them and returned to the report in his hand. "We can't emphasize enough how important it is—that the folks out there when they think they see anything suspicious—must let us know immediately."

"Doesn't that create a lot of loose ends to chase down?"

"Possibly—but, the Soo Hill kids called their teacher after they saw the fugitives, lemme see here, a Miss Agnes Gliech," he stumbled over her name. "But the kicker here is what seems to always be happening, she runs to the neighborhood store to call us, but the storekeeper talks her out of it." Frustration etched in his tired face. "He tells her not to bother us—they most likely are woodsmen."

The police report went on to say that the residents of the Wells area were terrified over the fact that the escaped felons were hiding in their area. Some kept their children home from school, while many others went to stay with neighbors.

Bernice Goodnaugh, a seven year old girl, spotted the convicts near her home in Wells Township. She called to her two sisters, Rita, 13, and Sandra, 10. The men fled into the woods when the girls screamed.

Their mother, Mrs. Clara Goodnaugh, a widow with six children, sent Rita to a store to phone authorities. The men were wearing tan jackets. Police were able to rule them out quickly based on the jackets stolen from the Idle Time.

At 3:30 yesterday afternoon, officers thought they had a good lead when a man was seen boarding a gondola on a Western Railroad Company freight train out of Escanaba. Officers in a free-lance patrol car near Powers were assigned to probe the report, and in less than an hour they discovered the men were just a couple of bums.

During the dinner hour, a Gladstone woman (Mrs. Francis Gobert) said she saw the convicts in a car on US-41, and identified one passenger as Charles Morrison. A Marquette state trooper investigated and found out that the motorists were tourists whose car had run out of gas. The out of state travelers noted that they had never seen so many law enforcement officers in the same day before.

Officers believed they had a real clue at 8:05 last night when a Harnischfeger Corporation worker saw a man near the tower at Radio Station WDBC. He turned out to be the station's engineer.

Plenty of tips were received daily. As they centered on Delta County's Wells Township, none of the tips materialized in a single capture. Frustration reigned...

"Okay men, let's get back to work. We got them on the run—now, it's just a matter of time. And, please—be careful. They're a bad bunch."

After leaving the Buick on Monday, the fugitives found themselves in a dense thicket that took them to a wide, thrashing river. From the river's edge they saw the feathery smoke plumes from the paper mill. Russell determined that they move in the opposite direction.

When they could no longer hear the sounds of pursuit, he called a halt to allow everyone to catch their breath. He recognized that his control over the men was reaching an end. A decision would be made. He had to be ready for anything—*if the mutinous decision proved to be violent.*

"We're gonna move along slow, find a good spot to lay low till dark. We'll find us something to eat when it gets late. The minute we get stupid, is the minute we get dead." He fixed a dead-eyed stare that stated—it was his way or nothing.

The revolt had begun, his hungry comrades were about to openly question his leadership. Keeping to the woods was contrary to their way of thinking. The rugged country with the unrelenting bug assault and endless dead ends were taking their toll.

"You know something? We're just going 'round in circles—soon we'll bump into a passel of cops just waitin' for us—ready for target practice."

"I know it's frustrating, Charles—we got to be patient. Layin' low is the only thing to do. They can't find shit, it we don't serve it to 'em."

"These fuckin' bugs, I don't even see them, yet I'm scratching my ass off. I can't take it much longer. What are these bastards?"

"Well, they ain't dog pecker gnats, otherwise you'd be scratching something else off. They call these babies no-see-ums, You don't see 'em, you just feel 'em."

"Dog pecker gnats? Don't that beat all," McDowell chimed in, "I'm starving, every time we get close to some food—we get run off."

Russell leaned back against a scrub pine whose sharp branches insisted on poking at him, first at his back, between the shoulder blades, then tearing at his bare arms. He scrambled back on to his feet wondering if the damn tree held a personal grudge against him, or was it that it didn't take to company. He stood there—staring—as the disenchantment took on a stronger voice.

"Shit," Morrison grumbled. "We ain't makin' it nowhere. We'll starve to death before we get the hell outta this state." The murmuring assent was a harbinger of things to come.

"You lissen up, I'm done telling you. We been planning this trip for a long time. I said we gotta wait for our chance—play it smart. I toll you to bring stuff wit you for a reason. You all told me you was tough, shit—you're a bunch a pussies..."

33

THE SPLIT

Thursday, June 4, 1953

Rosenbergs' Execution Set

NEW YORK—MARSHALL WILLIAM A. CARROLL announced today condemned atom spies Julius and Ethel Rosenberg will be executed at 10:00 pm (EST) June 18.

Headline—Grueling, Exhaustive Hunt

CAPTAIN THOR PERSON ORDERED ADDITIONAL TROOPERS sent to the Iron Mountain Post, to help extend and widen the blockade points in that area, in the belief that the fugitives may be attempting to cross over into Wisconsin through Dickinson County.

Tight blockades also have been set up on principal highways in Menominee County, and in Delta County, are still being maintained.

Under an intensive search this morning, was a heavily wooded area southwest of Soo Hill Grade School, off Delta County Road 414, in Wells Township.

In addition to the regular posse, additional officers were ordered into that section this morning, after a farmer reported that a tame rabbit had been stolen from a pen in his farmyard early today.

Lloyd Russell, probable leader of the escaped felons, is an expert woodsman and came from a farm, and officers believe he would be apt to try and get food for he and the other fugitives by stealing farm animals.

While hiding out by Yalmer the escapees ate several chickens. Those thefts were not discovered and reported until it was too late.

The search, which has reached the grueling and exhaustive point, is nevertheless being continued relentlessly by state police. Most of the officers, many of whom are from other posts in the state, are averaging 14 hours a work a day during the manhunt.

Captain Person, directing the pursuit, is at his desk at daybreak, and goes into the field periodically during the day and continues on the job until after nightfall.

"We believe the convicts are trying to get out of Michigan, by any means," Captain Person said, "and we are determined to stop them."

Captain Person issued a statement for the residents in the Wells Township area to report immediately any tampering with locks or doors of cars, as well as any suspicious incidents near livestock or cow barns. He believed that the local resident's vigilance could lead to the big break they needed to nab this bunch.

"There are other ways to get out of the state, rail or boat, but we feel they are waiting to steal a car. That would be their best chance to move quickly."

"We also determined that the burglary at the Walter Pragacy camp, in Menominee County, was done on May 31st or before the convicts got over here. The missing shotgun has also been recovered."

The Captain went on to detail other tips and area burglaries. Detectives found tracks near the camp of Charles Richards, whose camp had been broken in to the day before. It was located two and a half miles west of Escanaba's Holy Name cemetery. The detectives couldn't determine the freshness of the tracks due to the intermittent showers that had occurred during the day. The investigation revealed that the break-in had taken place three weeks prior, and the owners had not reported it to police.

The only report of consequence last evening was from Mrs. Fred Mattson, a Delta rural resident, who reported finding an empty king-sized pack of cigarettes and fresh tracks at a creek near the Soo Hill School. The area was near where other suspicious articles had been found earlier in the week.

"One of these tips are gonna be the real McCoy."

"You betcha."

Hutchinson Just Sits and Shakes His Head

Joe Falls

DETROIT—THEY USED TO CALL HIM "Fiery Fred." Now it's "Hutch the Hush." The reason is simple. There is nothing to talk about.

That's the way it was after the Tigers had been whipped by the Cleveland Indians 8-1. It was their eighth game without a win and left them gasping 18 and a half games from first place. Bob Lemon tamed the Tigers as Art Houtteman took the loss.

After dining on tame rabbit from the farmer's yard, the four thieves sipped on what remained of the booze and wine and discussed their options. As the liquor took hold, and tongues loosened, the discussion reached argumentative stages. The air was filled with a contentious behavior, with men used to settling disputes with violence. The men were teetering on the edge of a rage-filled settlement. The narrow escapes and the tortuous, hungry conditions were taking its toll as the seething cauldron was about to boil over.

"I'm sick a these damn woods, I say we follow the railroad tracks as fast as we can go till we boost a rod, then get out of here like a bat outta hell, and get our asses into Wisconsin." Charles Morrison's arms waved in further emphasis as his fury mounted.

"Take yer voice down," Russell spit the words, but maintained an outward cool. He knew what he had to do to survive. It was up to whoever wanted to stick with him. *I kin use 'em like I used the old men.*

Lloyd's right, lower your voices," McMackin cautioned.

John McDowell was agreeing with the dark haired "lifer" from the Market Basket robbery. "Charles is right, we been in these fuckin' woods too long. We ain't getting nowhere. We gotta make a run for it. Hell, they're gonna close in and corner us any time now. We gotta move."

Morrison wiped his lips with his sleeve, then belched, distorting his face after getting a second taste of the cheap, stolen whiskey. He passed the bottle on to McMackin, who took a slug, then swallowed like there was a lump in it.

He glanced over to Russell, who nixed both the whiskey and the idea with a quick shake of his head. "They got every road blocked going into Wisconsin, you kin bet your ass on that." He left the rest unsaid, nestled in the deep privacy of his heart.

Joseph "Jaybird" McMackin was caught in the middle. He felt that Russell was the one to lead them to freedom, but the urge to make a fast run was pulling at him, depleting his of his normal sense of caution. Not only was he facing the 10-30 year armed robbery sentence in Michigan, but the state of Missouri would then keep him incarcerated for the rest of his natural life. Red was his best friend and if they split up he felt a loyalty to follow McDowell.

"We gotta get the fuck outta Dodge. The heat is on..."

McMackin watched his pal hit the sauce with a heavy hand, and was now waving the rifle he had stolen with menacing gestures. Getting even more animated, he spat on the ground and handed the bottle back to Morrison, "I'm ready, if that little chicken shit won't get us the hell outta here, we'll do it our dammed self."

"Watch it, John. Lloyd's took us this far. Don't be calling him a coward. We all know he ain't that."

Russell kept his eyes hooded and unreadable. He spoke in soft tones, so that the man he was angry at could not see, until it was too late, when his eyes betrayed a striking snake. He stood there, weighing his options...

"Don't aim that fucker at me," Morrison pushed the rifle aside and grabbed the bottle. He finished it off, tossing it a side, the glass missile struck a rock and shattered into pieces as the crashing sound pierced the night air.

"Christ, that was loud," McMackin winced at the noise.

"Let's get moving, in case someone heard that," Morrison's whisper came out like the whistle of a leaking radiator hose. It was a sound that would carry far into the dark stillness of the night, and could reach the alert ears of their pursuers.

"He's gone."

"What ya' mean, Joe? McDowell asked as he swung the .30 caliber Marlin around as if expecting to be jumped at any second. "What you talkin' about?"

"I mean Lloyd. He's gone. Must of slipped off while we were yakking. It's what you were asking for, we're on our own now." Joe knew that Russell had washed his hands of them. He wondered if he had made a big mistake by not sticking with the experienced woodman. Something down deep told him he had.

"Move it, we got light." A pale moon cast its glow down for the three fugitives to be able to traipse down the railroad tracks like hobos looking to catch a late ride. "We stay on these tracks tonight, we'll make good time. Just like we did when we busted the joint." Morrison took the lead as the other two followed.

"I guess we got no choice. You lead, Charles. John can follow. I'll take the rear."

"I could use a drink."

They walked right on by Lloyd Russell—the estranged leader of the gang. *Good, those bastards are just the diversion I need.* He walked along slowly following the sounds of the drunken cons.

Yes. Russell managed a smile. *Good luck, boys. You're gonna need it.* The smile vanished as the next thought entered—*I ain't going back in, they'll never take me alive.*

34

Heading West

THE TRIO WALKED THE REMAINDER OF the night along the railroad tracks, taking them west of Escanaba. They hustled along as they believe they may have compromised themselves by not going to cover sooner. "I know he spotted us, Red," McMackin said. "We're gonna have cops all over us."

"We keep moving, by the time he gets back with the law, we'll be long gone." Morrison limped along at a quick gait. "These damn shoes are killing me."

"We've all worn out the leather," McDowell answered. "We better get off these tracks and get some distance away."

"Oh yeah. How far do you think we should go? Lloyd ain't here, you know." Charles Morrison grew edgy with the added responsibility. He was was vexed with the Upper Peninsula terrain.

"You're in the lead, Charley. You been wanting to be the boss."

"C'mon, John. Maybe, cause there's only three of us together—that could confuse 'em," McMackin said. "Four of us have been have spotted together recently. They may not treat this as such a big lead."

The escapees found the going relatively easy and made good time on their tired and sore feet. Morrison called a halt and said, "Listen, we got the jump on them. We kin take a five. My feet are falling off."

In the distance, sounds of the search reached their ears, a siren wailed fairly close, then drifted away as it headed toward the searchers. "Let's find a place to rest and lay low, it'll be light soon."

"Fuckin' A—I'm beat."

Lloyd heard the din from the search. He had wandered far from the tracks. He wondered if the others were now caught in the police web. This made him unhappy—it was much too soon, he hoped that they would have made at least one decent run at the border. The sky was graying, he worked his way back towards the track in an effort to learn if the three were still on the loose. He knew they wouldn't take to the woods, regardless of the circumstance.

Soon voices reached him. The southerly breeze was sending the indistinct noise to his trained ear. Keeping his senses tuned to the highest level, he edged in closer. The sounds did not appear to be that of a search party. The voices were becoming more defined. *McDowell's voice.* Audible with its high-pitched accent, made him swing to the north and skirt their position. They were going to lay low till nightfall.

Good. So will I.

He woke with a start, the cool darkness had just settled in. He had slept hard, waking with a start, momentarily disoriented. He found the branch he had broken and laid out to point him in a southerly direction so that waking in the darkness would not cause him to lose his sense of direction. He crept along silently, listening to the scurry of small animals retreating from his advancement. The quiet of the day told him the others had not been detected. Now, he was not sure if they were ahead or behind him.

A scraping of gravel reached his ears, soon followed by a muted curse. Someone had tripped. The moon had yet to arrive, making travel extremely difficult. It appeared that the Morrison led escapees were not nearly as careful as they should have been, judging by their noisy advance. *Shit, I gotta hang back further, they're moving way too fast. Like blind men walking right towards a trap.*

After starting out, they had crossed a river, which they determined to be the Ford, and had later passed a county road where a sign at an intersection just north of the tracks told them they were heading toward Hermansville.

There didn't appear to be any major roads interfering with their progress. Somewhere up ahead the cops would likely be setting up a roadblock. They made decent time despite the constant complaints about their blistering feet.

"Man, I gotta soak my dogs."

"Soon John, we're bound to reach water."

"Water? Sure, I'm thirsty too, but I gotta rest my feet."

"You kin soak when we reach water. That's better yet."

The moon was sneaking in and out of the cloud cover allowing for snatches of light. The strong south wind was keeping the mosquitoes at bay, as Mother Nature allowed the travel to become less stringent.

"Let's have a smoke and look over the map. We got some light right now."

They stood just off to the side of the grade, resting on a down-slope. They lit their cigarettes off Morrison's to reduce exposure and save matches. They cupped their hands over the cigarette glow when they drew in smoke. Russell had taught them that.

Morrison took a deep drag, then said in a strangled voice, "Damn, these boys can catch in your throat." He coughed twice, then lit another match to highlight the map. "See here, I think we're a little northwest of that burg called Wilson. We go about four miles and we should be right above here." He pointed at Spaulding, a little town nestled just to the east of Powers.

"Then what? Where do we go from there?"

The plan was to steal a car that they could safely get at, then make a quick dash to the Wisconsin border. McDowell stubbed out his cigarette, then picked up his burlap knapsack and rifle, and ever the impatient one said, "Let's go. Time's a wasting."

As they headed west they were unaware of a lone figure behind them, one who had watched them smoke and talk over their plan. *They'll never make town before daylight, I sure hope they hole up before they get spotted.* The odds of his escape went up as long as some of the other ones kept free.

He trailed along at a safe distance and watched the first discolored signs of daylight enter the sky.

"Dammit," Morrison groaned, "We ain't gonna make it, people are gonna be stirring soon. We gotta find a place to lay low."

"I need to rest my feet," McDowell swiped at his brow, "Damn, they're killing me."

McMackin pointed to a set of dilapidated buildings just revealing themselves in the first light. For all appearances they looked abandoned. "How's that look? Don't look like anybody would have business there." He hastened toward the old structure.

"Looks like an old brick yard," Morrison's stepped inside and looked around inside the deserted block building. "Don't look like it has been used in years."

"A good a place as any," McDowell added. "I'm gonna find me a place to take off my shoes and have me a good long snooze."

"Don't step on a rat, they love these old digs."

McDowell stopped and stared at the city slicker from Detroit. "Right now Charles, I see one a them bastards, I'll eat it raw."

The watchful eyes of Russell retreated further into the woods, a soft grin replacing his normal scowl. Now he could forage something to eat and rest himself.

Just before noon the whistles of a train announced its impending arrival coming down the Soo Line from the east. Morrison jumped up eagerly, "Hey, look at that. Whatya say we flip this train? Ain't seen a soul around here all morning. We should have a shot at it from this side without being seen by no one."

"I kin make it." John McDowell was always an eager beaver.

McDowell' noted with glee, "It's slowing down boys, this could be our chance. We could slip in before it stops."

"Whee, this could be our break."

McDowell, the impulsive, moved quickly toward the opening—hiding behind a crumbling wall that was now less than four feet high. Clutching his rifle as though he was leading a charge at Normandy, hissed, "On the count of three, get set—One—two..."

"Hold it, John. Stop! Christ, look at that." McMackin ever alert, noticed the action coming in from the south. He dragged McDowell back as he pointed at the vehicles heading straight for the braking train, **Michigan State Police** emblazoned on their doors.

They watched, mouths gaped wide, as officers jumped out and boarded the train, going rapidly from car to car, searching through them all. Two officers stayed on the ground, weapons at the ready, as the search took only minutes before the officers waved the train on.

"Did you see that? Damn, it was close. We almost ran right into them." Morrison exhaled a sigh of relief, realizing that he had been holding his breath through it all.

A nervous chuckle escaped from McDowell," We almost put our tits in one helluva ringer. Bet you won't follow my lead next time." He then added a summation, "I ain't never seen so many cops get in one place get there in such a hurry. They were everywhere."

"Ain't that the truth, John."

McDowell wiped his sweaty palms on his blue pants and then removed the cream-colored hat he had stolen along with the rifle, the spoils of a little excursion when the others had slept.

His red hair, damp and unruly from leaking his bodily fluids during the near fatal mistake, gave the impression of a mop that needed squeezing. He cupped his hands, even though it was broad daylight, and lit a cigarette. He puffed hard, three times, then sat back against a block wall and watched the end glow bright, as he slowly let the smoke out through his nose.

I'm going back to sleep," Joe said. "No sense just sitting here waiting for the sun to go down." He found a spot with cross ventilation to cool him and was soon snoring softly.

The three men watched as the village lights went out, one by one, as the townsfolk settled in for the night. "It's been a long fuckin' day, Morrison stated the obvious. Holed up here in this heat trap like a bunch a rats."

He had been pacing back and forth for over an hour. "But—we gotta make sure they're sleeping good before we make our move. By midnight the whole town should be down."

"I dunno Charles. What if there's a bar in town? Could be open till two, three."

"Not a chance, Joe. These small burgs roll up the sidewalks after ten, leven at the latest. After midnight, then we'll see what it looks like out there."

"Yeah," McDowell added, "If we kin get a few hours head start we could be across the border before they even know we was here." The thirty nine year old alumnus of Alcatraz and Leavenworth rubbed his tattooed arm before adding, "This is gonna be our only shot at it. We better make it a good one or we'll be back in the joint, or—dead trying."

McMackin wondered if all this was only wishful thinking.

35

THE NATHAN BRIDGE

THE FOUR DOOR KAISER WAS PARKED off to the side, away from the house. The doors were unlocked, but the keys were not to be found. The hood was raised with minimum noise and Joseph 'Jaybird' McMackin went silently to work while the others tossed in their articles of escape. Jackets, maps, and the rifle found their way into the auto. The burlap sacks were also tossed in to the back seat.

A dog, running free a couple of blocks down from them broke into a barking fit and was soon accompanied by two others. The engine joined them in the choir as it roared to life, putting a satisfied grin on his face. McDowell joined Morrison in the front seat as Charles revved the motor while McMackin closed the hood. Joe leaped into the rear seat as the purloined auto was already rolling down the tree-lined street.

They drove a couple of blocks before McDowell said, "Whoa—let's grab them plates off that car there. We kin switch 'em with this baby."

"Good idea. Why didn't I think of it?"

Morrison pulled up and McMackin jumped out and went about unscrewing the parked car's rear plate and removing it. McDowell had the plate off the Kaiser as Joe handed him the new one. They were back on the road a half minute later, all of them grinning at their slick move.

"Way to go Red. That was quick thinking." Bear Morrison congratulated him. "That just may be the trick we need to keep 'em from spotting us so quick. Let's keep using our heads." He pounded the steering wheel, adrenaline coursing through him. (Bear), was a name known to but an intimate few.

They headed south, creeping through the sleeping village of Powers as they turned off U.S. 2 and kept south on U.S. 41. Not a vehicle in sight.

"What time is it?"

"I dunno, must be well after midnight."

They had not gone five or six miles before they slowed for the village of Nadeau only to arrive at the Carney village limit a minute later. The two were virtually connected. "Hold it Charles, back it up, that sign says Wisconsin is that way, off to the right."

"Let's check the map," McMackin offered, as the Kaiser turned west on County Road 374. "Lemme see, this looks to be a straight shot, maybe 8-9 miles to the river that separates Michigan and Wisconsin," he calculated.

They continued due west as the night closed all around them. They drove past a sign telling them they were in Nathan, the wide-spot in the road was barely noted by the convicts in flight. They remained the only automobile on the road since they left Hermansville.

A blinking light ahead caused the Kaiser to slow as the occupants tried to determine the cause. "What ya think?"

"It could be the law, Charles. That could be the flasher from a patrol car's roof. Or, it could just be a warning sign. The bridge should be close."

"Or it's closed. You could be right, Joe. Gimme that gun, will you I say if they want us to stop—we make a run for it."

"Leave the gun in the back for now, we ain't shootin' it out just yet."

"We're screwed if we try to turn around and try to make a run back the way we come," McMackin said. Nothing indicating at this point, that the Kaiser was about to experience a nautical adventure.

"You're right Joe. They'll be on the radio before we get half way back. Dammit, I can't hit the woods again tonight," McDowell looked questioningly at Morrison.

"Well—that leaves only one way to go..."

The four-door sedan lurched forward as Morrison gunned the engine and charged ahead, hoping to slip around the flashing beam of the vehicle blocking its path. "Shit. Here goes boys, it's all or nothing." The vehicle on the bridge left no question as to its identity.

"It's the cops," McDowell shouted as Morrison veered to the left of the state patrol car partially blocking the bridge.

"Keep low—they're going to open fire. I'll see if I kin hit that opening!"

"Hit it Chucky," McDowell screamed. "What we got to lose?"

"Hell, it's a bridge," Morrison yelled in surprise as he realized they didn't have enough room to maneuver. He ducked down on the seat just as the Kaiser hit a guard rail, teetered momentarily, then was hurled into space. The big sedan slammed into the water with a teeth-jarring belly flop, delivering a mammoth billow with its landing. It rocked briefly in its wake, before starting its descent to the bottom.

The fugitives scrambled about unwinding the handles of their escape routes as the rear of the vehicle scraped against the large rocks, its bumper clacking in harmony with the rushing water.

McMackin was the first to slip out into the water as he allowed the current to lead him to shore. He climbed out of the river so close to the bridge that his movements went undetected in the frothy aftermath. He was able to keep hidden as the officers' focused further past him to the capsized auto.

He silently edged his way inland and out of the prying eyes of the law. He ducked under the glare of a spotlight, then caught a quick glimpse of someone in the water downstream, just off shore. He moved carefully in that direction keeping low and avoiding the searchlights above. *It looks like John—that's great. I gotta hook up with him.*

The lawmen up on the bridge were stunned by the quick turn of events. "Think we should have opened up on them?"

"No, how could we be sure? It could a been a car full of kids. We didn't have a choice. Let's get on the horn, call this in.'"

"Yeah, sure. You betcha."

Morrison sensed, rather than knew that he was the last rat off the sinking ship. He climbed out the window and heard shouts from the officers on bridge above. He started to swim toward the shore but the current held fast, taking him rapidly downstream, he didn't fight it and luck was on his side, as it sent him to the friendly confines of the river bank.

The swift current moved him over a hundred feet downstream from the sinking Kaiser. He clambered up the embankment ignoring the shouts to halt, then darting quickly into the cover of the woods. He dropped to one knee in the safety of the trees, just long enough to catch his breath. He dared not linger. Taking one deep breath he rose and urged his trembling body, fresh from its shock, to move on.

He slogged along, his sodden body weighting him down as he staggered ahead, almost falling. He turned too often to see if he was being pursued. He ran to a hard-packed clearing, the surface making his retreat easier as he raced for the shelter of the thick cover.

Trooper Ward Johnson shouted to his partner John Seppanen, "See out there—one's heading ashore, thirty-forty feet out."

"Yeah, I see him."

The figure scampered up the bank and continued its hasty flight into the shelter of the woods. "There's another further down, just getting out of the water," Seppanen pointed to the emerging swimmer, whose silhouette rose briefly above the black background of the trees. It disappeared as quickly as it had arisen.

"Think it was them? The Russell gang?" Johnson asked his partner. The startling and sudden encounter was still hammering in his chest.

"Hell yes, we couldn't fire the riot guns without being sure. What if it had been kids out for a joy ride?"

"No way we could a opened fire, John, we had to make sure. Hell yes, we did the right thing."

They quit second guessing and put in an excited call for reinforcements while anxiously scanning the river and the adjoining banks for more sign of the recent interlopers. Soon the wailing sound of their approaching support filled the once quiet night.

"Here they come..."

Friday, June 5

Stolen Car Plunges Into Menominee River—Two Flee Into Woods

TWO OF THE FOUR STILL-AT-LARGE convicts who escaped from Marquette Prison were believed to be surrounded by police early this afternoon on the Michigan side of the Menominee River, near the village of Nathan, 30 miles northwest of Menominee.

The fugitives were believed to be encircled after the stolen automobile in Hermansville early this morning had unsuccessfully tried to crash through a state police road block on the Nathan Bridge over the Menominee River, at 1:16 this morning.

State police said an automobile smashed into a wooden guard rail as the convicts tried to elude a check at the roadblock, and that it plunged twelve and a half feet into about six feet of water, landing with its top up.

In the car, a 1951 black four-door Kaiser sedan, belonging to Mr. And Mrs. Edward LaMaide, of Hermansville, were found three Marquette Prison jackets, a fully loaded 30-30 caliber Marlin rifle, a prison razor, a Michigan Highway Department road map and a book of matches from the Idle Time Tavern in Yalmer.

A fourth prison jacket was found later, floating in the water. Two of the men were seen swimming away from the car by the officers at the road block, and it was not determined what happened to the other two convicts, whether they had drowned or escaped into the woods.

State police are under the opinion that all four fugitives were in the stolen car. The river, which separates Michigan from Wisconsin at that point, has been dragged by officers throughout the morning with no success.

Michigan State police, Menominee and Delta County sheriff's officers, Wisconsin highway patrol officers and Marquette County sheriff's deputies encircled the wooded area where the convicts who fled the scene are believed to be.

Since both men who were seen swimming from the crash had hair, the most dangerous of the four convicts, Lloyd Russell, 31, who is bald, either went ashore unseen or drowned or was not in the car.

Troopers Ward Johnson, of the Sandusky Post, and John Seppanen of the Bad Axe Post, were manning the roadblock when the felons attempted to "run" it. The troopers flashed their patrol car blinker light on the automobile as it approached the bridge, and the car slowed down.

However, just before getting to the bridge, the auto burst into speed, and attempted to pass to the left of the patrol car, which was partially blocking the narrow steel bridge. The car caromed off into the water after striking the guard rail.

Johnson and Seppanen saw two men emerge and swim downstream. One, they said, reached the bank about thirty feet from the auto, while the other was carried by the current about a hundred feet. (Currents in the Menominee—are notably strong.)

"We should have shot them with our riot guns," they added.

"But we weren't sure the occupants were the convicts until we found the four prison jackets. We thought at first we might be dealing with drunks, or maybe kids on a lark."

As the bridge is more than twelve feet above the water, the men in the car must have gotten quite a jolt when the auto plunged into the river, the officers said.

Captain Thor Person, immediately ordered every available state police trooper and patrol car into the Nathan area.

Many men who had just completed twelve hour shifts were ordered into the area. It was not discovered that it was the LaMaide car which had been stolen until after the wrecker from Menominee had pulled it out of the river, and a check was made on its registration and license plate.

The license plate was registered in the name of Miss Marion Sprick, Hermansville, but when police checked with her she said her car had not been stolen.

After the registration number was checked with the secretary of state's office in Lansing, it was found that the stolen vehicle was owned by Edward and Lucille LaMaide.

36

Dragging The Menominee

THOR PERSON HUNG UP THE PHONE and looked up at the men gathered in his office. "What a helluva night." He shook his head in disbelief. "That was Lansing. Those clever sons a bitches did switch the plates on that car they took. You almost have to hand it to them." He rose and walked over to the large map of the area.

"We knew they were resourceful right from the get go, Thor."

"Resourceful, Earl? Those bastards are downright clever."

"They've been going to school a long time. Prison teaches them a lot—things they don't need to know, and what we never learn."

"Right—they teach each other all the new tricks. Classes are ongoing. Let's bring everybody up to snuff—our boys followed a track they found at daylight. It trailed southward along the Michigan side of the river, tracing a power line, then on to an old railroad grade. After that the ground became dry and hard, the tracks disappeared."

"What do you think, Cap? Was it one of our swimmers?" A gravel voice, filled with the phlegm of too many cigarettes and coffee waited for the reply, pen in hand.

"Our boys are pretty sure it was from one of the convicts. In places, the tracks were sideways, kind of dragging a foot along, as if the person stopped frequently and turned around. Apparently he was looking to see if anyone was following." He demonstrated the action by pacing a few steps, then walking sideways, "like this."

"The map we found in the car looked like one they're had for quite a while—long before they made their break out of Marquette."

"Why is that, Earl?"

"It was well-worn and tightly folded, like it may have been hidden for quite a spell."

"I see," Person moved along. "Let's go over the latest tips and reports. We've been getting a lot of help from the Wisconsin sheriff's department." He stood up and made introductions, "Men, this is James Spangler, Sheriff over in Marinette County."

The cooperation among the various law enforcement agencies owed a lot to Thor Person. They knew they could rely on the skilled lawman when the need arose.

Sheriff Spangler was a thick-bodied man who once had been in excellent condition. He had a heavily receding hairline and a face that just missed being interesting. One look—you knew he was the law.

"About five o'clock this morning, a new Buick went through our blockade at Amberg doing 90 miles per, and heading north on 41, me and my deputy took off after them"

"Where is Amberg?" a voice in back boomed out the question.

"It's about twenty miles south of Iron Mountain, but only ten miles or so southwest of the Nathan Bridge."

"We sent a state police car from Iron Mountain to intercept," Person interjected. "but Sheriff Spangler overtook the speeding car before hand."

"Yeah, it was just a couple of youths who apparently were out celebrating graduation night. Kids, I just don't understand 'em. My dad would waxed my ass." The room chuckled when he noted, "They're celebrating in my jail right now. "

"A picnic basket was stolen from Ronald LaCasse around noon yesterday while he was fishing by Hermansville. Now—that could be our fugitives," Person said.

"A sergeant stated, "We got a call yesterday that we also investigated, a woman over in Perronville, on M-69, between Schaffer in Delta County and Whitney in Menominee County said she saw two men who resembled the convicts." Again, it was a dead end, but one that had to be followed.

"They sure are busy. They're all over the U.P. like a week's wash." The room again broke out with tired laughter.

"We'll continue dragging the river tomorrow—Delta Sheriff William Miron is in charge of the two boatloads of men searching today."

Hathaway piped in, "Those jagged rocks and the swift undercurrents are giving the men a helluva time. It would be easy to miss a body down there."

"It would have had to gotten itself stuck, otherwise it would wash ashore," would be my way of thinking," said Sergeant Smith.

"There are plenty of places for a body to get tangled in the undertow," Sergeant.

Charles Morrison was alone for the first time since the breakout from the prison. He didn't like it. His night flight from the sinking car had left him disoriented and confused as to what direction he was heading.

Besides, he was a bug-bitten disheveled mess. He was a city boy. Now, the normally dapper thief was miserable. He had ripped off the stolen white shirt and buried it in the woods. He still wore his heavy underwear top from the prison.

Yet the most troublesome of all his miseries, was the hungry, voracious mosquitoes that attacked constantly. When not biting, they were buzzing around him with gleeful anticipation. And, the wood ticks, those ugly son of a bitches would burrow their way into his flesh and fester under his skin, sucking the very blood from his body. He was stopping on regular intervals to burn them off his arms and legs. They were everywhere in the dense woods, much thicker than they were further north. He had used up all the petroleum jelly that Russell had insisted they take with them from the prison.

He still wore the khaki colored jacket and pants, and would have readily traded them for darker clothing. He needed something that would blend in a little better in the thick, dark woods. A flash of blue slipped into his view. He crept ahead slowly hoping he had found a landmark. Luck was with him as he stared out at a vacant stretch of the river. Looking up at the sky, he guessed it to be about noon, the sun looking down from straight up.

The droning hum of an airplane reached his ears, search planes was his first thought. Of course, they'd have them out after last night's dunk in the river. He ducked under heavy cover, finding a spot a hundred yards from the river where he could hunker down till dark. A swim across the river and he'd be in Wisconsin. It was just him and the ticks to idle away the rest of the day.

Cedar boughs formed a pristine canopy for a large hollowed out tree trunk that lay uprooted. He nestled into the natural hideaway.

He dozed restlessly, his agitated state causing him to drift in and out of consciousness. Nearby voices woke him with a start from his fitful nap. *Shit. The found me, must be following the river.* He crawled deeper into his hole and spotted a set of legs walking within a few feet of him. Almost close enough to touch. Morrison had almost reached the point where capture would be a relief. Bug-bitten and starving, he shuddered involuntarily as he felt the wood ticks crawl under his clothing. His capture almost sounded good to him.

I could just yell out, hey I'm over here. He suppressed a giggle as he pictured their reaction. *They'd surely shit their pants.*

The posse passed on and all was soon quiet once more. Eventually the birds picked up a tune and the squirrels and other woodland creatures began scurrying for their next meal. Nightfall was a couple hours away, and then a swim across the river would take him out of Michigan. Wisconsin would hold the key to his escape. He grabbed a hairy legged bastard before it could sample his blood, trying to crush it with fingers but the hard shell wouldn't give in.

"I'll burn your ass."

"Ouch, dammit," the flame burnt his fingers as he finally ended the tick's life as he watched it curl from the heat in its death throes.

Dusk turned the woods into an eerie shadowy dance. Two critters scampered about on the forest floor, sounding larger than the chipmunks and squirrels. Nature encouraged Morrison to shorten his wait. He groaned softly as he stretched the day's stiffness from his tired body. He moved slowly making his way back to the river's edge.

He thought of looking for a log or something he could use in crossing the swift river. He made a cursory look up and down the bank but found no flotation device.

He allowed his desire to cross the river veto the call for precaution. *The safety of Wisconsin was so close!* A decision he would later recall with remorse.

He stepped out into the river and felt the biting chill of the late spring water, nipping at his ankles like a pesky terrier. *Damn, it's cold.* He stood and let the frigid shock dissolve before proceeding.

He waded into the current which grew more swift with each step. He slipped on a slick rock and soon found himself struggling in the full force of the river's wrath. He considered himself an above average swimmer and was in reasonable shape from working out in the prison daily. Russell had insisted on daily exercise and workouts to get in top physical condition for the arduous escape.

Had he done enough? He gasped for air as he came up fast from the craggy bottom. He tried to go with the stream's flow, instead of bullying his way through it. Instinct cautioned him to ride with the currents, especially the lung sucking undertow. *Hold your breath. Don't fight it.*

The river would tire him out and leave him floating face down in its wake if he let it. He stretched forward—feeling this surge could be his last. *Keep going. Keep...*

He managed one more gasp of air before the undertow sucked him back down, crashing him against the jagged formations. *I'm gonna drown...!*

The savage stream shoved him into the sandy shoreline face first. He struggled to his hands and knees as he spit our sand and water, gagging as he cleared his throat and lungs. *I made it, Jesus Christ— I made it.* He stared at the young whitetail deer standing on the bank.

"What you starin' at?" The deer shook its tail and wandered off.

The river had almost claimed the fugitive, but he had met the challenge, he stood on the bank savoring his close call. Soon, the night air chilled him to the bone and he longed for the warmth of a fire. He scrambled up the embankment, his water-soaked lungs screaming at him to go easy.

He had made it to the escapees' primary goal. Get out of Michigan. Yes, the very first thing you must do, before—you even have a chance in a snowball's hell of escaping the far-reaching tentacles of Little Alcatraz.

Welcome to Wisconsin, Charles Morrison—you've earned it.

37

STILL NO SIGN

Saturday, June 6

LAW ENFORCEMENT OFFICERS CONTINUED COMBING A five mile square wooded area near the Nathan Bridge in their search for the convicts who had chosen the wet route in their flight for freedom. Over 80 officers were used in the detailed manhunt that had started at day's break. They broke down the sections of coverage in an informal grid search.

The familiar brown jacketed county sheriff's officers mingled with the Michigan State blue. Each section of the dragnet was supervised by an officer of the State Police.

The work was exhausting, trekking through the thick underbrush, trying to examine every spot that would hide a man from his pursuers.

The captains, Person and Hathaway had surmised that the survivors of the river crash would stick together. "I see no reason for them to split up now, Earl, they have had a lot of good luck staying together. Just look how close we've come to grabbing them on so many different occasions."

"We are watching all bridges, Thor. This damn river will not be easy to swim across. There are undercurrents and jagged rocks that could render a man unconscious when he gets tossed about in there. I wouldn't try it, but then I'm not that desperate."

"What do you think Earl? Did the other two drown? We know there were at least three in the vehicle. How do they keep disappearing into thin air?"

"They sure as hell could have drowned. All the signs indicate they were all together in the car. It's possible our guys could have missed one or both of them escaping to the river's bank." Hathaway went on to point out what the officers had discovered when the stolen vehicle was retrieved from the Menominee River's lethal grasp. "There were four jackets left in the car, three blue prison issues and one, an army OD type."

The two men watched a boat filled with officers who were attempting to drag the river. The boat and its crew worked meticulously downstream and disappeared around the river's bend. The frothy waves were shifting the small craft from side to side.

"I'll bet that you're right in thinking they are still wearing those laundered white shirts they took from the Idle Time parking lot," Person said. "They should be easier to spot in the woods or along the river bank with those contrasting colors. The bugs were really out last night, I don't know how much longer they will be able to handle the black flies and mosquitoes."

"You said it before, Thor. They are a bunch of tough assholes."

"I never said it that poetically, did I?"

"Well—asshole is a fitting word for them."

"Right. In addition to the prison jackets, a loaded 30-30 caliber Marlin rifle, a prison razor, a Michigan road map and book matches taken from the tavern in Skandia were all recovered from the stolen automobile."

"I read that in the Mining Journal. They had to have taken them when they made their escape from Gladstone."

Hathaway excused himself to take a call. It was assistant 8th district commander Lawrence J. Baril. "Are you at the bridge in Nathan, Earl? I'm on my way over there. Have you pulled out the boats already?"

"Yes, I'm here, Larry. I haven't pull them out yet—waiting your word. Are they going to lower the dam?"

"Haven't gotten a definite on that—why don't we go ahead and suspend the operation until we hear."

"You got it—we'll have everything set for the grid survey by the time you get here. How soon can we expect you?"

"I would guess I'll make it over there in a little over an hour and a half."

The Wisconsin-Michigan Power Company had been asked to lower Chalk Hill Dam, which was about seven miles to the south of the Nathan Bridge. If this is done, the officers would be able to explore the river bed with much less conflict with nature. The swift undercurrents and ragged jutting that continued to hamper their search. The general feeling was, that one, maybe two of the escaped felons may have met their demise in the rushing waters of the Menominee.

Captain Person said he did not believe there was any connection between the car that ran a blockade on U.S. 2, at the Menominee Bridge near the Riverside Club in Iron Mountain around 2:30 this morning, and the convicts.

The car, a 1950 or 51 dark colored Chevrolet, went through a Dickinson County sheriff's roadblock, where a deputy fired one shot at the fleeing auto. The deputies thought that there were three men in the car.

However, no automobiles were reported stolen. It was believed to be young teens not wanting to be caught with alcohol in their possession.

Lieutenant Baril arrived and worked with the captains and local officers to make a thorough survey of the Nathan area. The grid work allowed them to intensify the search in the heavily wooded area. State Police airplanes were being used in the stem to stern probe. Officers in motor boats were patrolling up and down the choppy river looking for signs of the missing felons.

Larry Baril had moved rapidly up the ladder of the State Police since joining them in 1945. The tall, broad shoulder lawman was raised in the Upper Peninsula and was an ideal choice to plot the grid.

While Baril was busy sealing off the Nathan area, John McDowell and Joe McMackin were heading north. Their good fortune held once more as they soon found a beaten trail that took them quickly away from the Nathan Bridge area. They pushed on through the night, stopping only when the morning light started creeping through the trees. They then stopped to rest and attempt to find their bearings.

They had crossed a creek a while back and soon were out of the thick forest land and into terrain with stretches of cleared land. They found shelter in a large copse that offered a natural area that protected them from prying eyes.

The lights from a farmhouse had winked on, signaling the start of another day for the rural inhabitants. Tired and hungry, the convicts had surpassed the search party's exterior grid lines. For the moment—they were safe.

"Lately, I been gettin' the feeling we're wanted men," McMackin said, as he nodded in the southwest direction.

It was mid-afternoon, they watched the search planes float lazily in broad circles. McDowell removed a sore foot from his well-worn shoe and rubbed it briskly. "My tootsies are so tired and sore, they hurt when I look at 'em." He took off his creamed colored hat and swatted the air. "Ain't never seen so fuckin' many bugs. Every time it clouds up they come at ya' like kamikaze pilots. Ain't they got anything else they could chew on—'sides me?" He wiped a dead mosquito on his blue denim jeans and placed the hat back on his head, cocked at an angle. His partner ignored the solecism of his observations as he knotted the laces of his shoes.

Joe still wore the khaki jacket he had in prison, but now wore blue jeans and a pair of black shoes that were a size too big. "My blister's got blisters. We ever get someplace with a tub, I'm soaking in it for a week."

"I'd feel sorry for you—but I can't reach you."

"Up yours."

"We got no time for romance."

As the daylight flickered before going out, the two escapees gathered up their burlap sacks and headed in a northeasterly direction. About the time Charles Morrison was fighting the Menominee River for his life, his two mates from the Nathan Bridge episode were strolling leisurely toward food and water.

"We're far enough off the road so we just have to get down when we see headlights."

"Gotcha Joe. We take it nice and easy—yet we kin still make good time."

They skipped the areas that featured traffic and homes with lights on, fearful a barking dog could give them away. Unknown to the twosome when they skirted the tiny village of Faithorn, was that the railroad tracks they crossed would have taken them directly into Wisconsin. At that point, they were about eight miles from the brickyard that had hidden them in Hermansville.

The landscape consisted of wooded stretches with low lying swampy areas. Interspersed with cleared farming land, they vowed to remain alert so they could remain undetected. They patiently bid their time when crossing open land. Keeping a casual appearance when they were in the open was the most difficult task they had to do. They were well aware that any furtive action on their part would make the journey a disaster if someone was to report suspicious actions.

They kept to the wooded areas and stopped again to wait out the day. The problem was; farming country had to be cleared which created vast open spaces. They soon heard the noise of the traffic, unaware that they were near U.S. 2. Hunger was gnawing at the pair of desperate men as they spent yet another day in the rugged terrain of Michigan's Upper Peninsula.

They were sorely missing the foraging expertise of one Lloyd Russell. What they would give for a decent meal in the growling stomachs?

Time ticked slowly—like a broken clock...

"I'm sure gonna appreciate a hot bath and a change of underwear, Red. We been a long time without a few simple comforts."

"Simple? That'd be heaven. Who would a thunk?—when we was dreamin' of escape."

"Don't get philosophical, John."

"Shit—I can't even spell it. Did you really think we would a gone through all the shit we've been through? I might a stayed behind."

"Remember? I was the leery one about going in the first place."

Bitching about their plight seemed a good alternative to their discomfort. "There's another one of those little creeks, Joe. Let's soak our feet for a while," McDowell was already unlacing his shoes.

"Damn, it's amazing how cold the water is," McMackin said as he swatted at the latest arrivals. "Must be one a them spring fed creeks Lloyd told us about. He's about as smart a feller as I ever run across."

"Yeah, that Lloyd—the fucker's out there enjoying himself. Fat and sassy, just biding his time..."

"Ya' really think so? I always figured that was mostly boastful talk. Learn a few things in the library—then he could show us how tough he is..."

"Well, he's tougher than me—he can stand this damn place. I always thought you was closest to him, Joe. He picked you to work for him most of the time."

"That's cause I didn't argue with him. But, yeah...I had second thoughts, 'bout not stickin' with him."

McDowell quickly changed the subject. "These fuckin' bugs keep us moving. Hell, I'm ready to get going." The two fugitives rose and dried their feet as best they could, using the grass and leaves around them, then sulked off to continue their bid to freedom.

38

From Pembine To Vulcan

Sunday, June 7

CHARLES MORRISON HAD SPENT SATURDAY IN HELL. Wisconsin had not been the haven for escaped convicts, at least not for this one. It was a hell-hole of self-inflicted grief. Never had he imagined the cruelty that his tormentors were subjecting him to. This unyielding attack on his physical and mental well-being left the city kid from the streets of Detroit numbed by their relentless obsession to drain the very blood from his veins.

He rubbed his grimy, weathered hands on his dirty underwear top, running his fingers through his soiled hair in a gesture of defeat. He should get up and look for water to clean himself before he moved on. He ran his hand lightly along his thigh, passing over a pea sized lump. *That bastard is still there, embedded in my fucking leg, stuffing his ugly ass on my flesh.*

He had tried to check himself often; somehow he missed a spot and now the intruder had worked its way into the meaty flesh of his thigh and was nuzzling—feeding itself on his life's blood.

Lloyd said they'll hatch their eggs inside your body if you leave 'em in. Leave you an itchy lump, while it's making its way into your blood. Just livin' like cannibals inside you. He squirmed and gagged at the thought. Luck was with him for a fleeting moment as he found he still had dry matches.

He was about to light a petrified piece of ironwood that he had foraged, get some hot coals and burn out the demon that was invading his body.

Morrison was in the midst of pulling down his trousers when the dull drone of an airplane motor drew ever near. He scrambled under a large spruce using his stick as a cane to keep from falling headfirst. He waited under the large boughs until the plane had done its maneuvering and moved on. The incessant buzz from the voracious creatures gave him pause to think aloud.

"A guy could get all caught up scratching and thrashing at them fuckers and not pay any attention till the plane was right above, and with his pants down to his knees." A giggle escaped him, "There I'd be—waving at the fuckin' bugs...The cops in the plane above, saying, what the hell is he doing?" He burst out in full-bellied laughter at the absurdity of the moment.

"Man—I'm losing it."

It took three matches to get the dry, brittle stick, red hot and glowing. He turned on his side and looked at the crimson-bodied protrusion. He touched the stick to his visitor, yelping as the hot tip bit his leg. He gritted his teeth, sweat forming on his lip.

He saw his tormentor wiggle from the extended heat. The thought of the living thing inside him made his stomach churn, yet he kept the fire on his blood-sucking adversary. His pale, sun starved skin was glowing bright pink as he kept the stick on the invader until the retreating hairy vampire exploded his own blood back on to his charred flesh.

A perverted sense of satisfaction gripped him as he carefully wiped off the infected area. His blistering skin formed a bubble that his touch avoided. "How do you like me now?"

He rose, only then realizing that he was sweating profusely, at least until a cool breeze kicked up and caused him to shudder from the sudden temperature change. He wiped his brow with his dirty sleeve.

"Well, that's something I always wanted to learn. How to dig out a fuckin' tick from your ass. City folks wouldn't know where to begin. Would they?" He picked away at the tender area removing remnants of the tick and burnt stick, careful not to break the blister. He had nothing to use as first aid so he gingerly pulled his underwear and pants back over his slimming frame. Hooking his pants up over his bony hips, he cinched his belt another notch.

"Damn, I'm losing weight, gotta get something to eat before I starve to death." Yesterday, he had clung to the river's edge while staying out of harm's way from the human seekers who looked for him from land, air, and water. Yet, while avoiding them, he had suffered unbearable torture from the onslaught of insects that had entered every pore of his being, feeding and buzzing until Charles Morrison was on the brink of surrender.

The caw-cawing of a couple of ravens caught his attention as he lay resting from the removal of the tick. One landed on a branch above him—resting. It sat vigilant, appearing serene and contented, with an eye cocked in his direction, as if it had plenty of time to wait for its next meal.

"Fuck you—you old crow. Don't even think about it. You ain't pickin' my bones—no, you ain't eatin' me." He picked up a rock and hurled it in their direction.

"Damn, slow down John. We don't wanna wake up the whole damn town."

"We're in," a relieved sigh escaped into the opened front door whose sign above the store indicating that it was owned and operated by the **Marinelli Brothers.** They darted inside and commenced to shop. Pacing about rapidly, it was too much—as everything appealed to them.

"Careful, we kin only tote so much..."

"Gotcha, Joe. It's hard to decide what I want first."

It didn't take long to fill their sacks, hoping they hadn't overlooked a necessity. McDowell shoved a carton of cigarettes into his. "I'm gonna smoke a pack a these fuckers without taking 'em outta my mouth." He puffed the air and mimed his smoking binge.

"Hurry, John, we got all we can carry." He glanced around the store one more time before heading for the exit.

They made a hasty and uneventful retreat as they skirted the village limits and headed northwest to their temporary hideaway. "Did you grab some shit paper?" McDowell wanted to know. "By the time I get this belly stuffed, I wanna empty it and start all over again."

"Yeah, I got some toilet paper. My ass can use some pampering, too. It's funny, the little things we miss." McMackin let out a sigh, releasing the nervous energy that gripped him during their latest caper.

They reached their destination and sat with their backs against a couple of trees. They began to wolf down the favorites that had been missing from their meager diet.

"This is a regular fuckin' picnic." McDowell leered at the meal before him.

"I ate four dogs, a can a beans, a can a sardines, and a whole bag of chips." McDowell lay back rubbing his swollen belly while he sucked on a Pall Mall until his eyeballs almost joined together. He sipped his Granddad's root beer trying to force out a belch. "If I don't fart and burp pretty soon—I'm gonna blow up."

"Just make sure you fart down wind—I smelt your sorry ass before. I don't want to do that again."

"Joseph, ol' pal—what a hurtful thing to say. After all we been through."

"Well, if the truth hurts..."

"Kiss my ass, I ain't as bad as Mayberry—remember him? Stunk up the whole cell block, then laughed about it while we was gagging to death."

"No, you ain't that bad. Whatever did happen to him?"

"Sent him to Jackson—wasn't much of a threat to escape anymore."

"Why was that?"

"Sugar got him. Took off his leg—he had diabetes real bad."

"That's too bad, he was okay. I had a couple of details with him. Told a good story...

The days had been quiet for the fourth escaped felon. He spent days in a detached garage where he was able to watch the owner's house and comings and goings, making it easy for him to slip out the back should someone approach. Raiding neighboring clotheslines, he had shed his long winter underwear as the weather continued warming.

Concerned that the garage was also getting "warm"—Russell moved out and headed west for five miles or so and fashioned another lean-to hideout. He had some extra clothing and had also "found" some more bedding.

A creek was located nearby and it furnished him with water, and he was excited to find a patch of stinging nettle. His study of local herbs in the prison library had brought this herb to his attention as one of the finest and most nutritious foods in the whole plant kingdom. The truth be known, it had more nutrients than a lot of the vegetables he had located in kitchen gardens on his many scavenging trips. They offered a surprising amount of protein which was most difficult to obtain without raising an alert as to his whereabouts. This patch would be the alternative to a fresh cut of meat.

He learned quickly how to protect himself when collecting the nettles without being stung by the sharp leaves. He acquired a kettle and fry pan, which he used to simmer them and turned them into a tasty and nutritious meal.

There was plenty of food to capture, steal, and wild craft, if one knew what he was doing. Russell had mastered many tricks for his survival, and was always learning more. He waited as long as it took to move about the area—observing, learning...

He would also wait as long as needed before attempting to slip out of the state. Patience, that's what it took to make a clean break, patience—and a little luck.

Unknown to all, he slept in his make shift tent while his fellow escapees, known as the two M's—passed within a half mile on their way to shopping in Vulcan.

39

In Wisconsin

Sunday, June 7

THE UNYIELDING PRESSURE FROM THE INSECT attack had left Morrison with no option but to bug out of the woods. They flushed him out of deep cover forcing him to seek refuge. He attempted to enter parked vehicles, not even so much to steal them for a quick run, as was his quest to stop the attack on his tired and hungry body.

He discovered a car sitting alone in the driveway, unlocked, but without the keys in the ignition. A quick check of the house indicated that the owner was either still asleep or had gone off to church with a different vehicle. He pushed the car down the sloping drive, then jumped inside to pop the clutch in order to start the engine. Like everything else he had attempted this morning, the latest tactic—failed miserably.

He abandoned the vehicle, then worked his way down the road in hopes of finding something else. He hustled off into the nearby woodland when he became aware of a vehicle approaching.

He had ducked to safety on two other occasions to avoid being glimpsed by a passing motorist, possibly heading to church. Traffic was heavy, it being Sunday morning. He was disoriented by the quick reversal of scenery.

Unknown to him, his antics had not gone unnoticed as reports were coming in from many citizens around the Pembine, Wisconsin area. Officers were discharged and soon converged on the hapless runaway.

Officers were combing the woods near the Four Seasons Club where most of the morning's reports were centered, when Conservation Officer John (Jack) Shemky, of Crystal Falls spotted a figure dart back into the brush from a county road.

In accordance with a prearranged agreement, Shemky fired a shot into the air. He was immediately joined by Trooper Robert Dufort of the Marquette Post, and they converged on the spot where Shemky had seen the suspect enter. Charles Morrison, lying on the ground in a fruitless attempt to hide—offered no resistance.

"Get up. Do it slow and easy. No shenanigans."

Morrison shrugged at the vulturous mosquitoes as he followed orders.

"Got a smoke? I ain't armed."

"Get up now—real slow." Dufort voiced the underlying threat.

"How's this—for slow? Just get me the fuck outta this woods."

"Head out on to the road there—keep it nice and easy." The officers followed their prisoner to the two-track road.

The scene was soon a gathering of officers who had aided in flushing out the convict. State Police Detective Anthony Spratto, Detective George Strong, and Troopers Teddy Hanna and Raymond Rudman, all of Marquette, and Menominee County Sheriff's Deputies Edmund Hanna of Faithorn, and Andrew Vescolani of Hermansville were on the scene within minutes of the rifle's signal.

"Got anything to eat?" Morrison sucked deep on his first cigarette in days. "I could eat a horse, raw, right on the hoof."

"We're gonna take you to Marinette," Sergeant Spratto said. He had just closed his radio conversation with an elated Thor Person. "George, will you and Teddy ride with me with the prisoner?"

"To Marinette? We'll be glad to go."

The prisoner was loaded for the ride back to prison finish his life sentence.

Monday, June 8—The Mining Journal

CHARLES MORRISON, 31, THE FOURTH MEMBER of seven dangerous convicts—was being held in the Marinette County jail today until extradition procedures could be completed.

Morrison, lean, haggard and unshaven, and showing the effects of over two weeks in the woods, was seized by Michigan law enforcement officers at 4:55 pm Sunday afternoon near the Four Seasons Club, about nine miles southeast of Pembine, Wisconsin.

Morrison told officers who apprehended him that he, McMackin and McDowell had split from the other escapee, Lloyd Russell, after a row in Wells Township last Wednesday.

Russell is still believed to be in the northern part of Menominee County.

The latest development in the convict chase was the robbery of a store in Vulcan, Michigan, and only 18 miles from where Morrison was captured. Troopers said quantities of food were missing and the robbery had been carried out by very hungry men.

The officers said Morrison was in bad shape, and that the woods and nature had taken their toll on the fugitive. He was badly eaten up by flies, bugs, and ticks. He had not shaved for about three or four days, and had not eaten in four days.

Morrison said he was willing to wave extradition but he was brought to Marinette first—he had $74.00 in his possession, but did not disclose anything about the robbery in Skandia Township. Under interrogation by Captain Person, and Detectives Spratto and Strong, Morrison poured out his tale of the break and subsequent events.

Morrison's Account:

I DIDN'T DO ANY CUTTING WITH the torch in the prison, because the prison authorities would not let me get near a torch, knowing that I did that sort of work on the outside. I got lotsa experience in the use of 'em. The prisoner was talkative and plainly relieved to be out the tormenting woods.

"We planned to break out together—all of us, but there were no plans beyond that. It was every man for himself once we got out." He shrugged at Detective Spratto's raised eyebrow.

"We camped near the Idle Time because we thought that if they (the officers) would drive (search) the woods, they wouldn't bother with a little patch like that. Lloyd was pretty sharp—he knew how the cops thought." The slim escapee lit another cigarette.

He had been virtually chain-smoking since his capture His fatigue was playing against him.

"It rained the other day, and we got soaked. We were wet all the time. We had some candy bars, and the food situation was pretty rough. Once—we ate a muskrat." He shook his head, "Wasn't that bad—just the thought."

Morrison said he hadn't eaten in four days prior to his capture, and officers attested to that fact, by reporting that he devoured a whole loaf of bread, two pounds of cold meat, and two pounds of cheese, and drank two quarts of water during the ride from Nathan to Marinette.

The convict told the officers that the car he and the others stole from Theodore McMaster, had "quit" on them while they were in Deerton and that they stole the other car (from Edwin Peura) after abandoning the McMaster's automobile.

McMackin, Morrison said, was an "old hand" at crossing wires of cars to get them started without a key, and that job proved no difficulty for him in the escape. "He's a wizz at crankin' them (deleted) up."

Morrison said they drove toward Munising and picked a lock from a filling station to fuel up. "We then drove south and didn't have any idea which road we were on. Our only object was to get out of Michigan as fast as we could. After we left the Buick (Peura's car) near Escanaba, we hit the woods, taking everything we could grab. Russell wanted to stay there, in the woods. He was a country guy. The rest of us are from the city and we wanted to get out by following the railroad tracks."

"Wednesday? Yeah, it must a been around Wednesday night (June 3rd), we had a helluva argument with Russell, because he wanted to go back in the woods and swamp. That's when we split from him. We were all weary from dodging the police and everything had added up to cause the argument."

Morrison admitted—as state police last week had surmised—that the convicts had the Michigan road map in their possession before they broke out of prison. "I toll ya'—Lloyd was a schemer, he had it all planned to a tee.

Skilled and practiced in the art of lying, the officers would sift through the information that Morrison had provided, and try to recognize fact from fiction in the pursuit of the three remaining fugitives.

Morrison said the three of them, after splitting with Russell, followed the Soo Line Railroad Company tracks into Hermansville—walking in the brush and woods along the tracks. They had decided against "flipping" a train after watching state police go through a freight train (while stopped) in search of the convicts.

"Before leaving there," Morrison said, "McDowell left camp one night and went into the village. He came back the next morning with a rifle, but no food."

The rifle, (the 30-30 Marlin), which was found—fully loaded—in the stolen car after it crashed into the Menominee River was not reported stolen to State Police. They were unaware of its existence until the car was pulled out of the river. "We didn't ask him where he got it; we just knew he had it."

The felon said they spent one night in an abandoned brick yard, before taking the LaMaide car and heading for Wisconsin.

Morrison said he was driving the car as it approached the Nathan Bridge, which, he added, none of the convicts knew was there. "We saw the sign pointing west to Wisconsin—it looked the quickest way to get there."

He spoke of their surprise at the roadblock. "I ducked for shelter," Morrison said. "In case they (the state troopers) fired into the car. I thought the bridge was wider than it is (16 feet). The next thing I knew we were sailing into the river."

"At first I thought it was just a creek, but soon found out it was a river—swift and deep. I was the last to get out of the car. I tried to swim back to the bridge (possibly to go across the river), but the current was too strong and I stopped and turned around. I was lucky to make it to the bank. The other two must have had a tough time, because I am the best swimmer, and I was in the best shape of the three."

Morrison said he did not see either McDowell or McMackin after the car plunged into the water. Morrison said he saw the search planes and also searchers but managed to keep out of sight. He said he swam across the river Friday or Saturday night—he wasn't sure—and that he "damned near drowned."

"I should have taken a log across with me, but I hit it alone."

He said he wasn't trying to steal a car, but simply looking for a blanket and a roof. "I hit the road Sunday, the ticks and bugs were getting unbearable."

Joseph Fisher, of Pembine, riding with his family on the Four Seasons Road, reported that he saw a man who appeared to be Morrison, duck into the woods. The tips on all the tampered cars led to the search where Morrison was apprehended.

When taken, Morrison was not wearing any prison clothes. He was dressed in heavy underwear, a bluish sweater, a khaki colored jacket and pants, and had a blue blanket. Asked by officers if he was glad the chase was over, he replied, "Yeah, I guess so. I couldn't have stuck it out much longer."

Then—there were three...

40

The Longest Manhunt

Tuesday, June 9

THIS MORNING THE STATE POLICE AND Conservation Officer Clarence Lienna of Stephenson were making a check of approximately thirty five deer hunting camps in the belief that one or two of the convicts might be hiding out in one of them. It just stood to reason that a break-in of a vacant cabin would provide the most comfortable accommodations, along with a possibility of some canned goods and other provisions.

Law enforcement officers returned Morrison back to Marquette Prison and were now concentrating their search for the remaining three felons in the Vulcan and Nathan areas. The search spread to Vulcan, due to the break-in of a local store in the village.

Officers in charge of the search said this morning that it is "quite apparent" that one of the felons drowned after the crash into the Menominee River, and they were dragging the river again today. Police believed one convict drowned because of the report by the troopers at the scene of the blockade.

Adding to the theory was the fact that Morrison said he was the best swimmer of the trio and that he hadn't seen either one since the wreck. It was easy to believe that the untamed river could have taken at least one life.

The big question confronting officers today was the whereabouts of the other escaped convict at large—Lloyd Russell, according to Morrison, split up with the other three following an argument as to what course to take after abandoning a stolen car.

Russell, born and raised on a farm, is an accomplished woodsman, as well as a dangerous criminal.

The robbery of the Marinelli Brothers store in Vulcan was discovered yesterday morning when the owners found the lock on the front door had been forced open by use of a heavy bar or stout piece of wood.

Meanwhile, two trained bloodhounds brought in by Marinette County Sheriff James Spangler from the Winnebago County sheriff's department in Appleton, were being used in the search on the Wisconsin side of the Nathan Bridge.

There is no provision by the Michigan State Legislature for the use of bloodhounds in hunting escaped convicts. An immediate dispatch of the bloodhounds would in all likelihood have led to a quick resolution in the dramatic escape.

It was very possible that some of the ninety troopers from lower Michigan assisting in the search would have to be ordered back to their posts because of the tornado damage near Flint. The report stated that the National Guard was being used in the storm area.

Monday afternoon State Police Lieutenant Lawrence Baril, Sergeant E.C. Goldsworthy, Gladstone Post Commander, and Corporal Barney Froberg of Lansing, took Morrison from the Marinette County jail to the county courthouse, where the convict waived extradition before Judge William Haase of Marinette.

The officers then took Morrison to Gladstone. Lieutenant Baril, State Police Detective Leonard Bartelli and Sergeant Ralph Sheehan, Marquette, and Trooper Marvin Anderson of Manistique took him to Marquette Prison.

The prisoner was quiet and the officers did not extract any more information from him that would help expedite the capture of the three remaining escapees. "Shit, you guys know more than me now," he said before nodding off to sleep.

The prisoner missed the spectacular view that Lake Michigan offered that sunny afternoon as they motored along M-35 passing through Cedar River on the way to Gladstone. The fifty five mile stretch from Menominee to Escanaba was traveled in relative silence as the accompanying officers were content to enjoy what nature had to offer.

In Gladstone, the switch of officers was made and after a quick visit to the rest facilities and a chance to grab a fresh cup of coffee. Morrison was escorted on the final leg of the trek back to lifelong incarceration. Sergeant Sheehan was behind the wheel as Baril and Bartelli chatted quietly in the back seat with their prisoner.

"Got anything to add? Something that will help make your stay back inside a little more comfortable?" Baril, being cordial.

"Not an effing thing." Morrison, once again, Mister Tough Guy.

"Let's go over it again, one more time. Sometimes a person remembers something he overlooked." Bartelli, putting in a sharper edge. "Think it through—real hard. You're a smart guy, smart guys live easy in the joint." He slipped a cigarette between Morrison's lips. "Always got enough smokes, things they can use..."

Here's the way it was, I went swimming, almost drown, pulled ticks outta my ass..."

"Okay, that's enough." Baril closed the session.

There were a few inconsistencies in the re-telling, but no new information was gleaned from the hardened criminal, a veteran of an uncountable number of grilling and other tactics from law enforcement officials.

While Lloyd Russell was staying put and laying low in the Faithorn woods, the Mac duo was angling their way toward the border. Keeping to the woods during the day, resting and staying out of sight, they waited till late night before making their move in what they believed was a mostly westerly direction. They picked their way around the village of Norway and were now following a set of railroad tracks they believed would lead them to the promised land of Wisconsin. The clouds covered the moon and stars and made the trek slow and meticulous. A sense of achievement was setting in.

"All those lights up ahead, that's gotta be Iron Mountain, John. It wouldn't be the other town, Kingsford. That should come after."

"Kingsford, Smingsford—we're getting close, I kin smell it. If our luck holds out, we kin get real close before the sun comes up. We find a place to hole up for the day—you know, check things out real good before we make a run at the border."

"Like Lloyd would do? Now—that's smart. Damn, it's dark. I almost fell head first. I'd a landed on my face."

"Hush, Joe. We're getting kinda loud."

"Yeah—you're right." He hissed.

"I know. It's them falls, they're so noisy, we ended up talking above them." Joe stopped them and leaned in close. "You got it right. We'll take cover before first light and look things over real good. You know they got the roads sewed up tight."

A sense of urgency seized them as they neared the village of Quinnesec. It may have hampered their ability to be alert—and to be aware. Soon they were moving rapidly, without caution, as if the nearness of the border was pulling them.

"Damn, them waterfalls—sure is noisy. I reckon no one can hear us either."

"I don't like it John. The darkness and the noise—we could be walking right into an ambush."

"And—never know it." John McDowell finished the ominous statement.

The Mining Journal

NEWS FLASHES

SEOUL—NINE PLANES FROM THE NORTH swept over Seoul tonight in the biggest Red air raid in the war, dropping bombs that shook President Syngman Rhee's mansion and injured seven persons. Some of the bombs barely missed the Eighth Army press billits.

Washington—Sen. Knowland (R-Calif) today called on South Korea's President Syngman Rhee to accept the Korean armistice. Knowland, chairman of the Republican policy committee, spoke out in the Senate after Secretary of State Dulles had briefed a group of senators on the latest developments. Knowland previously supported Rhee's objection to a truce leaving Korea divided.

LONGEST MANHUNT IN STATE

The search for the convicts still at large is the longest sustained manhunt in Michigan's history.

The previous longest manhunt was in 1938, when state police chased a bank robber for seventeen days before catching him in a swamp in Lower Michigan.

The fugitive at the time, Tommy Hunt, stole $18,000 in bonds and cash from a Hillman bank after he had gone to the bank president's home and ordered the president to go with him. After the theft, the bank president was locked in the vault.

Today the search for the three remaining fugitives still free from the confines of "Little Alcatraz" is in its 18th day.

41

Fumee Falls

Wednesday, June 10

TWISTER DEAD—111 IN FLINT; DAMAGE OVER TEN MILLION.

Flint, Mich. (AP)-As the second dawn rose on the wreckage left by a string of Michigan and Ohio tornadoes, crews resumed cleanup work and the long search for more dead.

Worst hit Monday were the northern outskirts of the industrial city. The dead were numbered at 111. But twisters took at least eight other gigantic swipes to kill a total of 139, injured more than 1,000 and do possibly fifteen million dollars damage.

Eight died in the Cleveland area, eight in Wood County, Ohio, and one each in Elyria and Ceylon, Ohio.

In Michigan, four were killed in Eric, just across the Ohio line, four in Tawas, a northern resort town, and one each in the Ann Arbor area and the tiny Lapeer County village of Brown City.

The Flint twister swept through a tightly packed area of modest factory worker homes in the Beecher metropolitan district, leveling everything but a few stark naked trees in a four mile by four block area.

Midnight on the railroad tracks was a particularly noisy as the two convicts worked their way toward Quinnesec by passing the noisy crescendo to their right. In the ebony of the moonless night, movement was slow and tedious as they guided themselves by feeling their way over the railroad ties. They heard the cascading roar of the water falls in the still June night long before arriving at this point.

"I bet we're only but a couple a two-three miles from the border," John McDowell attempted to hurl his voice to his partner without sending it beyond them to unseen lawmen who may be stalking them.

"What? I can't hear you."

"Never mind. Keep going."

McMackin was guided forward by McDowell's light hat which made the going slightly easier for him. Although both had tripped and stumbled several times in the extreme darkness, sudden stops by his cohort had caused a couple of minor collisions in the cave-like conditions.

"Watch where the fuck your going."

"Sorry, I wish I was a bat."

Unknown to the beleaguered twosome, trouble awaited their next step. With the roaring of the falls still fresh in their ears, they approached a railroad car sitting idle at a railroad siding.

"Carl, did you see that? Look straight down the tracks." Roy Christianson nudged his fellow trooper as he eyed the bobbing hat that was closing in from the east. They couldn't pick up the scraping sounds of gravel from the escapees' shuffling footsteps due to the animated sounds from the falls.

They waited a few minutes in silent communication honed by years of tactical training and experience, snapping their flashlights in choreographic union on the unsuspecting convicts.

"Freeze," their voices blended in perfect harmony.

"Don't shoot, we ain't armed."

"Put your hands straight up to the sky."

"Jesus, I can't reach that high."

"Do the best you can, and do it quick."

The fugitives complied without hesitation and were soon wearing familiar jewelry on their wrists. They were squired silently to an awaiting squad car and placed unceremoniously in to the back seat.

For John McDowell, 39, alias John H. Kelly, and Joseph "Jaybird" McMackin, 35, their springtime odyssey had come to a roaring end.

McDowell-McMackin Captured—Police Hunt Russell In Delta

TWO MORE CONVICTS WERE RECAPTURED EARLY today by Michigan State Police near the village of Quinnesec, five miles east of Iron Mountain, leaving only one of the seven felons who fled Marquette Prison in the sensational break of May 22, still at large.

They offered no resistance when spotted by Troopers Roy Christianson of Escanaba, and Carl Stromer of Chassell, both assigned to the Wakefield Post.

The officers had been on duty since 8:30 last night, but were able to see practically nothing in the pitch black of the night, and couldn't hear footsteps due to rocky waterfalls, the twenty foot Fumee Falls, on the north side of U.S. Two. The tracks were on the south side.

It was the first time that more than one of the felons was seized at one time.

The only convict still being sought this morning was Lloyd Russell, 31, thought to be one of the ringleaders in the break, and believed to be the most dangerous of the seven.

Police were in hot pursuit of him today.

This morning police thought Russell was in the Menominee-Delta County area, probably in the vicinity of Hermansville, where a pack sack bearing potatoes, cigarettes (Lucky Strikes), candy bars (Hersheys and Babe Ruths), and a rear view mirror from a car, was found shortly before midnight last night.

The articles were found in a private, two car garage near Harmansville, and the owner said to state police this morning that he suspected something wrong there for a couple of nights, but he did not think it worthwhile to report.

Officers also found a suit of prison-issue winter underwear, with Russell's serial numbers on them, in the garage, and also a partly built lean-to not far away from the garage.

Police believe that Russell stayed in the garage one or two nights, and that he was scared away by the owner.

All available state troopers were being sent into that area this morning to conduct the search for the fugitive.

When captured, McDowell and McMackin each had burlap bags which they were using as knapsacks. In the sacks were two long (about one foot), home-made knives, groceries, cigarettes, bottles of drinking water and two blankets. They also had a $150.03 in cash, including several handfuls of silver.

"We caught them by surprise," Christianson said. "They didn't try to run away—they didn't have a chance. We snapped the cuffs on as soon as we could."

The officers had been assigned to that point by Sergeant Graham Pebbles, Iron Mountain Post Commander, formerly of Marquette, who had gone over the blockade points with Captain Thor Person, who is in charge of the longest sustained manhunt in the state of Michigan.

They were brought into the post at Iron Mountain and were stripped and thoroughly searched. No additional weapons were found.

Sergeant Pebbles was in charge of the shake-down search in preparation for their return to prison. They acted nervous and camera shy while chain-smoking throughout the process.

"Get outta my face wit that thing, you got enough pictures awready." McDowell flashed up his hand in protest. "Ask the coppers for their takes, I ain't posing for youse newspapers guys." He had reverted to gangland slang, or—at least his perception of it.

At 1:00 am, they headed back to where their twenty day trip had begun. At Marquette district headquarters, they were interrogated by Captain Person and Lieutenant Baril. Hoping to take advantage of their fatigue, they were questioned together at the onset, then split, and interrogated separately.

They asserted that they had split up from Russell and Morrison, "after about four or five days," and that they had followed the North Western Railroad tracks practically all the way, walking in the brush near the tracks most of the time, keeping the rails close at hand, and on the tracks the rest of the time.

"It was pretty rough in the woods," McDowell said. "But shit, we almost got to the border."

McMackin added, "We would a made it, too, with just a little luck on our side."

They denied having entered Marinelli Brothers store in Vulcan and burglarizing it, saying that they had purchased some things in an "out of the way grocery store." Further adding, "We don't even know or remember the name of the place. Hell—for that matter, we don't even know what county we was in."

The two new returnees also branded the parts of the story given to them supposedly by Morrison, as least concerning them, was false. (They did not believe that Morrison had been nabbed until seeing the pictures of the capture during individual questioning.)

Both were reluctant to discuss their experiences, and professed their innocence to all the crimes committed since the break.

"I'd rather not say anything," McDowell said—and McMackin chimed in, "I haven't anything to say either."

They denied having any dispute with Russell.

"Joe and I went off by ourselves. I won't do any yapping; and I won't do any denying that Morrison told you what you boys says he did."

McDowell kept on his cream-colored hat of detection and was wearing a blue sweater with blue denim jeans and black shoes. It was the hat that stood out in the black night near Iron Mountain.

McMackin had a khaki jacket, blue jeans, and wore the large black shoes one size too large for his feet. The shoes were well-worn, and their feet, although showing the affects of the twenty plus days in the woods, were in better shape than Morrison's.

Both were clean-shaven (they said they had just shaved Tuesday morning), and that they got the "horse blankets) and hat in a barn in Marquette county. Neither appeared hungry, and they only asked for cigarettes during questioning.

They were shown the Mining Journal's Photographer Lou Armstrong's picture of the break, from the air (taken without his knowledge that an escape was taking place). The convicts said, "Sure enough, there it is." They both recalled seeing the plane as it circled over them at the time of the break.

Both convicts denied having had a part in any crimes since the break and said they "did not ride in any car," other than the patrol cars that brought them to Marquette.

The officers thinking was, then the moon really was made of *green cheese.*

42

GRILLING THE RETURNEES

AFTER THE INITIAL INTERROGATION, THE PRISONERS were separated, then left to stew in their own juices while the interrogating officers sat down to discuss the individual questioning. "These guys are experts at this sort of grilling," Thor Person cautioned Baril and Spratto. "It's important that we get what we can from them. Anytime you spot an inconsistency, interrupt me, jump right in and hit 'em with it. Question it right away."

"Who we gonna start with?" Spratto said.

"Let's start with the redhead. I think we have a better chance of him slipping up first. He's a talker. McMackin chooses his words carefully. If we get McDowell to loosen up, we can throw that at his partner."

"I'll watch real tight, let you two do most of the grilling. If I spot any-thing—I'll jump right in." Baril suggested. "That way he'll concentrate his answers on you two and I may rattle him when he starts making things up."

"Very good, Larry. I like it."

"That should throw him off. He's a talker—not a thinker."

"Okay—let's get started. I lead in, try to set the tone."

"Good Captain, he'll expect you to take control."

"Hello, John. How you doing? Everybody treating you right? We'll chat a little before we let you get some rest." Person, almost sympathetic.

"Say—I could use a smoke."

"Soon as we get a few things out of the way, we'll all take a smoke break. What you say? Let's get the work done first, then we can relax." He nods to all at the conference table, including the stenographer who sits in almost silent fashion, as if she's part of the furniture.

McDowell shrugged, "Hell, it's no biggy. Been without 'em before. Sometimes for weeks at a time."

"Your shoes sure do look like you walked a good long way in them," Thor Person, ever so caring. "We'll fix you up with a new pair and those feet soaked in the infirmary. First, we need to know exactly what you did and where you've been since you left here."

"I'm okay. I've had sore feet before." Again, he shrugged.

"Where did you go after the break? Start at the beginning—that Friday afternoon."

"Gee, we gotta rehash that old shit?" McDowell thought over his answer, "We took off following Russell and Morrison. They were heading south for—I dunno, four, I think maybe five days."

"What happened then? Where'd you go? Was it four, or was it five days? Think hard now. I said it was important."

"We split up, me and Joe headed out on our own. We figgered two-somes stood a better chance of getting away."

"Did the four of you have a falling out?" Spratto interjected for the first time.

"Naw. We jest wanted to keep moving. Lloyd—he wanted to wait it out. Guess Charles did too. Though he figgered he could talk Lloyd into boosting a ride."

"The evidence says there were four of you in a lean-to in Yalmer." Captain Person pointed the facts out to his uncooperative witness.

"Oh, where's Yalmer? Never heard of it. Yeah—we stayed some wheres for a night or two, wit them." Attempting to sound more convincing, he added, "We split up by mutual consent. Was no trouble. You kin ask Mac."

"Oh, we'll ask him alright. Why don't you just sit back and visit with Sergeant Spratto, while Lieutenant Baril and I visit with your partner."

"How about that cigarette?"

"Sure, go ahead, enjoy."

Baril, for the first time spoke, with a hard edge to his voice, a sneer forming on his lips. "John, while you're smoking, think about those lies you been telling. Remember—life is easier inside when you cooperate..."

"Sorry to keep you waiting Mister McMackin. May I call you, Joe?"

"Like you won't call me what the hell you please."

"As I was saying—your friend John has been bringing us up to date on your activities and events since your escape."

"Really? Yeah, sure he did. What can I add to that?"

"Care for a smoke? Here, I have a light handy. Larry, I've been doing all the talking. Joe, have you met Lieutenant Baril?" Person leaned back in his chair, rocking on its hind legs. He puffed contentedly on the unlit pipe.

"Hi Joe, could you give us a quick take on what you did after you busted out of here? Let's have your version now. Cut out all the shit, we'll get to take a break sooner that way. Where did you head, and with who?"

"Well, John and I—we just followed Russell and Morrison for a few days—you know, from a distance. I ain't much on direction, I think we was heading west—to Wisconsin. Maybe started out going south."

"West, huh? That's interesting. Did you stay with them in a lean-to?"

"A lean-to..? Oh, you mean that shack Lloyd built? Yeah—yeah we did. Just for a couple a days. Then Red and I blew out by ourselves one night cause we was in a hurry to get to Wisconsin. Lloyd—well Lloyd wanted to wait it out. But the bugs was real bad. We wanted out of the woods."

"We see you left your prison issue jackets near the camp. What did you fellas eat while you were there?

"Eat? Oh, some berries. Lloyd was good at finding food. Once, he fed us some chicken, and be brung us some fresh milk and eggs. He was good at finding stuff. Mostly, Red and I laid low, played cards, a little gin, and some, ah—canasta."

"Oh—that takes a couple of decks of cards, doesn't it? Funny, we didn't find any cards. Not on you two, not on Morrison. Do you suppose Russell is out there somewhere playing solitaire?"

"I dunno. We didn't take the cards. Maybe Lloyd, he burned them."

"Say Joe," Baril's voice pitched upward an octave. "Why did you boys have those Michigan maps with you? If you boys took the tracks all the way?"

Joe McMackin felt the denials and downright fabrications catching up with him. "Oh, we used 'em to give us a general idea, you know—as to where we was going. It was tough though, as we were lost most of the time. But—wait, the other boys took 'em wit dem."

"You know what I notice, Joe?"

"What's dat Lieutenant?"

"I notice you talk like a punk when you're lying to us. You speak pretty good English when you're not."

"Huh? Zat so?"

"Yes. I think that is so. You insist that you didn't take that ride in any of the stolen cars. Yet—Morrison says you hot-wired them, Joe. Said you were the only one that could. Morrison's a tough guy, too, Joe. And—I believed him. Captain, did you believe Morrison?"

"All the way, Lieutenant. Morrison was very candid. I promised to put in a good word with the warden."

"I still don't believe you caught Charles. Even if you did, it had nuttin' to do wit me. I didn't steal no cars. Look at my sheet. I never boosted no cars. Shit—I can't even drive."

"Why's that, Joe?"

"It's my sight, I'm practically blind. Blind as a bat."

"Excuse me, gentleman." Thor Person rose from the table and left the room. Returning in less than a minute, he lay the day's Mining Journal on the table. "Look at this, Joe. Can you see? That's a pretty good picture of Morrison, don't you think?"

"Shit."

"Morrison says you fellas took the car in Hermansville. Just the three of you. Even switched the plates from a neighbor's car. John's idea, and—you helped." Person was again in charge of the interrogation.

"We skirted around Escanaba, we didn't know where that Hermansville place was. Never heard of the place."

"There seems to be quite a few pieces that just don't jive here, Joe. We're having trouble fitting them all together—you know, the chain of events. The way you fellas mumble, and downright lie, we're getting mighty curious as to what you're hiding."

"Me? I ain't hiding nothing."

"Nothing, Joe? It seems to me you're being purposely vague."

Baril rose and pointed to a map on the wall. "It's a little strange how you took the track all the way and nobody spotted you. See? We had checkout points, here, here, and over here."

"I dunno, like I said, we was real careful..."

"We'll help somebody that helps us put this all together—add up all the pieces. Starting with—how did you and McDowell end up together? You were just strolling along—in the moonlight? No wait, it was pretty dark when the troopers arrested you."

"We become mates, back in the stir, cause we knew each other better than the others. You know how it is, when we was in the joint."

"No, I don't know how it is. See Joe, I've never been in the joint. Not on your side of the bars. How about the rifle we found in the submerged car?"

"Rifle? There was never no rifle. I don't know nuttin' about no rifle."

"We understand McDowell had it in Escanaba, before you got to Hermansville."

"Red and I never had no firearms at all—if he would a had one—he would a used it to shoot a squirrel or something." Trying to switch the topic, he alluded to the search of the train. "Say, I never saw so many cops in one place. They were everywhere, but we still thought we'd make it to Wisconsin. We was close."

Yes, you were close. Just three miles short."

"Excuse me," Baril said, "If you were never in Hermansville, how did you know about the big search? Look again at the map, Joe. It happened right here, in Hermansville."

"Huh? See—I toll you I didn't know where we was."

"Okay, Joe." Person again took over. "One last time, how did you get to where you were when you were apprehended?"

"We were gonna go on into Iron Mountain, maybe lay low, try to blend in a little, then slip on over to Wisconsin—when no one was looking—I mean."

"How'd you travel, without being seen?"

"We slept during the day, then walked three, four miles, sometimes nine or ten miles, but just at night." Turning to Person, "We might as well get back in the joint, we got a lot of bull pen time ahead of us."

"Wanna tell us about the car in the river, Joe? What you did after you went down?" Baril said, "Were you ever worried that you might drown. That river was rough."

"Shit. We wasn't in no car in no river. Besides, I got nuttin' more to say. I'm all done, I got rights..."

The interview ended for Joe McMackin. Person buzzed Sergeant Smith. "Take him back to the prison, we'll know where to find him when we need him."

The Oklahoma City native, first arrested at sixteen, knew how to do hard time.

"Hello John, we're back again. But we're just about finished here, too." Person burst into the room, tossing the Mining Journal on the table. "Take a good look, I think you know the star on the front page of today's edition. Maybe you busted out together?"

McDowell's eyebrows raised as he scanned the newsprint, trying to glean anything he could get from it. "Shit, that sure does look like Charles. Where'd you nab him?"

"Why, just across the river from where you boys went in. He actually made it into Wisconsin where the bugs got him real good. There were lotsa nasty ticks. Seems like you two picked a better route."

"If I was a woodsman like Lloyd, I would a made it, too. All the way to Wisconsin I would a been free."

"Morrison did make it to Wisconsin, John. Why didn't you swim over with him? He almost got away, don't you think?"

"It's just about useless to grill me, Captain. I been through the mill before. Sorry, but yer just wastin' yer time." McDowell winked, "Honest—I kin play real dumb."

Sergeant Spratto said, "Why didn't you stay with Russell? He's so smart. He's a helluva woodsman—he'd have taken care of you."

"Well, I admit it was tough to beat the woods and all the cops, we gave it a good try, I'd say. What the fuck?" He threw up his hands in mock surrender.

"Morrison said that you went out one night and came back with a rifle."

McDowell set his hat further up his head, "Lissen up, our stories ain't ever gonna match up, so I'm not sayin' another word."

"Let's finish this up. Back to where you started from, John. I wanna hear your story one more time—top to bottom."

"I think I was pretty thorough last time, Chief. How about I think a something new? My memory's not as sharp as it used to be."

"Sometimes, John, it goes like this. You tell it again, you remember something new, or—better yet, you forget the lie you told before. You ever hear that before? The worst thing about liars is their memories." Person waved a hand of dismissal—then whirled and faced the prisoner. "John, don't you ever call me chief. If you can't remember Captain, you can call me sir."

"Sir? Catch this one. It's belt high and down the middle. You ain't never gonna catch Mister Lloyd Russell.

Captain Person stared at the convict and mulled over his last statement. Smiled and said, "We may not be the Mounties, but we most generally get our man. Get him out of here."

After McDowell was removed, Person turned to the other two interrogators, "I'm not sure how much I wanna believe Morrison's tale, but there was an element of the truth there. Maybe it was his sorry condition when we captured him. One thing for sure though—we'll never get the whole picture."

Obviously pleased with the recent days' events, he adds, "Now, we'll continue to beat the bush for Russell until we get him or we're sure that he is no longer in the state of Michigan. Anthony, it is now your case. Let's get him. It would be a real nice feather in your cap."

"Yes, Sir, I'll do my best."

43

Down To One

June 12

SIX DOWN AND ONE TO GO. It was the thinker, the planner, the leader. Just one to go, but this one was the deadliest, the smartest, and—the most dangerous. Most people believed that he was the driving force, his name synonymous with the infamous break from Little Alcatraz.

The searching officers were concentrating their efforts in the Faithorn vicinity, setting up points at the intersection of Menominee County Roads 537 and 385, some eight miles west of Hermansville.

Articles belonging to Russell had been found in a partially constructed woodland hideaway yesterday morning. His lean-to style construction was fast becoming his trademark signature. The articles found at the site included his prison-issue underwear, stamped with the identifying serial numbers. Leaving no doubt that the inhabitant of the structure had indeed been the last remaining fugitive. It appeared that the occupant had made a hasty departure. Something, or someone had put Lloyd Russell back on the move.

The river separating the border states were but a mile west of the village. Law enforcement agencies were keeping a vigilant eye on the Soo Line Railroad tracks and the trestle that spanned the Menominee River.

"We're working on the assumption that Russell is still on the Michigan side of the river. We believe him to be somewhere here in the Faithorn area." Thor Person briefed Earl Hathaway, "There's a chance that he isn't because there have been no reports of any auto thefts or recent burglaries."

"I don't think he'd boost a car, or raid any place where he'd get noticed. We are dealing with a very patient man. He'll wait it out."

"I agree Earl. Boost a car? What you been doing is watching too much of that television outta Green Bay. Yes, my money is on that he'll go 'er on foot. For as long as it takes."

"A woman reported last night that she saw a man answering Russell's description running out of a barn near here, Thor. She said he was wearing a long overcoat."

"We've had several other sightings reporting much the same thing. You'd think that attire would make him stick out like a sore thumb."

"So—he's got himself a nice long coat, helps ward off the bugs, and these U.P. nights just haven't warmed up much."

"Plus—he appears to be getting fashion conscious after all the years doing time."

"That's it, Thor. Maybe he's watching some television movies. Some of those mobsters are downright fashionable."

"I do think he's moving only at night, holing up before the first light. Those rare sightings are the result of his lack of knowledge about the area." Person glanced out the window, noted the time of morning and the gray, hopeless skies. "Yes, the nights are still cool—unseasonably cool. I'd appreciate warm duds."

"Me too. It's been a funny spring. A lot of weird stuff, extremely hot a few days, then terrible cold, I think it's global cooling. Those tornadoes in Flint, my oh my, the devastation."

"I feel for those people. So—bring me up to snuff, Earl. What we doing?"

"We're maintaining roadblocks in the Menominee and Dickinson County areas, and Wisconsin HP and the Marinette County sheriff's officers are going to continue their blockades on the other side of the river."

"He could be anywhere, Earl. But, I'm inclined to believe that woman's sighting—I think he's still around in the Faithorn—Hermansville area. Don't ask me why, it's just a gut feeling."

"Trust your cop's instincts, Thor. That's what got you this far."

Observation points were maintained in the hopes of spotting the elusive Houdini-like Russell. Bloodhounds were used in Marinette county Sunday and Monday, then returned to the Outagamie county sheriff's office in Appleton.

Opinion was divided among officers as to whether McDowell and McMackin, or Charles Morrison was close to telling the truth about the escape and subsequent events. Did the disagreement between Russell and the other three occur? Later discoveries provided proof positive that he was not in the stolen vehicle that drove into the Menominee River off the Nathan Bridge.

Five miles north of the village lay a thirty five mile area of dense swampland. It was the perfect habitat for the foxy, elusive con. Should Russell enter this great swamp, the officers felt the odds of capturing him in there were slim to none, but that Russell's odds of survival were even slimmer. Not many who had experienced even a brief visit to this thick, bug-infested swampland, could envision a lengthy stay there.

"How many of the troopers have been sent back to Flint and to the surrounding tornado area, Thor? We gotta be working with a lot less men."

"I don't have the exact figures in front of me, but a number have been released to critical areas pending further developments." Reiterating, "Our police strength here in the 8th District will be concentrated on the hunt."

The belief was that Lloyd Russell was armed and dangerous, vowing never to return to prison life. Officers were repeatedly cautioned to be especially careful and alert during their search. They were under constant vigilance as they scoured the fields and woods maintaining but an arms length between them. The systematic stalking was time consuming but effective in keeping the fugitive from slipping past them. The problem with this was; they couldn't maintain the pressure up at night. The elusive Mr. Russell could slip out anywhere he chose.

Flint Prepares To Bury Their Dead

FLINT (AP) – DAMAGE FROM THE TORNADO which devastated an area on the northern outskirts of this city was estimated at $Two Million Four Hundred Thousand today.

The living residents of the seven mile by seven block stricken area took time out from their jobs of grimly digging into the debris to prepare to bury the one hundred and twelve that were dead.

The bodies of a girl between eight and twelve years of age with terrible head wounds and a man about thirty are still unidentified.

The Red Cross issued an appeal for blood donors to replace its dwindling plasma stock. More than two hundred pints of plasma were used in one day at Hurley Hospital, where the largest part of the injured were taken.

June 13

ANOTHER DAY IN SEARCH FOR RUSSELL proved futile. The roads blocks would be continued in the Upper Peninsula until there was solid proof that he had slipped into Wisconsin. In what form the proof that was needed to declare this was anyone's guess.

The search, in its 22nd day, was now the longest sustained search in the annals of Michigan crime lore. The previous longest was Tommy Hunt, a bank robber from Hillman.

"We are working on the assumption Russell is still in the Faithorn area," Captain Person said. "Sooner or later he is bound to come out, although we have found nothing definite of late to prove that the convict is or is not there."

Several reports from the Hermansville-Faithorn area of a man resembling Russell being seen last night were being investigated, and declared to be unfounded. In one case, the investigation yielded nothing but a harmless hitchhiker.

Police said that no tips of consequence have been received since Tuesday night, when Charles Koehn, a conservation fire warden, reported finding a burlap bag Russell had left in his garage.

Monday, June 15

NO NEW TIPS OR CLUES TO the whereabouts of Lloyd Russell were obtained over the weekend. Captain Thor Person stated this morning that it is "difficult to say" whether or not the fugitive is still in Michigan.

Captain Person also informed at his morning press conference that the 30-30 caliber Marlin rifle, discovered in the car that attempted to crash the blockade at the Nathan Bridge belonged to Edward Hurtubise. Hurtubise, a farmer, apparently did not discover the theft and report it until the past weekend.

Tuesday, June 16, 1953

FBI In Hunt for Russell

LLOYD RUSSELL, FUGITIVE FROM THE MARQUETTE prison was added to the list of criminals wanted by the FBI.

Announcement that the FBI has joined forces with Michigan and Wisconsin law officers in the hunt for Russell was made this morning by Fred H. Mcintre, special agent in charge of the Detroit office. A federal complaint has been filed in Marquette against Russell with Roscoe Baldwin, United States Court Commissioner for the district.

Action by the FBI was interpreted to mean that Russell was hiding out in Wisconsin. The search for him on the Michigan side is being continued.

The FBI pointed out that its action in filing a Federal complaint against Russell means the entire organization has been put on alert and all the manpower will be used in the hunt for the Marquette Prison felon.

The conjecture as to his whereabouts touched all the citizenry of the Upper Peninsula and northern Wisconsin. As the summer heated up, the most popular children's games became "cops and robbers" in the hunt for Lloyd Russell.

And every mother warned her kids not to "stray off" as Lloyd Russell may be hiding and, "he's gonna get you." Yes—the quiet, meticulous bandit who eluded all law enforcement agencies had become the "Boogie Man."

Part Two

44

Lloyd Reed Russell

SUMMER DAYS—AS JUNE ANNOUNCED THE summer solstice a solitary man worked at leisure, improving his new living quarters as he allowed the world around him to buzz and conjecture as to his whereabouts. He was fairly certain of one thing, the posse searching high and low for his capture would not venture into his kingdom.

Studying the antics of a squirrel as it slipped in to steal a morsel of food that was set there to seduce him, was teaching the fugitive much about nature's ways. Enticing the little rodent into approaching ever closer to the snare, was both useful in catching the day's meal, as it was entertainment for the trapper. The little paws held the seeds while its teeth broke open the pods and in staccato fashion made short work of its contents.

A grin flashed across his face as he realized the quarry was about to make its fatal mistake. The thin wire sprang into action with blurring speed that soon had its victim dangling from its noose. The snare had worked to perfection. "These little red ones are small with too many bones, but what the hell—it's supper," the cagey woodsman spoke aloud.

A sense of pride, of that long forgotten ability to survive on his wits alone welled inside him. There was no rush to move on, no urgency to cower and hide, for this fleeting moment, Lloyd Russell had gained his freedom.

He felt safe from the risk of capture, trusting in his abilities, knowing that he was deep in the north woods, far from where any posse would dare to venture.

He was virtually surrounded by a large swamp—penetrable only by the finest woodsman, adept in living off the land. No one could come sneaking in on him—and, if such a man existed, he welcomed the challenge.

He cleaned the squirrel with rapid efficiency, going about gathering what he could muster for the night's supper. There were the seasoning herbs—tonight's fare would be far from elegant, but it would sustain him.

Off in the distance, the outside far from his world, speculation as to his whereabouts was the topic of the day. World and current events remained foreshadowed in his wake. He was unaware of the intense manhunt that had scoured the fields and woodlands in an all out effort to capture him.

He guessed it was the twentieth of June, trying to keep score of the calendar days was reassuring, a way to measure his success.

On the twenty four of June, attention was withdrawn from him, as The Mining Journal chronicled the wild pursuit of capture of an honor camp runaway.

Trustee seized by Police After Wild Chase On Highway M-28

FORREST CONRAD, A THIRTY-FIVE YEAR OLD trustee who fled Marquette Prison's Honor Camp early last evening was apprehended by state police in the woods three miles southwest of Watton, in Houghton County, following a wild chase on Highway M-28, during which officers fired several shots at the fugitive.

Conrad's stolen 1952 Olds 88 from the garage of L.B. Hadley at 420 East Hewitt Avenue about 3:40 this morning was jump started, a common practice among inmates.

At 7:45 he crashed the road block south of L'Anse, Troopers Horace Hosmer and Edward Raisenen fired at the auto as it whizzed by. They then took pursuit. Between Watton and Kenton, the convict zipped off onto a county road, and the officers were able to follow the trailing dust.

Officers fired at the speeding car several times, and two blasts pierced the rear window and emerged through the front windshield but the convict was unhurt. The convict then turned onto a farm road that was a dead end. He attempted to turn around again to elude police but lost control of the car and crashed into a ditch.

He ran into the woods where he was captured by Troopers Max Little and Russell Soyring as they the fugitive as he was trying to hide behind a log about a half mile off the side road.

The convict admitted pilfering several automobiles, stealing a jacket out of one and a bottle of whiskey out of another, before finding the one he wanted.

He stated his goal was to reach Wisconsin.

Had Russell been aware of the escapee's flight, he would have offered this advice. Lay low, fella—don't try to make a run to the border. Instead, he studied the sky—it didn't offer him the slightest hint of the upcoming weather. Nor did it offer him any insight as to what and where his pursuers were plotting. The only certainty—they were still doggedly pursuing.

Keeping track of the days was a constant problem. He tried to keep count by marking a nearby tree, but this turned out to be more difficult than he thought. He should have selected a specific time of the day to do so, instead of pondering if he had already done so for the day.

One thing for certain, it was time to take a foraging trip to the nearest town and the surrounding farmhouses. He needed to gather food sup-plies to sustain him through the summer and also to snatch anything that he could use for comfort and warmth. He suspected it was too soon to raid local gardens, except for a few of the earliest crops that were ready for consumption. Sweet peas, lettuce, etc., should be ripe for the plucking. The cool nights would have slowed down the vegetable season's growth. He had read enough about the upper section of Michigan to know that this summer had started out unseasonably cool. And—that was saying something.

He stopped to make camp for the night when he was close enough to a road to hear the vehicles passing within earshot. "I'm hungry for some real food," he mused aloud before settling in to his makeshift accommo-dations. The night under the summer stars was pleasant and peaceful, the world's strife benign to his thoughts.

He woke early to chew on a cold breakfast of last night's left-overs, sucking his teeth to rid himself of the porcupine's tallow-like aftertaste. He gathered his bedding and hid it in a hole of a nearby stump, then proceeded toward the nearest farm. After an hour of careful plodding, he neared a paved road that offered him cover from detection in the form of a brush-covered ditch.

Traffic was heavy, certainly for a rural countryside. *What was going on? An event of some sort. Could it be a holiday?* In the distance—he heard shouts, heralding trumpets of revelry. Indeed a party was going on. *Maybe a wedding celebration, naw—too early in the day, and too boisterous.*

A thought formed...*I got it—it's the Fourth of July.*

He sat in the protection of the clump of brush—thinking, soon he was thinking out loud, "Now is the time to go into town. There'll be strangers everywhere—moving all about—no body will be paying me any attention." He had on his best, cleanest set of clothes. In a rare burst of spontaneity— he threw caution to the winds and headed up the road.

Russell had walked but a quarter of a mile before he heard a vehicle slowing down behind him, the gears whining as it slowed. He didn't turn around, just kept walking at a steady pace, until a voice hailed him. "Hey buddy, lookin' for a lift into town?"

Lloyd turned to see a single man behind the wheel of an old Ford pickup, a prewar heap of rust, with parts of the rickety fenders missing as it waited for its new passenger. He gave a slight wave, ready to shake off the invite, when he changed his mind. *This might work even better—I'll blend right in, be one of them.* He looked to see if any other vehicles were approaching, seeing the road clear, he reached for the door...

"Thanks," he acknowledged as he jumped into the shuddering convey- ance and tried to shut the door. The latch protruded, stuck in its open position. "Giver 'er a slam. Pretend it's the old lady. Ha. The sonovabitch is crooked and bent, getting old like me."

Lloyd gave the door a determined slam and to his surprise it remained shut.

"There, that's it. She's still tighter than the valve on a virgin."

Lloyd looked over at his new friend and guessed him to be between fifty and sixty. The man was already into the spirits of the celebration and he thrust a bottle of sixty cent wine at Lloyd while pulling out a package of smokes from his shirt pocket. "Have a Raleigh, I ran outta Pall Malls and I found these in the glove box. Must be my buddy Eino's. Who else would smoke this shit?"

The unfiltered cigarette had a bite that Lloyd had to choke down as he drew it into his lungs. "I know you could use a little holiday cheer." The driver winked as the Ford hiccoughed twice and then leaped forward. A patch of toilet paper hung from his chin where he had nicked himself shaving.

"Thanks for the smoke, and—the drink. I do appreciate it."

"Names Harold, here, have another belt—it gets tastier. Besides, we gotta celebrate the day." Harold winked—delivering a drink with fingernails that needed trimming, and the dirt and grime removed.

"Thanks Harold, I'm, uh,—James. Call me Jim."

Harold stalled their ride. Unaffected by the mishap, he ground the starter to fruition, wincing when it screeched in protest, popping the clutch, the old Ford gagged and sputtered before leaping forward toward the village ahead. The day was filled with anticipation as revelers crowded the streets as they entered the village of Hermansville.

Their auspicious and noise-filled arrival went mainly unnoticed, a blessing in disguise. His newly found friend, Harold, was blitzed and boisterous, which made people notice him, and ignore his companion, which was much to Lloyd's pleasure.

Harold waved and hollered at faces that he recognized—yelled out a few names of those he knew, and generally announced their arrival in a most celebratory manner. *We're sneaking in here under all this commotion—perfect.* Lloyd chuckled under his breath, enjoying the great irony. The last thing this town was expecting—was a visit by the most wanted man in the state.

He pulled hard on the drink that Harold offered, growing confident in the warm mid-morning sun, He was about to enjoy himself—what the hell. It had been years.

Sure, he knew, he could be recognized at any time, even though he tugged the baseball cap down almost covering his eyes. His bald head was concealed—making his long sideburns appear as though he had a mop of hair. He trailed Harold into a tavern and bought the first round of drinks, picking a dark corner at the end of the bar to sit in. They moved to a small table, that was covered with a checkered cloth that just sat the two of them.

Lloyd strode up to the bar, that was busy in the forenoon celebration and bought a pack of Luckys and a couple of beers. Handing over a beer, he offered his new friend a cigarette.

"Thanks Jimmy, lemme get us a couple a shots. Let's toast the Fourth, and toot our flute. Brandy okay, or are you a whiskey man?"

"Brandy is fine, just fine."

"Toby, we need a couple a shots a brandy, we have to toast our independence."

Independence? Yes, guess I am celebrating that. "Harold, let's drink to freedom too."

"Freedom? Hell yes, Jimmy. It's great to be free. Ever spend any time in the hoosegow? I spent a night in a drunk tank in Chicago once. Drunk and disorderly, it was a long night."

"I did once, Harold. It was a long time ago."

"I got pinched for drunk and disorderly once, Jimmy," repeating himself. "Can you picture that? Ol' Harold Sweeney disorderly? Hell, let's have another, pal."

They had another drink, then Lloyd slid away from Harold, promising to see him later. He hustled out the tavern door, feeling the buzz from the drinks.

"Okey dokey, Jim. I'll be right here or just a bounce or two off the corner. I may put the old Ford in the parade. See ya' later."

Lloyd heard the echoes of Harold's order. "Say—bartender, you think I could get another beer with a side-car of brandy?"

With his head down to protect himself from the wind and recognition, he bumped into a man as he turned the street corner—glancing up, he first saw the patch of a uniform shoulder, *Sheriff.* His heart muscle cramped, a spasm of animal survival shot through him. *I can take him out with this knife.* Lloyd clutched the handle.

"Scuse' me."

"No problem, Buddy. Just take 'er easy today. We got lotsa folk wandering around—not paying attention."

"Yes sir," Russell glimpsed up from the brim of his cap, shielding the better part of his face as he spoke.

"Have a happy Fourth of July," the officer moved on—greeting people by name. "Hey, George, congrats on the new grand kid..."

He took a deep breath and moved along—careful, but not acting suspicious. Keeping to the inside of the walk, he found the local Co-operative grocery.

He quietly went about shopping—purchasing canned goods, powdered milk, two loaves of bread and a small bag of flour, along with oatmeal, something that would stick to his ribs. He wanted to keep his purchases within his ability to carry them. An overloaded tote would attract attention. He'd buy items that would keep—that was the key. He chose one small roast for immediate use and also bought salt and pepper, in convenient shakers.

Crossing the street, he entered a package liquor store, tossing his grocery sack on the counter and ordered a carton of Luckys and a bottle of Jim Beam bourbon.

He slipped out of town in a manner much quieter than the way he and Harold had arrived.

He would now find a cache for his grub, and wait until it became dark before raiding a garden or two.

45

The Ten Most Wanted

THE SUMMER WAS MOVING TO A rapid close as Lloyd moved at a slow pace north, and then east of Hermansville. He continued to feed himself off the land, his clever snares and ability to forage the land, plus his silent raids on neighboring gardens, kept him subsisted. Although the new diet was making him lean.

August turned to September—the search for food becoming difficult. His newest lean-to was further north, and deeper into the swamp. The cold nights had forced him to layer his clothing—in an effort to keep him warm with a minimum of fires. The fires had to be small and discreet. He waited until well into the evening before he allowed a warming fire. Soon, the weather would force his hand, wintering in the Upper Peninsula was not an option.

He readied himself for a trip to visit "his gardens," this time to gather root vegetables. He had acquired three burlap sacks to tote the potatoes, rutabaga, and carrots back and was still expecting to find an onion or two, and a head of cabbage. Meat was plentiful—when he could fire his gun. He had acquired a .22 caliber—one a farmer had left in his milk shed to deter raiding critters.

He headed east in the early morning prelude to dawn. His plan was to raid the first garden on his list at the break of day, digging in to the second one at leisure, for he he knew the owners were absent the whole day.

Careful of not taking more than he should, he helped himself to filling his bags, confident he was only cheating the other invaders. The farmers would suspect the local predators, not the most wanted man in the state of Michigan.

Let them think it's the deer, the coons, and the rabbits that are helping themselves. If the truth be known—they were more competition for the local gardeners than he was. The deer were constant foragers this time of year, as were most of the vegetarian animals.

The landscape was a revolving mix, swampland mingling with high ground—leading to open fields, harvested for the grass that turned to hay for their milk cows. Wooded copses—led back to swampland, thick and bushy. A habitat that served a vast array of animals. Many members of the rodent family survived in the environment, making Lloyd Russell's living room large and diverse. In this environment—he thrived.

He followed the creek—running along the edge of his campsite that went nowhere. As it led him deeper into the swamp's recesses, the earth soaked it up, dissolving its existence. The shoreline, the water and the creek bed itself disappeared somewhere into the swamp's vast underground. Would it reemerge with dark waters that would hold the biggest trout? Today would not be the time to look, as the thick branches from a windfall altered his route.

August 19, the Record-Eagle out of Traverse City, ran an article on his impending climb up the criminal status charts.

East Lansing-(UPI)-Michigan may soon have two men on the list of the "ten most wanted" criminals in America.

One Michigan man, Fred Bryant already is on the infamous list and state police believe

Lloyd Russell, who made good on his boast to escape from Marquette Prison may be added as soon as there is a vacancy.

Bryant, who escaped from Southern Michigan Prison in Jackson, January 24, 1952, replaced Izat (Frenchy Beausolle, who was wanted by Monroe county authorities for questioning about the murder of Mrs. Rose Trahan. Beausolle was captured in Chicago on June 26, and three weeks later Bryant took his place on the FBI list.

Bryant will be 47 years old August 25. He was serving life for armed robbery at the time of his escape. He fled while being taken to the main prison from a trustee camp when he stuck a knife to a guards throat and ordered the driver to take him out of town.

Bryant has spent more than half his life behind bars. He was sentenced to Jackson Prison from Grand Rapids in 1924 for assault and served four years. In 1929, he received a life sentence after pleading guilty to eleven armed robberies in Western Michigan.

Three months before his escape, the parole board considered releasing him under the "lifer law" but decided to wait "until his attitude was better."

Bryant is 5-feet 8-inches tall, weighs 138 pounds, has blue eyes and receding auburn hair, a slender build, and a ruddy complexion. Parts of two fingers on his right hand are missing and he has scars on his right ear and upper lip.

Russell, who is Michigan's second best known prisoner (Earl Ward, leader of the 1932 Jackson Prison riot) was born on Christmas Eve in 1921 in Youngstown, Ohio.

Police believe one of three things may have happened to Russell—he may be dead. He may still be running loose in the vast Upper Peninsula swamps, or he may have escaped to neighboring Wisconsin and could be anywhere.

Lloyd Russell made his way through the dawning light, unaware that he was the 11th most sought after felon in America, and quietly moving up the chart. His thoughts centered on the day's foray, hoping it would prove fruitful.

Tuesday, September 8, 1953

WASHINGTON—LLOYD RUSSELL, 31, WAS ADDED to the FBI's list of ten-most wanted fugitives.

Russell, who figured in a number of daring escapes, is the last man remaining at large from a group of seven convicts who burned their way out of a Michigan prison.

Russell has a long criminal record, largely involving robbery, dating back to 1938, when he was sixteen years old.

He is a native of Youngstown, Ohio, is of medium height and weight, and has a number of scars of his face.

The FBI noted that he nearly always wears a hat because he is self-conscious about premature baldness.

Russell replaces Jack Gordon White on the "most wanted" list. White, a southeastern states bandit, was picked up in Seattle, Washington, August 27.

The nights were getting increasingly colder. He roamed the area and found he had worked his way off the beaten path, traffic on the roads he neared were very light and sporadic. The nearest paved highway was noted on a sign as M-69. He had seen a "village limit" sign a little further up that told him he was camping outside the village of LaBranch. His map informed him that he was a good 15-20 miles northeast of Hermansville.

I worked myself quite a ways back north—means a longer trek back to Wisconsin. Again, he cautioned himself to wait...

He had lost a considerable amount of weight, even though he had not been starving. His diet was naturally low in fats and his stomach had shrunk. A haircut would have come in handy, his naturally thin hair, looked scraggly and unkempt at its present length. Yet, he kept himself clean-shaved, and bathed often in a pool in the nearby creek, regardless of the temperature.

He spent considerable effort to dam it up so that he could have a deeper pool that would warm during the sun of the day.

The staples he purchased on the Fourth of July were depleted and he was living on a diet of potatoes and carrots extracted from local gardens. An occasional snowshoe hare would enter his snare along with the squirrels, added some protein to his meal.

The night before, a fresh muskrat had been his treat. They would be more plentiful as winter made its approach. The trick was—to make sure he didn't bust a musk gland during the cleaning of the meat. He had trapped them in Ohio during his youth. *I could use a little anise oil, that brings 'em right to the trap.*

His scavenging had been on the meager side. The last cold, damp spell had done damage to the root vegetables. The slugs had entered them in their weakened state, and some were rotting in the wet, mostly clay soil. Cleaning them became time-consuming, as the dirt clung stubbornly to their toughened, scaled skins.

He woke up the following morning, the sound of a baby crying. *What's that? A baby way out here? Screaming?* His sleep had been deep. A loud, insistent, demanding wail pierced the still of the early day. It was not yet light, just an illusion of morning gray creeping into the morass, sending gloomy shadows among the trees and awakening the small woodland critters who scurried away from the shrill screams.

Rabbit. He was awake in an instant and on his feet. Grabbing his club he found the hare hanging by an unlucky foot from his snare. One solid tap on its snout brought the silence back into his woodland hideaway.

Fresh meat, potatoes, and carrots—I'm going to have me a fine stew.

He painstakingly kept a count of the days, ever since the Fourth of July. It was important to him to do so. He would have to leave before a brutal UP winter set in.

He could no longer blend into the citizenry and shop at any local store. Yet a craving would linger, it was odd how something simple, taken for granted, could become so important. It would be a wonderful addition to his stew. It was a staple—since the beginning of man...Bread.

Damn—Lloyd Russell shivered in the early morning dew. A nascent thought was forming. *I sure as hell would give my right arm for a loaf of fresh bread.*

That night he ate the stew, savoring the hot meal that would stick to him and add warmth throughout the night. He looked at the bottom of his bowl, listening to the thought of the bread as it returned. "Son of a bitch, I would sure love some bread to mop this shit up."

He was speaking aloud more often, to practice—for the time when he would again be moving around the populace, conducting business with other people. At least he hoped that was the reason. *Was he becoming one of those old-time hermits that lived alone in the woods and talked only to themselves? Will I et crazier than a shit-house rat?* He chuckled—"Naw, I ain't been out here that long." A chilling breeze reached in underneath his canopied hideaway and he kicked at the dying embers—shivering as he crawled back inside his lean-to.

The following morning brought fresh rain, followed by a shift of wind to the south so that by noon the air was crisp and bright, renewing the hermit felon's spirits. He moved about his forest retreat for the next week, searching for fishing holes and fresh herbs.

The middle of September passed—for this he was sure. The meager supplies from ten days before were now depleted.

He reached the highway's edge, looking both ways before crossing the road. *What was that?* Something lay up ahead—in the ditch. He circled the prey, making an arc away from it as he entered a copse of trees that sheltered him from view.

He stood—waiting... A car went past, a vintage Chrysler, tail fender rattling, blueish-gray smoke indicating the burning oil. He waited until it disappeared around the bend, waving goodbye with a puff of blue.

He spotted the road-kill flicker of white lying at the edge of the ditch. Creeping to the fresh-killed animal, he again glanced both ways before grabbing the doe's front legs and dragging its carcass into the shelter of the wooded area. He grunted with the exertion yet did not stop until he was hidden from the view of passing motorists.

He stripped to the waist, not wanting to bloody his clothing. Naked, his belly was flat, looking as though he had been fasting.

The broken neck, lying twisted in death, was skewed to one side, a bead of bright blood at each nostril. He brought out his knife, finding the deer still warm—he drew it along the back... *Damn, I wish this was sharper.* He tore into its backside following along the first cervical vertebra, peeling back the skin as he went from front to back revealing the line of meat...

Standing—he shook his hands, coppery with blood—and looked around for some way to clean them. Thick grass and surrounding leaves served as a towel to wipe him dry so that the morning's work didn't drip on his clothes. He put the meat in his sack and prepared to cross the road with the fresh venison. He left the butchered carcass under a maple, retracing the arc he had made coming in.

Lloyd made an uneventful return to the morning's vegetables, and laid the venison sack next to it to catch his breath. He spied the wisp of smoke from a house a couple of hundred yards up the road. Again—as his thoughts turned to a venison stew, a desire rose up in him. *Bread—maybe I kin buy me a loaf of bread.*

He brought the morning's catch further west, pausing briefly, before heading back toward the house at the edge of town. His mind was made up. He would take the risk for a loaf of fresh bread to soak the grave from his stew. A treat Paul and he had enjoyed in those carefree days of 'growing up.'

It was a story and a half bungalow, with asphalt lap siding. He came in on the north side which featured a small porch that led down the drive. The front door was open, with a screen door protecting the occupants from the fall house flies—his blood beat in his wrists as he approached the door and knocked.

Anxiety rose in him like liquid from a straw. He saw movement from within the house. *I dunno—maybe I shouldn't be doing this...*

"Yes, can I help you?" A pleasant voice was trailed by a matronly woman, armed with a fly-swatter. Her face did not completely relax though her tone was neutral. She gripped the fly-swatter as she appraised the stranger.

He would take no risks—he was just a bum passing through the landscape. A use of force was not an option.

"Howdy, Ma'am, I was just passing through, and I was hoping that per chance you could sell me a loaf of bread—I have the money—right here."

"I'm sorry Mister, but I'm out myself, but—there is a store just up the road a bit." She looked at the sun and wind-burned stranger, his face peeling—like the paint on the house across the road.

"Why, thank you Ma'am, I'll be off then. Have a good day. Just up the road, you say? " He hesitated—then turned away without another word.

The lady watched as the heavily-dressed man walked away, not toward town and the store, but to the west, back toward the woods.

46

A SIGHTING

Tuesday, September 22

THE SEARCH FOR LLOYD RUSSELL WAS revived following a report that the fugitive had been sighted in northern Menominee county.

State Police Detective Sergeant Anthony F. Spratto had always maintained the theory that Russell had never left the Upper Peninsula. After the massive manhunt was abandoned in late June, Spratto was among the lessening few who believed the escapee was holed up somewhere locally.

He spent as much time as he could afford driving through all the towns and villages along the Michigan/ Wisconsin border asking the public about any unusual or suspicious behavior.

Receiving information from a confidential informant that Russell had been spotted, his suspicions were rewarded. The informant stated that he had positively identified the felon. Russell was believed to have been in the village of LaBranch, just off of Michigan highway 69.

It seemed logical to Spratto that the wily convict, last sighted in Hermansville, could have headed northward. That certainly was the proper move to make—and an accomplished woodsman would stay out of harm's way. He was also a survivor who could have entered the swamplands and built another lean-to while foraging for his food.

Spratto sat and discussed the previous day's trek to La Branch with Captain Person and other ranking police officials. Stating his source reported that the man he later thought to be Russell was wearing about six shirts, at least three pair of pants, and a baseball cap. With the unseasonably cool evenings, a man living in the woods would need extra clothing, especially if he was averse to lighting fires.

The man also had long hair going down on his neck, was severely sunburned and appeared thin and hungry. It was noted that the description maintained that he had recently shaved, even though he appeared in dirty attire.

"The suspect went to a house last week and asked if he could buy a loaf of bread. He was told by the lady of the house that they were out, but there was a store a short distance away where he could purchase some." Spratto said. "The suspect thanked her, but declined a trip to the store and instead—retreated back into the woods to the west. She believed it was the way he had come." Spratto rose and pointed at a map.

"As she watched him from behind a curtained window, her suspicion's rose. She said his actions made for a furtive departure. Her words. She described him as having dark, piercing eyes and acting nervous."

"What's your take on the suspicious stranger, Anthony?"

"As you know, I was in LaBranch all day yesterday," Spratto wanted to let the others in the room aware of his trip. "In my investigation I concluded that the man who attempted to buy the bread was Russell. He hair was long and unkempt, but I believe he would have shaved. He always made sure the others did."

"You're right, Tony. He always kept the other three fugitives clean-shaved when they were hiding in Yalmer. Even made them shave and cleanup before they stole the car and left there. You've been conducting a quiet search all summer in the Menominee county area, so I believe you have a better grasp of his habits than most."

"Yeah, I have a real strong feeling that he's still hanging around."

"Trust your instincts, Tony—they've always been good."

"The description given to me in LaBranch by my informant, coincides closely with the one on the FBI circular."

"What's the circular say? I haven't had a chance to look at it yet."

"It's right here—says Russell is five feet, five and a ½ inches tall, weighs a 147 pounds, has brown eyes, and dark brown hair and is partially bald across the top. He is an experienced woodsman and has escaped custody several times by taking to the woods."

"That's pretty close, alright. Can you imagine—not even five and a half feet tall, and causing all this trouble?"

"Dammit, there's a lot of man stuffed into that small of a package."

"Yeah, they say he's as strong as men twice his size."

"He's kicked a lot of ass, and most of the time, they were a lot bigger. They say he won't back down from anyone."

"He's a survivor, I give him that." Spratto then added, "Well, just look at his record, it sure proves that."

"Is that what he is, Tony? A survivor? Yes, he sure has proved that..."

"One more thing Captain, I tried to alert everyone in the area, the Conservation Department, the fire tower men, and asked them to notify state police or any other law officer of any suspicious person that they run across."

"The Forest Service tower men—that's a good idea," Sergeant Smith stood up, "if you need any help from me, Tony—just gimme a yell."

"Thanks, Jim. I'm hoping we get another spotting that we can act on."

Good work, Tony. Thanks." Captain Person shuffled the papers on his desk. "Next? What else we got?"

Russell worked his way back to his hideout, sans the bread. A gnawing feeling entered while simmering the venison stew. It was an uneasy feeling—that kept gnashing at him throughout supper. *That woman may call the cops. She looked at me—real suspicious-like. Like she suspected I was on the lamb. I better think about moving on.* He had looked back over his shoulder and found her behind the curtain—watching him...

Maybe I should a headed toward town a ways, acted like I was headed to the store. Then pulled off and headed back.

In the morning he broke camp. It had been his home since a little after the Fourth of July.

He started out in a northwesterly direction, fully knowing that the landscape would determine much of the route. It occurred to him that he had no sure way of knowing where he was going, since this was the way it was—it was impossible for him to get lost.

Wednesday, September 30, 1953

UNKNOWN TO RUSSELL, THE SIX OTHERS who went out with him were sentenced. In addition to the disciplinary measure already taken against them, the convicts learned their ultimate penalties in court yesterday, when they were sentenced by Judge Glenn W. Jackson, Gladstone, to a total of fifteen to eighteen years of additional time in prison.

Hunger forced him to break in. He found a general store at a place called Foster City. After lying low and moving slow, he guessed it had been ten days or so since leaving the LaBranch area. It had been dark for many hours and he guessed the time to be well after midnight. His entry was quiet, managing to find an unlocked window, he forced it open with a minimum of noise.

There was a dull glow from a night light in the front of the store, his eyes were adjusted to night vision helping him work his way around the store. It was a typical country store, with narrow aisles holding everything from 'soup to nuts.' He caught a stack of motor oil cans that were out in the aisle before they could topple over.

Catching his breath, he crept slowly inching his way to the front of the store where there was more space in front of the counter. He waited until he had his bearings, scanning the darkness to plot his shopping spree.

"What the hell?" Lloyd swung around knocking over boxes of Cheerios with his elbows. "A fuckin' cat. You scared the piss outta me." The night mouser was most likely curious about who the intruder was as it rubbed itself against his leg. "You scared me outta a year's growth," he stroked its back briefly, "Now, go catch a damn mouse."

He stacked the cereal boxes back up and continued shopping—wiping the sweat from his brow. He stuffed his sack with canned goods that he determined would be least noticed by their absence. He took but one package of bacon and another of sausage.

He opted for a jar of Sanka coffee, noting it was brewed in an instant. He read by the dim light. *Just add boiling water. What will they think of next?* A bag of toast caught his eye, cinnamon rye made in Trenary, Michigan landed in his sack. He adjusted his load, so he could add two cans of condensed milk and a box of oatmeal to it. He topped his load with a family-sized loaf of Bunny Bread, and tossed in a package of sweet rolls. *The cigarettes—where are they? Okay, I see 'em.* He spotted them behind the counter.

That's enough. He headed to the open window, then back-tracked a couple of steps and reached over to grab yesterday's Iron Mountain Daily News. *Catch up on the doings, a little something to read with my morning coffee—catch up with the news.*

He lowered the sack to the ground with care, climbing out after it. Standing on tiptoes, he slid the window down to where he'd found it, hoping his night's work would go undetected. Moving out at a cautious pace, he came to a junction that indicated that the road went south to a town called Loretto. He hesitated, but continued alongside M-69, ever-ready to take to the nearby brush.

He guessed it was two miles from the store to an unused logging trail heading off to the south. He followed it for an hour before it died in a circle, typical of a forest 'lumber jobbing.' The second growth was well established and he found ready cover for the remainder of the night. He slept on the bare ground, hoping the night would not turn frigid.

Shivering, he rose at first light, finding a deer trail that carried him further into the woods in what he felt was a northwesterly direction. The going was easy, and he moved at a rapid pace, the damp leaves allowing him to travel in relative quiet. Certain he was safe from prying eyes, he stopped to build a breakfast fire.

He ate a breakfast of oatmeal and bacon with bread he toasted on a stick. He cussed when his first slice slipped into the flames but with a little adjustment by splitting the stick and squeezing the bread in between, he was successful with his next attempt. He settled back with his instant coffee and a sweet roll as his eyes settled on the front page of the newspaper.

"Let's see what's going on in the world."

Dateline—From The Marquette Mining Journal

THREE YEARS IS THE MAXIMUM SENTENCE provided by the state for a prison break. In McDowell's case, a judge recommended that he be required to serve the minimum.

The sentence will commence at the end of their current sentences.

Charles Morrison, 31, considered along with Russell, to be the ringleader of the plot, two and three quarters years.

John L. McDowell, 39, two and three quarters to three years.

Joseph Saunders, 55, two and one-half to three years.
Joseph McMakin, 31, two and one-half to three years.
John Podolski, 51, two and one-half to three years.
Lloyd Burgdurf, 59, two and one-half to three years.

"Shit," he spilled his coffee on his leg, "they've all been caught—every damn one of 'em. They just wouldn't listen to me." He rubbed his leg and thought about it more. "Well, I guess the old-timers did listen, I just steered 'em wrong."

He refilled his cup and continued to read about the plight of his fellow escapees, shaking his head as he read on...

Morrison Makes Statement

WHEN HE MADE HIS CUSTOMARY QUERY if the defendant wished to say anything before being sentenced, the judge heard Morrison state indeed he wished to say something. "I've been in the hole" on bread and water. I am in the "hole" today on bread and water and I'll continue to be in the "hole" as far as I know," Morrison complained. "I feel I've been punished enough as far as escapees go."

That 7 X 7 Cell—To which Judge Jackson said, "You are now serving time for armed robbery. You caused a lot of trouble and caused the county a lot of expense by demanding a trial when you had no rebuttal."

"Well," Morrison replied, "I'm not saying I'm not guilty, but I've been punished enough. That seven by seven cell..."

Morrison is serving a life term for armed robbery in Lansing, where he shot three policemen in a supermarket stickup.

"Shut up—Charley, you got caught now do yer time till you kin work a plan to get out again. Don't be making useless noise, it just draws attention to yourself." He read on, wiping frosting off his chin.

McDowell—Professes Innocence

MCDOWELL, TOO, HAD A STATEMENT TO make before being sentenced—and his was prepared and written out on paper.

McDowell asserted that he was serving a sentence on a crime in which he was innocent and that "circumstances" led to his misfortune.

"I was just walking down the gallery in Cell Block C minding my own business when I lost my balance and fell out an open window. When I got up, I was so goofed up I walked off in the wrong direction. I spent three weeks looking for the prison and two state policemen were good enough to help me find it."

Then he added, "I was placed in a disciplinary cell—15 days on bread and water—and kept in the bull pen after that." McDowell said.

"I am asking that you issue a restraining order on the warden (Emery E. Jacques) to keep him and other prison officials from taking further disciplinary measures against me."

No Control over Prison—The judge replied as follows:

"The court cannot accept the word of any prisoner who comes in here. Most of them think they are being mistreated. Furthermore, we have to assume that you were rightfully sentenced."

"You, McDowell, were one of the leaders in that sensational break. You also were dissatisfied with the attorney the court appointed for you."

McDowell was originally sentenced from Kalamazoo for breaking and entering and escaped and was captured on a Federal offense.

He served time in Leavenworth, Kansas, and Alcatraz, San Francisco, both Federal Penitentiaries, before being returned to Southern Michigan Prison in Jackson and later transferred to Marquette Prison.

"What a bunch a babies. I better get moving—I think I'll save the rest for later."

47

THE RIVER

THE TERRAIN WAS MUCH EASIER THAN he was used to traversing. The natural forest trails wove around, going left to right to left, sometimes almost circling itself. He often came upon a thick windfall that he would have to circumvent, the trees too long to go over or the branches too thick to crawl through. Except for the barriers, it was almost like a walk in a park, considering some of the places he had been.

The leaves of the maple and poplar, though spectacular in color were already falling to the ground. To Lloyd it was another sign of an early winter as he made his way through the noisy trail.

He stopped for a break when the sun was as high up as it got at this time of the year in the northern skies. He checked the date on the newspaper—Wednesday, September 30. *Let's see, that was a day-old paper, that means today is the 2nd of October. The hunters will be coming. I gotta get out of these woods—soon.*

He folded the paper back into his sack, and moved on after eating a can of sardines with a cigarette for dessert. He went less than fifty yards when a partridge popped out in front of him in a rush of thrashing feathers that took a year off his life expectancy. He stopped to let his heartbeat get back to normal. *Damn, they'll be hunting these birds soon—if they aren't already.* He didn't relish the thought of living amongst the animal prey.

He knew that by nature, most hunters would be too lazy and out of shape to trample very far into the woods. However—a road could be close or even a logging trail that could deliver a hunter in a jeep or truck.

He stopped early for the night when he found a natural campsite with thick, overhanging boughs of a spruce that would offer a canopy to shelter him from the morning dew.

After the fire was down to a bed of solid coals, he laid the rest of the bacon into his fry pan, adding a potato and onion to complete the sizzle. He would save the beans for another meal, rationing his grubstake. It was plenty to eat for his stomach had shrunk to the point where he filled himself up with less food, even though he was so very active. He stirred the evening meal before unfolding the paper...

Had First Pleaded Innocent

SAUNDERS WAS REMINDED OF THE FACT that he had pleaded not guilty to prison break, and then had an attorney appointed by the court (at county expense) and that he later changed his plea.

Saunders is serving a life sentence for armed robbery in Genessee County (Flint).

McMackin actually went through the entire procedure yesterday—being arraigned and sentenced, inasmuch as he originally entered a plea of not guilty.

Prosecuting Attorney Edmund J. Thomas, had the action in the case delayed because of the late arrival of witnesses.

Wanted In Missouri

"I UNDERSTAND YOU NOW WISH TO change your plea to guilty," Judge Jackson told McMackin.

"Yes sir," he replied.

"You are now serving time for armed robbery, and you are wanted in the state of Missouri and also by the U.S. Marshall," the judge commented, adding he was giving McMackin the two and a half years because of "the seriousness" of your situation.

McMackin is presently serving a 10-30 year term for armed robbery in Detroit and was sentenced in Wayne County.

Killed Officer In Robbery

TO PODOLSKI, THE JUDGE SAID: "The court accepted your plea of nolo contendre on condition that it would be treated as a plea of guilty."

Podolski is serving a life sentence for first degree murder. He killed a policeman during a jewel robbery in Detroit.

Burgdurf, serving a life term for fourth offense burglary, was the first convict to be recaptured. He was told by the judge: "You honestly admitted you broke prison, and pleaded guilty—and that's in your favor. However, you took part in a break from within the prison with others."

"I'm not surprised you were first, Burgy. That's what I put you out there to do, get your ass caught first. It might have been better to spend a day or two a free man. I doubt you'll ever see the outside again." He checked his supper, stirring the meal and scraping the burnt potatoes that had stuck to the pan. "It's done, smells good enough to eat."

Lloyd set a stone to hold down his paper as the breeze had picked up. He was soon filled as he soaked up the remaining juices with one more slice of bread. He belched a sour essence into the late afternoon air, lit a cigarette, and picked up the paper once again.

Three Seized Quickly

BURGDURF WAS RECAPTURED THE SAME NIGHT (Friday) of the break, Saunders, the following night, and Podolski on the following Monday afternoon. All three were caught in Marquette County, two in this city. (The other in Negaunee.)

But, the other three were free longer, Morrison was not apprehended until Sunday afternoon, June 7, near Pembine, Wisconsin, and McMackin and McDowell were recaptured Tuesday night, June 9, in Quinnesec, near Iron Mountain.

So—Charley made it into Wisconsin. He should have got away if he got that far. Hell, looks like I'm headin' toward Iron Mountain. I better be luckier.

Russell

THE LAST TRACE OF LLOYD RUSSELL was obtained near Hermansville, and he is believed to have gone northward, into the vast swampland.

They figgered I been here...

Russell, wanted in Ohio, was serving time for assault less than the crime of murder. The sentence was imposed after he shot Detective George Strong, Marquette, in a running gun battle between he (Russell) and his brother Paul 27, and the state police near Shingleton.

Paul Russell is now behind bars at Jackson Prison.

Someday, Paul—I'm gonna spring you.

He was finished with the newspaper. He would later be using it to start his fires. He tossed his cigarette and prepared to bed down for the night.

The clear night brought out the stars, staring up at their different configurations, he was not at all sure what he was looking at. His astral view was limited, yet he searched the Milky Way looking for the dippers, big or little, for he didn't know one from the other. He watched as a star erupted in temporary brightness, disappearing just as quickly into the galaxy. He rolled over and went to sleep not knowing that he had witnessed a nova.

Lloyd Russell shivered in the heavy morning dew. Although the day promised to be warm and sunny, the early chill was first to be endured...

He headed directly opposite of the morning sun, moving due west. It was quiet at this time of the year, no crickets chirping in the grass or grasshoppers thumping ahead and leaping in front of his footsteps. After an hour he picked up the rush of water, and as he closed in on the sounds, he entered a thicket that was dark as dusk in the blocked out sun. Pine saplings and a variety of leafless brush closed in on him and made his progress torturous.

With quiet patience, he extracted his sack yet another time before it was ripped wide open. It seemed to keep getting lured by the protruding arms that forced him to stop often to free it from their possessive embraces. A glimpse of blue—he kept working his way through the maze and stood gazing at the molten river below.

The water cascaded down a series of rocks and outcroppings to a deep ebony pool below. He left his sack at the top and slid down the bank to stare into the foaming water. Fish, large brightly colored fish were darting in and out of the deep pool, chasing crawfish and minnows among the rocky bed.

Trout—rainbow trout. I gotta catch me one of those fat beauties.

He needed something to use to catch the big fish, something that could catch and hold a powerful trout. It would require a trip to a nearby town to acquire the necessary tools. He would need something better than a safety pin and a length of string. He made himself lunch, then cached his sack in a natural dugout in the side of the bank.

They outta be safe there.

He filled his pockets with the remaining can of sardines and a couple of candy bars then headed upstream following the river north.

The woods were thinning just as he heard the far off rumble of thunder harmonizing with the closer sound of a moving vehicle. He worked his way to the edge of the forest where an open field lay straight ahead. It had been cut short, a recent crop of hay had been harvested, most likely a second crop.

His eyes followed the forest outline as it swept to his right and seemed to extend a long way, possibly forming a natural snow barrier. He guessed he was facing to the west, looking at an outbuilding, possibly a hay barn that stood in front of him.

He looked at the sky. *It's gonna rain—hard.*

The wind picked up as if cued by the thunder. The sun, a tarnished yellow, started down from the clouds as if it had been flushed from the sky, draining into the barn roof in a lifeless swirl—turning the structure into a sinister looking retreat.

He headed toward the barn, his head down he half-ran, half-walked, into the teeth of the quickening breeze. His speed picked up as he felt the prickles of half rain, half sleet as it beat down in a quickening frenzy.

The shadows cast by the tree line shifted and shortened, then became more agitated as the wind picked up. Lloyd had reached the mid-ground between the barn and the woods—swirling bits of hay chaff and dust scraped at his face and probed into his eyes.

He whirled to turn back, retreating from the teeth of the wind, hesitating—then deciding he would seek the long term safety of the barn. He dismissed the meager cover that the trees would offer. He faced the direct force of the wind as he charged for the protection of the barn. The barn was getting closer but still seemed too far to reach before he'd be totally drenched.

Pellets of cold, frozen rain bounced off him just as he reached the hay storage shed. *Hail. Damn, that hurts.* He rested against the wall, gasping, trying to catch his breath. His thoughts were drowned out by the explosion of thunder that preceded the blinding flash of lightening that was arcing across the sky like a giant welder spewing a volcanic eruption. He ducked in reflex when the next thunderclap slammed his ears.

Made it just in time. He entered the barn through a south side door, just as another bolt of electricity lit up the barn showing him it was unoccupied except for the loose hay that made it three quarters filled. *This place will be snowed in once winter hits. Good—they shouldn't be using this hay till spring.*

Throughout the remainder of the afternoon, the wind blew through the cracks between the slatted pine walls with enough force to shake the entire building as it clutched to its cinder block foundation. The hail rattled off the roof, sending rounds of buckshot pellets that chased the critters, who called the barn home, from the safety of their nests. Their harried frenzy only added to the racket of the storm. A barn owl flew down from the rafters and screeched and scolded Lloyd for his part in the commotion.

"Man, this is just dandy." His voice was drowned out by the onslaught. The hail storm was reaching its crescendo, pounding against the walls and roof in a deafening roar.

He found a ladder nailed to the wall and climbed it to the top, then worked his way toward the front of the loft where an opening faced the road. The window/door was kept closed by a handmade wooden latch that swiveled to open and close the portal from both sides. *That's clever.* He appreciated the maker's ingenuity.

The hailstones had dissolved into rain that drummed persistently against the tar-papered roof. Lloyd ate the sardines and saved the candy bars for the next day. Digging a comfortable hole into the hay, he quickly fell asleep to the music of the rhythmic downpour.

He woke at daybreak to a quieter version of yesterday's storm. The rain continued throughout the day and Lloyd wiled the time preferring to stay in his dry aerie. The traffic on the road was sporadic and the closest house was at least a half mile away. He had plenty of time to find a hiding spot if someone should come out and poke around the barn for some odd reason or another.

Sometime during the following night, the rain had died and was replaced by a distinct drop in temperature. He shivered as he left his snug loft bed, deciding it was time to head back to his woodland lair.

On his way out, he grabbed an old pitchfork that was leaning against the barn wall. A weather-checked gray, he tested the handle's soundness. It showed the character of its tensile strength by springing back when he thumped it on the ground. He also took a roll of twine that hung from a forty penny nail sticking out of a rough-sawn six by six post.

He poked his head outside, as was his cautious nature, checked in all directions before heading across the open field.

48

Going Fishing

HE HUSTLED BACK TO CAMP, the brisk morning hurrying him along. He spent the day making firewood and hauling it back to his campfire. The brisk air suggested that it would hang around for a while. He didn't want the weather to force his hand so he wanted to have as much wood to burn as he needed to keep him warm.

On the next afternoon, he found a cave cut into the hillside below a small falls. A large fish broke the surface from the pool below leaving a water ring of impressive size. He stood and watched, waiting for its return. The pool was deep, deeper than the water that was at his current campsite.

He spent the remainder of the day hauling the wood to his new site. He built a fire near the entrance making sure the wind wouldn't blow the smoke inside and choke him out. A little search of the cave proved to be a serious stroke of luck. He spied the light shining in—he would have a chimney. He could make a fire inside—and make his new home snug and warm. The trick now was to bring in dry hardwood that would burn freely making less smoke.

The weather stayed dry and cold for the next three days before it started warming up. *What I could use—is an old fashioned Indian summer.* He decided that it was about the tenth of October which would make the timing about right.

His food cache was about gone. His staples were depleted, and he had only supplemented his supply with a couple of rabbits and a spruce hen. He had fashioned a hook with part of a tine off the pitchfork and used the twine to tie it to. He carved a sturdy pole out of an oak branch, but had no luck inducing the fish to bite, even with the juicy night-crawlers he found.

This weather ain't gonna last. I gotta get some grub to hold through. He decided the next day that he needed to make a trip for supplies. His vigil near the deep pool lasted until he couldn't see and none of the big trout came within his range.

He headed north at dusk, wanting to make the wood's edge before nightfall. He reached a point where he could watch the citizenry in the town of Felch. He could see rugged highlands to the north, and having been in this terrain for what he guessed was a month, he was getting used to the ups and downs of traveling. It was much different from his earlier swampy existence.

As the lights of the town began flickering and waving goodnight, he edged his way closer to the town limits. The trees he stood among were pine, adding to the scent of the night. Faintly were the kitchen sounds, a hint of a radio, some barely audible music. In the distance a dog barked. The net effect was to emphasize the quiet.

An automobile entered town moving along at a slow pace. It pulled into a driveway and a couple got out and entered the house. He waited until the lights went out in the house.

Closer. He felt his heart was strong and his senses were keen. *Now.*

He dug at the back door hasp of the store. It was sloppy, already loose. Working carefully, he wriggled the screws free from the aged wood. He entered with a minimum of disturbance, sucking his breath and edging his way through the store. After all, he was a Class A safe-cracker. The store offered little illumination, he searched for a flashlight to help him guide the way.

He heard a sound. Was it a door slamming? Was he too early? He had waited for what he guessed was an hour after the last light was out before making his move. Yet—he could still be too early. The house in back— could it be the owner's? *Shit. Why didn't I wait some more?* He didn't need a confrontation. Not this close to the border.

It was so still in the darkness he could hear his own breathing. It no longer felt deep and quiet to him. Now it seemed to beating as noisy as a jackhammer. He waited...Whatever he had heard had quieted back down. He moved down an aisle, gingerly—*careful now...*

Shit. He knocked a box off the shelf. *Corn flakes.* The box burst open spilling the cereal onto the floor. *Shit, now I got a mess to clean up.* He crawled around on the bare hardwood floor, scooping up the chips into a circle too big for him to gather in with his hands. He had to find a light. He worked his way along the aisles, there were but four, until he found the limited hardware section. He grasped the handle of a flash light, lit it, pointing the light toward the floor, away from the windows.

Let there be light. He allowed himself a grin of relief, then set about seeking supplies he could tote back to his lair. He filled his sack with essentials, topping it with a carton of Luckys. At first he was apprehensive about making such a large purchase, yet realizing that would be noticed as a theft that kids would make.

He borrowed a broom and dust pan, scooping up the corn flakes and hiding them in a corner in the back of the store. He put the open box in his bag. Reaching the back door, he paused, listening to the sounds around him. A clock was ticking loudly somewhere in the store, which added to his anxiety. The more he avoided people, the more he was uncomfortable being around them. Even when they didn't know he was there.

He screwed the hasp as tight as he could allowing for the possibility of a return. If he could make this shopping trip unnoticed to its owner. Except for the cornflakes—he was sure he had.

The night was still, the chill urging him forward, he hugged his overcoat to him as he returned to his lair at a hurried pace. He wished he could have found a fishing pole—something he could set out overnight to catch the big trout.

The store had yielded but little meat, little canned sausages, tuna fish, and sardines. He couldn't take but a can of each, again hoping his visit would go undetected.

This weather won't last long. I gotta think about moving. First—I gotta catch me a fish. Just to say I done it. Who was he kidding? His meager supplies he took from the store would not last long. The morning air was brisk. He pissed away from the fire, the steam that rose told him how cold the ground was. He couldn't stop thinking about the trout. He suspected the day would be cold—yet sunny. "I need some clouds," he said aloud as he skirted the embankment looking for the multi-colored fish.

He spent a leisurely day, "My shadow will give me away. Dammit. What the hell was time?" again, he caught himself voicing his opinion aloud.

Five days passed since his raid in town. He was out of food.

Late that afternoon. Grinning out loud, he watched the dark clouds hover above him. "Tomorrow, I'm going fishing." He fixed his spear ready and held it ready to catch the monster trout.

"Now's the time." He looked at the dark sky knowing the dawn had already arrived. He wouldn't be casting a shadow as he worked his way along the river bank squinting carefully into the dark pools.

The force of hunger empowered Lloyd with a quiet desperation to take chances to land the big trout. He followed the stream bed watching the river grow deeper along its bank, the great fish holding themselves head-on into the dark currents. He crawled up a tree branch hanging over the river, dangling over the broiling surge of water, he clutched the wet branch with one hand, sighting into the depths below.

He raised the farmer's pitchfork and heaved it downward like a spear, lost hold of the running line he had attached, although just for a moment, he lost it in the tumultuous river. He teetered perilously grasping a small limb attached to the one he rode. He saw the graying tip of the ash handle growing out of the greenish water, colored there by the weed.

Without hesitation he left his perch to retrieve the pitchfork, gasping as the frigid water washed over him. He hauled himself and the pitchfork to shore and stripped off his wet clothes, shivering and sucking cold air into his lungs in an effort to stabilize himself.

He ran up the bank, stubbing his toe he cursed and yelped, "Sonova-bitch, I'm gonna freeze my balls off." He reached the campfire and rushed about stacking wood on top until he had the makings of a funeral pyre.

He hung his clothes near the fire in an effort to dry them. "I'm gonna need dry clothes when I get done." He turned and headed bare-assed back to the river.

He stood shaking with cold in the late morning gloom making clumsy strikes while his feet tangled in the hairy weeds. He stabbed once more at the fish. *This time I got him!*

"Now, you bastard you're mine." He looked in shock as the mighty fish ripped itself free of the tines, almost pulling Lloyd with him. "God damn you, I'm gonna get you if it's the last thing I do."

He trembled some more, blowing on his frozen fingers, waiting for the fish to return—settling the mud clouds—saw the bubble of his last breath—waiting for that great fish to rise from the bottom and roll there. He flung the makeshift harpoon once again connecting into meaty flesh. He knew he had sunk the makeshift harpoon deep into the fish.

Yes—he's mine. This time he staggered up towards the embankment through the soil and stone tripping on tree roots as he heaved the magnificent trout onto the shore.

The late season nettles still flourished along the river's edge and stung him with a relish as he scrambled barefoot up the steep incline. The trout wiggled mightily on the end of the pitchfork bending its tines until it worked itself free. Ignoring his skinned knees, he pounced on the slippery fish, found a stick for the fire and beat the monster rainbow to submission.

He added wood to the fire, grabbing a dry shirt and using it to towel wipe himself off.

Adrenaline was leaving him, replacing it with a cold that threatened to numb him senseless. He dressed as quickly as he was able, rubbing his fingers in an attempt to make them warm enough to work his buttons.

After donning every dry piece of clothing he owned and standing hunched over the fire as close as he dared, he gradually warmed up. "You crazy bastard, you almost killed yourself." He shuttered involuntarily once more before grabbing his knife to begin cleaning the catch of the day.

The sputtering sounds of the fish being seared over open flames heightened his thoughts and even as he turned the fish over to cook evenly on all sides, the normal evening extracts were taking on a new, more meaningful reverberation.

It came to him and left no doubt. It was time to leave his safe little nest. Before he even had a bite of the succulent flesh nearing completion, he grew wistful. It's time to go. I can't spend a winter here. He shook this rare penchant for self-pity and dug into the evening meal.

49

The Storm

HE WOKE TO LARGE SNOWFLAKES DRIFTING DOWN, at least four inches of snow already on the ground. He stepped outside to relieve himself surprised that the gray sky of the morning seemed so threatening.

"I gotta move out. There's a big storm coming in."

He hustled about, getting ready to leave the cave. He ate cold trout, packed what was left and set out into the rapidly thickening snow. The four inches had already changed to six. He pressed on, the drifts being soft and fluffy.

He guessed it was still October, near the end of the month. Soon it was ten inches deep, but he was still able to walk with relative ease. The snowfall was increasing, thicker flakes were falling at an alarming rate—yet all he could think of was getting out of there. At this point, he had but one thought—beating the storm and getting out of the wooded lair.

The wind kept picking up. He was soon wading in snow above his knees. The snow was soon thicker, forcing him to squint to see ahead of him. Soon the trees, the rocks and his surroundings became vague shapes he could barely make out.

"Shit. I'm in a whiteout." He had heard of such a storm, but had never come close to experiencing one. "I'm in deep shit."

There is something fiercely insensitive about an Upper Peninsula blizzard, something hateful and shocking in its brutality. It ripped at him now, pounding him with smashing fists of wind, and raking his face with claws of blown ice.

He couldn't tell the land from the sky. Everything looked the same. The snow was now gray and so thick around him he had trouble focusing. *I gotta go back!* He was caught in a storm that left him but one option. He turned around hoping to return to the safety of the cave.

He walked right into a tree—scratching his face during the effort. He felt the warm blood slide down his cheek. *How am I gonna find my way back?*

The wind and snow cut into his back, thankful now he wasn't facing it. "Where am I? I didn't go all that far. Did I?"

He decided that he'd never find the cave. The drifts were up to the crotch of his trousers. He was moving up hill which helped him against the drifting of the onslaught of snow. Exhausted—he pressed on...

The river! He heard it, the rushing of the water tumbling down and over rocks. The cave had to be near. It just had to be. He turned in to his left, away from the river, stumbled and fell to his knees. His knapsack pulled away from him. He huffed and puffed, gasping for breath.

"Gotta find my sack." He was afraid for one of the few times in his life. "Gotta find it, quick." He managed to work his right hand until he found a frozen strap. "Got it."

His hand grazed through ashes as he retrieved his burlap sack. "Ashes, I feel them, the cave is right ahead. I'm gonna make it." He struggled to regain his feet.

He looked ahead, determined to locate the way to his den. The swirling snow took a brief rest enabling him to see a dark spot directly in front of him. He headed for it, determined to stay in a straight line.

He fought another huge drift before he pawed his way into a hole in the rock formation. He had made it. He tossed off his knapsack, rolling onto his back to catch his breath. "I can't lay here long. I have to keep moving."

He needed a fire. He forced himself up, happy that he had left dry wood in the cave. He soon had a warming fire going, realizing only then that he could have been dead. The storm howled on throughout the night. His fire was warm enough, though his food was limited. He had never seen such a storm. The ferocity of its onslaught was overwhelming.

Lloyd didn't know what time the storm subsided. The cave was blocked with fresh snow. He started digging out a hole, surprised how the snow bank had become so firm. He finally cut a hole big enough to wiggle through, checking out his surroundings. The sun hit the new snow, blinding him with its brightness.

"Shit. I can't handle this."

He gathered more wood that he had outside the cave, banging the sticks against each other to shake off the wet snow, then dug into the snow enlarging the entrance hole.

He would have to stay at least a couple of more days. That was all the fish he had left, his only sustenance. Then, come what may, he would be forced to move.

Luck was with him, for the next two days were filled with unseasonably warm weather and nighttime rain. The snow melted to a negotiable slush that would be gone in another day. He moved out before dusk on the following day and headed back to the store in Felch. Again, he waited until it was reasonably safe to enter.

This time Lloyd Russell was not so careful. His entry would be detected. Luck was still on his side though, as word would not reach Detective Anthony Spratto for another week.

On the day before the deer hunting season was to open, Russell had stolen a hunting outfit that a hunter's wife had hung out on the line to clear the mothball smell from the woolen garments.

He bid his time hiding out in an abandoned farmhouse waiting for just the right moment. Again, luck showed him the way. He caught a ride with a hunter at a gas station on the corner of M-95 and US 2 after going in for cigarettes. The gas station was filled with hunters loading up on last minute items for hunting camp. He was wearing his newly acquired hunting clothes.

"This here's a 52' Willys-Overland, Jim," the hunter told Lloyd. Kaiser bought them out this year. "I got the 4-wheel drive for hunting season. I go places the other boys can't get to."

"Nice pickup. I never rode in one before, Ernie. I sure appreciate the lift." Lloyd had found a bag for his meager belongings and put it in the back with Ernie's camping gear.

"You're welcome. Have a beer." Ernie handed Lloyd a can of Goebel's beer. "It's nice and cold, I just picked it up at the store. We don't have Goebel's in Milwaukee."

"Thanks. Milwaukee—that's where your from?"

"Yup. Originally from Crystal Falls, north a here. Me and three other fellas originally from the UP come up every season. The other boys will get here tomorrow."

"Where do you hunt?" Lloyd felt a need to be friendly. Being too quiet could arouse suspicion.

"Ha. Up on mahogany ridge. That's where we end up doing most of our hunting." Ernie winked at Lloyd. That's why we stay here in Iron Mountain, more bars and action 'round here."

"Mahogany ridge? Oh—the bar tops are made of mahogany. That's a good one."

"You got a place yet, Jim?"

"No. I told you my car broke down and will be fixed by tomorrow. Then I'll meet my group. If I kin just get dropped off near any motel with a vacancy sign."

"Say...I can do better than that. We got two cabins for us boys. One will be vacant tonight. How about you pay me ten bucks and stay next door to me for the night. We can grab us a couple brews and get the hunt started. What you say?"

"Sounds good to me." That worked out well. Lloyd wouldn't have to expose himself by registering himself.

He took a long hot shower, then shaved and trimmed his own hair in the mirror. He had picked up a pair of scissors at the store in Felch. It looked passable when he put his hunting cap back on. He put the hunting clothes back on, sans the jacket, and waited to hear from Ernie.

Ernie soon rapped on his door. "Let's go get a bite to eat. I ain't had but a donut all day."

"Good idea."

They got back to their cabins around five o'clock. Each man had bought a cold six pack. Lloyd grabbed another pack of smokes and Ernie bought a package of rum-soaked cigars.

After drinking most of the cold beer, and passing a bottle of brandy back and forth, Ernie got a wonderful idea. One that Lloyd jumped on immediately. "Let's take a trip to see the dollies in Spread Eagle, Wisconsin. There's this place called the Green Door..."

"Lemme grab my jacket from my cabin, Ernie, I'll be ready to go." Lloyd wasn't going to give Ernie a chance to change his mind. He had drunk more than Lloyd so he didn't want the man getting sleepy and wanting a nap.

A light snow was drifting down when Lloyd slipped into the truck, tucking his bag between his legs. "What's that for, Jim? We'll be coming back."

"Well, it's for just in case I like it there, Ernie." He winked at Ernie as he was handed him a beer. *Yes, Ernie. I'm gonna like Wisconsin real well.*

50

Welcome To Wisconsin

THE SNOW WAS COMING DOWN A bit harder, dropping down large, heavy, flakes. The warm weather made the snow wet and would make the roads slippery when the temperature dropped. They crossed the bridge in Wisconsin and were soon stopped in front a bar in Spread Eagle.

The bar was already thick with hunters. It was November 14, the eve before the start of deer hunting season. Wisconsin's season was later, so the place was packed with Michigan hunters.

They stayed for two rounds of drinks before Ernie decided to beat the crowd to the Green Door. "Let's get over there before we have to wait in line."

A big surly looking man dressed in hunting garb shouldered Lloyd at the door. He was going out of his way to start trouble. Lloyd sucked it up, holding his breath. He wasn't going to be baited into a senseless brawl. Lloyd could taste real freedom after months of being on the dodge with hundreds of lawmen on his back. He wouldn't blow it now.

He went with Ernie to the Green Door, mentally counting his remaining cash. Ernie was well remembered as he greeted several ladies with a robust welcome. He hugged and twirled them about, "Hey, Sheila, I missed you honey."

"It's Shirley, Arnie."

"Ernie, Honey, it's me, Ernie."

"Whatever, wanna take a trip 'round the world?"

"Let's go baby, I got enough cash, let's go 'round twice."

Lloyd sat on a synthetic velvet couch, content to sit for a minute contemplating his next move. He already knew there were no hotels or boarding rooms in the little town. He wasn't going back to Michigan, so he needed to catch a ride further into Wisconsin. The snow was still coming down, the weather expecting it to reach freezing temperatures.

"Hi, mind if I join you?" The voice was soft, not brash and pushy like most whores.

"Sure. Go ahead, I'm just waitin' for my friend." He turned to look at her, noticing the mouse under her eye.

"I'm Annie, are you looking for a good time?"

"I'm a little strapped for cash, I'm really looking for a ride south, wanna find a room for the night,"

"Where you headed? I go south when I get off of work." She didn't know why she blurted that. He was a perfect stranger. He could do anything, be anything...

"What time do you get off work? I mean, how far south are you going?"

"Probably late. Why don't you hang around? I'm having some trouble with this guy that thinks he owns me. He's the one that gave me this shiner. If you're here, I doubt he'll get rough."

"Why not just quit? Do you need the money that bad?"

"After tonight, I'll have enough to pay back my folks for their help. They need the money bad."

Lloyd shook his head. He couldn't quite figure how a woman would lower herself this far just because she was so strapped for cash.

"Where did you say you was heading?"

She didn't get a chance to answer. Her ears perked up as she listened to the bellowing voice from the front room.

"Quick. Come with me. It's Thornapple." She grabbed his hand and led him down the hallway to a bedroom. "C'mon," she hissed, "we should be safe in here. Maybe he'll go away if he thinks I'm busy."

Alas, he didn't. He followed them right in to the room, bursting through the door. "There you are, bitch. You're my wench, to use as I please. You forget who I am?"

"Yeah, I suspect you're a dickhead who has trouble with woman. Can't get it up?"

"Who's this shrimp?" The intruder made a move to throw Lloyd out of the room. It was a major mistake on his part.

The movement seemed casual. But, it was a blur. And cat quick with fierce intent. The blade struck—hard and deep, tearing through the flesh of his thigh before hitting the femur as Lloyd yanked it back out. Thornapple gasped, his knees buckling as he toppled over face first. He lay on the carpet moaning in obvious distress.

Russell bent over him with a look of blank disinterest and grasped Thornapple's hair with his left hand and held his head up, putting his face close to him as he spoke.

"You're all mouth," he said gently. "If you ever come near this woman again, you're dead meat."

"Look," Annie said," his leg is bleeding, real bad. It's all over the carpet."

"Lucky I didn't stick it in his guts. Oh shit, he needs a tourniquet. I must have hit the artery."

Annie grabbed the sheets off the bed and ripped some strips six inches wide. Lloyd was impressed with her ability to handle a crisis.

They soon had the flow stopped. "We have to go,"Annie said. "I hear a siren."

"Mister, that's all I kin do for you. Count to a hundred, then loosen the tourniquet, otherwise you'll lose your leg."

"You bastard, I'll get you."

Russell bent over once more, "Where I come from tough boy, you'd be used for a pet."

"Follow me," Annie said. They went out the back door into an ally to a 48' Plymouth parked on the side.

Annie drove expertly, slipping through the forming ice for three blocks before spinning out and finding an outlet to the highway.

They met two more police vehicles and an ambulance as they darted south as fast as the slippery highway would take them.

"You drove on ice before. That's good."

"But, it's turning to slush. It's gonna get worse."

And, it did. They bounced in and out of a ditch a half-mile later. "Jesus, slow down. We gotta weigh down the back end. It's too light. Stop. Don't pull off the road."

"What you gonna do?"

"Hurry. Open the trunk. I'm gonna jump in." He lugged everything out of the car with him into the trunk. "Drive as slow as you can."

The Ford straightened out and Annie drove until the road cleared. The pavement was bare when she pulled off and helped Lloyd out of the trunk.

"Where we headed?"

Annie smiled sweetly, "You are going to spend a few days on an Indian reservation in Lac Du Flambeau until you tell me who you are."

"Let me out here. You're better off not knowing."

"We're in this together whether you like it or not. Or—are you gonna stab me too?"

"Lac Du, what?"

"I want to thank you. I've thought it over on the ride here. You saved me a bad beating by stickin' your neck out for me. I always help those that help me. I think it's a Chippewa thing."

Lac Du Flambeau was on an Indian reservation where Annie had been raised. Most of the locals worked in the resort business that was booming, especially in the summer. She had a little cabin in a remote area that gave them the seclusion Lloyd required.

They hung low for four days—Annie just going out for food and supplies. She gave him a real haircut and found a new set of clothes that fit him. Whoever had bought them must have been on the short side—or a kid.

After four days, Lloyd grew restless, itchy to get further west. "I appreciate all you've done, Annie, but I best get going so you can get back to your life without an escaped con to worry about." For Lloyd, it was a long speech. He was fond of the slight, dark-haired girl.

They were lying in bed, both naked from the waist up smoking cigarettes. She eyed him with a mixture of curiosity and sadness. This quiet, troubled man had treated her better than most men she had known in her twenty four years.

"Where are you going? I can give you a lift."

"I'm low on cash, I need to get away from here, get a grubstake and head to Fargo."

"Why, Fargo?"

"I heard the pickings were easy there."

"The pickings?" She ignored him for a moment before speaking. "It's going to get colder—my car's got a heater."

"Annie, yer a good kid—don't get caught wit a man on the lamb."

"What do I have here, Lloyd? Just more abusive men to call me a whore and use me up? So when they get tired of me they kick me out in the street? That's what I have here, Lloyd."

"Life on the run is a bitch, Annie. I want you to know one thing. I ain't going back in the stir. Right now's your chance to get a way clean, I'd guess that no one knows you helped me. That may change..."

"I don't care, take me with you."

"It's yer funereal." Secretly he was pleased. "We gotta head north—go up to Duluth. Then head west to Fargo."

"I'll pack up what I'm going to take. It won't take long. But—first..."

It was another hour before they rose to eat and pack their meager belongings. Annie then went over to visit her parents and give them the money she owed. It had been a tearful good-bye.

They waited till dawn the next morning to start their journey.

51

FARGO

November 23, 1953

THEY PULLED INTO FARGO IN THE early afternoon after spending the night before in Brainerd, Minnesota. Minnesota had been good to the two fugitives. After breaking into a gas station/grocery store in Cloquet, Lloyd found a safe in a back room office that held over two hundred dollars cash. Along with the money from the till, he had netted over two fifty.

In the safe was a .32 revolver with a box of shells. It was an ideal 'carry' gun as it could be slipped into a jacket pocket without worry of detection.

Annie was waiting in the car, she owned a 1948 Plymouth. In the rush to build post war cars, few exterior changes were made from the 1942 models. Engineering improvements were: a new gasoline pump eliminating the glass sediment bowl, and a long-life gasoline filter that was placed in the fuel tank. New, low-pressure super-cushion tires, introduced in 1948, gave the five year old Plymouth an easier handling ride.

"Pull over here." The gray sedan eased over to the curb in downtown Fargo. "See that big hotel across the street. They're the best places to stay in. Lotsa people moving in and out, we won't stick out."

They rented a room on the sixth floor of the Excelsior Hotel paying for a week in advance. Lloyd woke up before dawn drawing a robe around him as he plodded over to the window and looked down at the main street.

Big flakes of snow swirled down on the lighted street, the wind pushing it south from Canada. He didn't have to go outside to know it was frigid. He put a cigarette in his mouth, firing it up before realizing he was smoking one of Annie's Chesterfields. He hacked the morning congestion from his chest and went into the bathroom to freshen up.

When he returned to the room, Annie had the electric percolator brewing the morning coffee. 'Are you all right? You look pale."

"I'm fine. Just slept like shit. I think I caught a cold. One day it's warm, the next day I'm freezing my ass off." He walked back to the window. "Weatherman says we're gonna get six to eight inches of this shit."

"We can stay in bed and cuddle..."

"No. I'm gonna case a joint. Once the streets are messed up, I'm gonna go in an make a score. Less cops will be out on patrol, they will be lazy and just trying to stay warm."

Lloyd's take from the evening break-in of a liquor store would keep the couple comfortable through the holidays. Lloyd's birthday passed without comment. They kept a low profile, doing their shopping and daily outings during the slow times until New Years Eve...

He started drinking hard early. Whatever was bothering him, festering like a boil, was transferred to Annie keeping her quiet, not wanting to add to his mood. She didn't fear him, she was certain he wouldn't hurt her. Yet, she suffered his pain. The holidays had been hard on him.

He left the room without a word. Annie cried softly at the window watching him disappear down the snow covered street with the night closing in fast. He had turned up his collar as the wind pushed it tight against his cheeks.

Midnight—she wasn't much of a drinker but at midnight she poured a glass of blackberry brandy that Lloyd had bought for his cold. The dark purple colored liquid burned a trail down her throat. She sighed, waited for the heat to die down, and pulled a bigger chunk from the glass. This time—it went down much smoother.

She sighed, "well, Happy New Year, Annie," as the clock on the bed stand glowed with the hands straight up declaring midnight. *I love him. What have I gotten myself into?*

The brandy in her glass had been emptied so she refilled it, lighting a Chesterfield as she sipped. At 1:30 she went to bed, crying herself to sleep almost instantly. The almost empty brandy bottle silently mocking her as it had not offered the solace she had hoped for. What it promised was—a New Year's morning hangover.

3:30 am—she didn't hear Lloyd come in. He had left drunk, but now appeared sober. He poured himself a whiskey, drew on a Lucky before glancing over at the near empty brandy bottle. "Well, Annie, we'll celebrate together, tonight." He shook a paper sack he extracted from his jacket pocket and spoke softly. "It's our best score yet." He stubbed out his cigarette and joined Annie in bed after shutting off the light. He was snoring two minutes later.

"I met a fella last night." Lloyd sipped his coffee and bit into a donut he had gone across the street to pick up after he woke. He licked the sugar from his lips and continued, "A guy named Floyd, we had a mutual friend from Ohio that he had done time in the stir with."

Annie broke her silence. "He must have been better company than me."

"Hey—none a that. I offered you no promises. Anytime you don't like how I treat you, there's the door. I'll give you gas money back to Wisconsin."

"I'm sorry, Lloyd. My feelings got hurt, is all. You don't owe me any explanations. So, what does Floyd do?"

"Have a donut. Last night, actually this morning, me and him hit a bar after it closed. We got the whole New Year's Eve take out of a cheap safe. There's tougher piggy banks. Took a coupla g's a piece. Tonight, I'm gonna take you to a fancy joint for steaks."

"That's wonderful, Lloyd," she got up from the edge of the bed wrapping her arms around him hugging him tightly to her breast. She kissed the top of his head. "Thank you, Lloyd."

"First, I'm gonna take us shopping. You need a new dress, I need a new suit."

The month of January passed without incident. Floyd was the opposite of Lloyd. He was tall and brash, constantly talking. He was a flashy dresser and sported a new lady every week or two. They made an odd couple.

They had been meeting and plotting for over a month. This was going to be the big heist. The score that would send them from Fargo and keep them tracking further west. Floyd had got a hold of two .38 caliber revolvers. Lloyd was cleaning his when Floyd knocked on the door.

"We got a wheel man, name a Lester Boyle. He's been outta the joint since Christmas and is getting hungry. He did three and a half in Nebraska for a job he did there. Kind of a cowboy, but says he kin take orders. Still drives stock cars in the summer."

"You think we kin trust him? This caper's got to take brains and guts. It's a three man job, no question. When can we meet him? Have a couple drinks—get a take on the guy. I ain't going back to the stir, I toll you that."

"Good idea—I'll set up a meet, let you know..."

Annie sat silent through the discussion. It was clear this job was going to be big, a strong-armed robbery. She shivered, "Don't get yourself killed, Lloyd. That's all I'll say on the matter."

"That's good, Annie. Otherwise—I wouldn't have let you be privvy to the confab. We ain't gonna hit it till the end of the month, that's when they'll have the most cash on hand."

"Can I ask, what are you robbing?"

"A little bank on the west end of town, almost to the city limits. We rented a storage garage where we'll stow the getaway car. We'll divvy up there, then you and me are gonna head west. Fargo's been good to us but we gotta move on before we feel the heat."

52

THE BIG HEIST

FRIDAY, FEBRUARY 27—THE MINER'S STATE BANK. At 4:45 pm, two masked men entered the bank brandishing weapons. Fifteen minutes before closing time, there were but five customers remaining and some of the tellers had already closed and were counting the day's transactions.

"Give us cash, no funny money or checks." Floyd waved his .38 in the face of the head teller while Lloyd stuck his pistol in the manager's face. "Hurry, be quick, all a you. You can keep the change."

Lloyd rushed the bank VP to the vault, "open it, and be quick." Lloyd had the biggest sack. "Get the lead outta yer ass. Move it."

The head teller hit the silent alarm...

The Fargo police cruiser turned slowly around the corner radioing his command post for further instructions. "There's a 52' Ford, no front license, parked in front of the bank. Over."

Proceed with caution. Do not enter the bank until other officers arrive. Over.

"Got you. I'm parked across the street from the suspect vehicle."

Lloyd followed Floyd out of the bank door in time to see a police cruiser turn a corner and stop a car length behind Lester. Lester reached across the seat and flung the front passenger door open as Floyd yanked open the back door.

"Cops, Lloyd," Floyd raised his .38 as he shouted, "across the street and behind us." He fired at the new police arrival behind Lester as Lloyd tossed in his bag and slid across the seat to shoot at the tires on the cruiser across the street. Fargo response time had been too good...

"Get in, Floyd. Hit it, Lester." Floyd threw two sacks on the back seat and clutched the third to his chest, shutting the door as the Ford lurched forward. He coughed a gurgled gasp and pushed against the dash as Lester whipped around the corner on two wheels.

"We ain't being followed, we did good—shootin' their tires like we planned," Lloyd yelled above the din. Lester hit the city limit sign doing eighty, thanks to the bare roads.

Lester found Lloyd in the rear view mirror, "Floyd's hit—it looks bad. Real bad.

"Slow down, do the speed limit. We turn in a mile or so." Lloyd shook his head, this wasn't supposed to happen.

They stopped at the rental garage, Annie was immediately out of her car. Concern etched on her face.

Lloyd was out first, opening Floyd's door, speaking softly to his fallen partner. "I'm gonna stop the bleeding, then we'll get you to a doc."

Floyd coughed blood, choking briefly, "It's too late. In my billfold is an address for Eleanor, send her my share of the take."

"You sure have your wimmen. Don't worry, you'll get to spend it yourself." Without opening Floyd's shirt he knew the wound was a bad one. Foam mixed with blood as Floyd struggled to speak.

"Eleanor's my kid sister. She can use the money." He coughed his last, more blood leaking down his chin. A pall clouded over the successful heist...Floyd Loman was dead.

"What we gonna do, Lloyd? The cops kin tie him to us."

"Let's get the car in the garage. Then we hide him in the woods out back as far as we kin. We'll cover him up, best we kin." He didn't mention the coyote and other predators.

It took them an hour to take care of Floyd and the dispersal of the day's take. Lloyd kept Floyd's take vowing to send it to his sister in Iowa.

"Lester, you spend a penny of this loot before the heat is off, I'll hunt you down and split your throat. In fact, get outta Fargo. Go back to Nebraska."

"I got my parole officer here."

"You just went in last week. Tell him you're going home. He kin transfer you. You got a bundle, just cool yourself."

The two shook hands, Lester leaving in a dilapidated ten year-old Chevy.

Annie and Lloyd drove out without looking back. Leaving the stolen Ford locked in the garage, wiped down for fingerprints. It wouldn't be found until the rent became due in May.

It was dark when they left the garage heading west toward Jamestown. Stopping for fuel and a bite to eat at a truck stop, they didn't halt for the night until they found a flea-bitten motel on the west side of Jamestown. They had traveled about eighty miles from Fargo.

They slept five hours and were back on the road before 6:00 am heading for Bismarck. An early news broadcast informed them of the daring armed robbery of the Miner's State Bank in Fargo. A state-wide search was taking place looking for a dark-colored Ford with three male passengers.

A Fargo police officer who responded to the bank's silent alarm was certain he had hit one of the fleeing bandits. A spot of fresh blood at the scene confirmed his assertion. "Let's get off the road and hole up in Bismarck for a couple days. Then we'll head north to Minot and follow US 2 west," Lloyd announced after studying the map.

"Good idea, Lloyd, the radio is calling for a major snowstorm starting this afternoon."

"That's great, Annie. It won't cause suspicion if we hang out a hotel waiting for the storm to blow over and the roads to clear."

Lloyd bought a bottle and spent the afternoon brooding over the loss of Floyd. He sent Annie out for hamburgers and a newspaper instead of ordering room service. The downtown Bismarck hotel was a step up from the room they had at the Excelsior in Fargo.

When Annie returned, she was surprised and happy to see that most of the bottle Lloyd had bought had hardly been dented. She handed him the newspaper that featured the robbery on the front page. The local and state law enforcement officers were under the opinion that the trio was holed up in the Fargo area.

Lloyd smiled briefly before setting down the paper and eating his hamburger, washing it down with a beer that Annie had brought back. The red-labeled bottle had a picture of a Canadian Mountie on it. He had not had a Drewry's before. He reached for the 'church key' and opened another.

He sipped on the second one, ignoring Annie as he grabbed the Western pocket book he had asked her to pick up. He read the first few papers, set the book down, and somberly spoke. "Thank you, Annie. You been good to me."

He set the empty beer bottle down and lay down on top of the bedspread, leaning on the head board and read.

Annie understood, Lloyd was dealing with the loss of a loyal friend in the only way he knew how. Of all his good and bad points, Annie had discovered that he was loyal to those who were loyal in return. The brash, reckless Floyd Loman was one of those men.

A week after the day of the bank job, Lloyd paced the room after listening to the morning news and weather report on the local Bismarck television station. "Looks like we kin get started north, first we got a coupla things to take care of."

"Good, Lloyd. I'm getting real antsy sitting around here." She was at the bathroom mirror combing out her long black hair. She had wiped the mist off the mirror after a hot shower and was applying the little makeup she used. "Are we leaving today?"

Lloyd studied her for a minute, liking the looks of the small breasted, slim-hipped woman who shared his bed. "Naw, most likely tomorrow. First off, call me Ray. From now on I'm Raymond Kidd. Second, we're gonna trade the Plymouth for a new ride."

"Raymond Kidd? Where did you get that?" Then… "We're going shopping? What kind of car are we going to get? Tell me Lloyd, this will be fun."

"It's Ray, babe. Don't forget, call me Ray." He tossed a colored add from Sunday's paper, it was folded to the new Fords. "Ray Kidd was in that book I read last night."

"Ray Kidd," she tasted the new name on her lips. "I like it." Annie brushed her hair from her eyes before returning to the subject at hand. "A new Ford. This one really looks spiffy. Can we afford a new car, Honey?"

"Look at this, the new Ford has an overhead valve V8. When we had a flathead 8 in Michigan back in 50' we beat the cops outta town hands down. Course Paul could drive as good as a race car driver at the Indianapolis 500."

"We're going to trade in the Plymouth? I have the title in my suitcase. I'll dig it out." She dug around in her partially packed suitcase and came out with the title. "You think of everything, Lloy—er, Ray. It's a good thing you had me get that release of lien from the bank before we left Wisconsin."

Lloyd waited for Annie to dress, she did so quickly every time she knew that Lloyd wanted to go somewhere. "I'm ready, Hon, whenever you are."

Lloyd walked over to shut off the television, stopping in front and shaking his head. "Did you see that, they're gonna start selling color television sets this summer. What will they come up with next?" He was still shaking his head at the new Zenith commercial.

After stopping at a diner for a late breakfast, Annie drove them to the local Ford Dealership. An eager salesman soon had them going through the showroom.

"So you want something with a little pep, huh? This new "Y-block " V8 has a 256-cubic-inch V8 rated at one hundred and thirty HP's, that's horsepower. That's when it's breathing through a two-barrel carburetor, and goes a full one hundred and sixty horses when the air comes through a four-barrel Holly carb."

"Lemme see the blue one here, Jerry." The salesman had greeted them with an overly friendly, "Hi, I'm Jerry, your sales consultant." They were the first customers of the day for him.

"The new Crown Vic, a helluva ride, Raymond. It's got power, class, and is a super ride. Has a new radio system, best in the market. This baby's ahead of its time. I'll get us a plate and we can take it for a spin."

They returned from their demonstration ride, Lloyd deferring on Jerry's offer to let him drive. "How soon could you put in the four-barrel carburetor, Jerry?"

"I'm sorry, Ray, we no can do. They say it's too powerful for the average public, so it's restricted to our law enforcement force. The state cops ordered a bunch of them, fastest cars on the road." He winked, now a fellow conspirator, "There's a fella I know that could do it for you, but he ain't cheap. Just save the old one so you don't lose your warranty."

They came out of the sales office all smiles. "Congratulations folks. You got one on the best cars on the road today." He shook hands with Lloyd and Annie after handing them both set of keys.

The four-barrel carburetor had been installed by 4:00 that afternoon and the couple made plans to leave at first light in the morning. The morning was chilly although sunny and bright as they left Bismarck heading north to Minot.

53

WEST TO THE ROCKIES

THEY COVERED THE 120 MILES TO Minot by mid-morning, then, after circling along the west side of town they were soon on US 2 heading west to Montana. They spent the night in Wolf Point, Montana near the Fort Peck Indian Reservation. The weather had stayed above freezing, the road dry and free of ice and snow. The new Ford handled the road with ease as both Lloyd and Annie took turns driving.

That night as they lay in bed reading about the local area, Lloyd read this item he found fascinating. "It says here that Lewis and Clark camped near Wolf Point on May 5, 1805. They noted in their journals that Clark killed a large grizzly bear on the banks of the Missouri. The bear was described as being 8 feet 7.5 inches long and weighed between 500 and 600 pounds. Don't wanna meet one of them in the morning."

"I'd guess they'd be hibernating still. This is interesting. Says how Wolf Point got its name." Annie read on...

One account of how Wolf Point took its name stems from an event which occurred in the trading days. During harsh winters trappers had success trapping and poisoning wolves, but the wolves froze before they could be skinned. The trappers piled the wolves along the banks of the river until spring, when they could be skinned. When the trappers returned for their skins the land had been taken over by Indians. The trappers were forced to leave and the spot became a landmark for steamboat crews, hence the name Wolf Point.

"Interesting place. The Missouri riverboats refueled their big wood burners here."

Two days later they were in Kalispell, rising into the Rocky Mountain Range. Lloyd had chains installed on the rear tires to help them drive through the steep, treacherous winter roads. That, and the fact that the car was heavy and handled well made their trip less hazardous thus far.

"Put the radio up, haven't heard this one for a while," Lloyd said as he steered carefully on the many sharp curves of US 2. Red Foley's "Chattanooga Shoe Shine Boy," sang through the speakers on the Crown Victoria's new, improved radio speakers. That was followed by "Stranger in Paradise," a new hit by Tony Martin that Annie liked. She thought of Lloyd every time.

Lloyd had decided to chance moving on and up in the Rockies even though the weather forecast was for more snow and the highway could get impassable quickly. He had promised Annie that they would stop in any of the small villages along the way to Libby as soon as the weather was threatening, no matter what the size of the town.

They ended up stranded in Hoppy's Inn, Montana. It was named after a stagecoach stop back in the days when gold fever had struck the whole Montana Territory. The population was less than three hundred but featured a saloon, general store, and post office.

Annie was reading a brochure for guided tours from May to October. They featured treks to abandoned silver and gold mines, including a chance to pan for gold. "It says here the trading post was burnt down by Indians three times. I would have just given up and moved to a safer place."

"We're thirty six hundred feet above sea level and still climbing. Let's see—that's over a half mile up. We're at the edge of Pleasant Valley, that's why there's all those scenic turnoffs."

"How high up is Libby?"

Lloyd let out a low whistle, "Whee, it's sixty two hunerd feet before we get there, hon. Drops down after that. Libby's only about 3,000 feet. Lessee, there's fifty two hunnerd to a mile. We're going up over a half mile in less than forty-fifty miles of twisting road. We got some climbing to do."

Annie whirled around to look at Lloyd studying the map. He had never used a term of endearment before when addressing her. She smiled, a loving, tender smile. Yet—it was a smile filled with foreboding and sadness. He was again talking of making a score, a big one. The cost of the new Ford had got Lloyd thinking about money again.

"We have to wait for a break in the weather fore we try that, Honey."

"Yup, let's go down to the saloon and grab a bite to eat. Hear they got good steaks for cheap. Maybe find out when a group will start out together. They travel up and down the mountains like coyote packs in the winter time."

"That's a good idea, if one gets stuck the rest can help them out or at least give 'em a ride to a safe place."

"There's cars and pickup trucks that sit till spring before they kin get 'em out. We can't afford to do that. Hate to have to rob some little burg cause we're stranded."

"You're right, we can't do that, Lloyd. We'd get caught for sure."

"We ain't getting' stuck." The conversation ended as they entered the Midway Saloon. A half-dozen cowboys in fur-collared wool jackets sat at the bar turning to look at the new arrivals.

A heavy-set waitress with flabby arms ambled over as they were the only ones seated at the tables. "What kin I getcha to drink?" She thrust dog-eared menus at the couple.

"Beer is fine, get a round to the boys at the bar, too. On me."

She grinned, displaying a dentist's nightmare. Missing teeth made the tobacco-stained remaining ones crooked to compensate for the gaps. "They'll appreciate that for shore. Works been might slow this winter." They were most likely running bar tabs until spring.

She came back with two bottles of Rocky Mount beer. She slopped it into their glasses before informing them of the beef stew special with fresh made cornbread.

"Sounds good to me, Lloyd said." He looked at Annie who nodded her approval. "Says here on this label that Rocky Mount is brewed up in Libby, outta cool mountain springs. If we end up holing up till spring, we kin get a couple of fishing poles and go trout fishin.' Nothing I like to do better."

"They're good eating, too, Ray."

"Damn sure are," he gave her a nod of approval for using his new alias. "Though, when we was kids in Ohio, pan fish and bass were all we caught. Weren't no trout."

The next week went by agonizingly slow—with Lloyd pacing the two room cabin that only had a radio for entertainment. They had borrowed a hot plate from the owner of the rental cabins so they didn't have to eat every meal at the saloon. Werner and his wife Hulda were a congenial Scandinavian couple who fussed over them to make their only guests content. They normally had only seasonal rentals but kept a couple cabins available in the winter for stranded travelers.

On April 1st, the weather broke, and the plows headed up and down the highway starting in the south at Kalispell, and from the north in Libby. The entire route was about ninety miles. It took over three days to clear the pass before the state police deemed it safe enough to travel.

A convoy of twelve vehicles started out from Hoppy's Inn at noon on the fourth day, expecting to be in Libby before night fall. That gave them close to five hours to travel the forty eight miles.

They arrived in Libby without incident and Lloyd rose early the next morning to plot their route out of Montana.

54

IDAHO

IDAHO WAS A NARROW STATE AT the top and Canada could be reached easily in a day if Lloyd chose to do so. They were on the west side of the Purcell Mountain range when they entered the state arriving at a point where US 2 veered back south toward SR 95 and on down to Coeur d' Alene. Creston, in Canada's British Columbia lay a short distance to their north.

Over hamburgers at a roadside cafe'—Lloyd made his decision. "We're goin' south—I would a liked to head up into Canada, but if we get checked at the border, we could both have to show ID, even if you was driving. I don't wanna take the chance."

"Where we going? Do you have a town in mind?"

"Yeah. One I can't say." He pointed to Coeur d' Alene on the map.

"Coor d' Alene. I think that's how it's pronounced. A lot of the breeds back in Lac du Flambeau were French descent. It goes all the way back from the early fur traders."

"It's near the Washington state border. We lay low in Idaho and we kin hit a few joints in Spokane. It's a big town, all kinds of crime to keep the cops busy already. We won't be noticed."

"You have to be careful, Honey. Sometimes I get some awful bad feelings. I get scared for you." She shivered in the warm cafe.'

"I'm always careful. It's when you go off half-cocked you get in trouble. I ain't going back in the joint so I gotta be double careful."

They stayed the next three days in Hayden, just outside of Coeur d' Alene before making their first ride to Spokane to gain a feel of the area. Lloyd grew animated on the trip back to Hayden. "This is great, Annie, we got pickin's all around us. The Spokane area, plus we kin go down south to Moscow or back southeast to Missoula, all within easy driving distance."

"Take it easy, Honey," this was as excited as she'd ever seen him. "I could get a waitress job that would buy us groceries and help pay the rent."

"If we need to, I won't stop you. But, till I meet someone, you gotta be my wheel man. We gotta find us a straight stretch someplace outta town, I wanna see what this baby can do." He patted the dash, a big grin on his face.

April turned to May as Lloyd concentrated on small break-ins that kept them from digging further into the bank job money. He seemed content enough for the time being, allowing Annie to relax a little, yet not completely able to ignore the nagging sense of doom that hung over her, crowding into her thoughts.

"Hey, Baby. Let's go fishin' for a couple a days. The weatherman says the days are gonna be warm and the trout are biting."

"The weatherman said the trout are biting?"

"No, that was the guys down at the Stumble Inn—they do a lot a fishing from their bar stools." He had started going down to the nearest bar to pick up any useful tidbits. He got up and padded naked to the bathroom.

Annie stretched and lay back watching her man climb into the shower. The afterglow of their lovemaking left her drained as she sighed contentedly. *This has been perfect. Maybe too perfect. How I wish it could stay this way—forever.*

The last month had been mostly carefree and blissful. Though nagging doubt often broke through the pleasant days to vex her and cause fear to rear its ugly head. She could not will him to stop his criminal ways, yet she believed in the old adage, 'Crime does not pay.' She told herself to enjoy the day—for it would not last.

Annie had been raised by the Chippewa and their influence was present in her everyday life and her way of doing the day's tasks. Superstition and trusting one's instincts were an important part of that upbringing.

They spent three idyllic days fishing several tributaries of the Snake River, camping out in the awesome scenic backwoods of Idaho. Their diet consisted mostly of fresh trout. Although they had brought potatoes, eggs, and beans among other necessities required for a three day camping trip.

They lie on their sleeping bags outside their tent watching the spring evening light up with stars aglow and a bright full moon. "You know, hon," Lloyd reflected on their recent travels.

"I would a liked to have lived back in the days of Lewis and Clark, blazin' trails west."

"Why is that, Honey? You'd be long dead now, nigh on a hundred and fifty years. I wouldn't have ever got to know you."

"What's the dif? Dead is dead. A hunnerd years from now I'll be just as dead. Lewis and Clark discovered a lot of herbs and medicines still used today. They made a lot of good discoveries and found interesting things to see."

"How do you know so much, Lloyd?"

"I read a lot about 'em, when I was in Marquette. They taught me plenty. What I learned helped to get me this far. Otherwise, I would a starved to death in those UP woods."

"You're a smart man, Lloyd."

"Not really, I'm a survivor. Look at that sky. It's every bit as big as Montana's."

55

Norman Wyatt

ON THE THIRD OF JUNE, LLOYD received a letter postmarked Lincoln, Nebraska. It was from Lester Boyle addressed to Raymond Kidd. He wrote that the law was sniffing around trying to nail him on some stupid petty shit he had pulled. He couldn't come out west, probation was on his ass.

"It's a small world," he wrote, "my cousin Norm Wyatt is in Spokane, he said it's not far from you, Lloyd. Look him up, he's a good man, forget his youth, he's been around the block. He can be found..."

Interesting—Lloyd mused, *he just might be the partner I need.*

The next morning Lloyd left Annie in Hayden and went off to find Norm Wyatt. He stopped at a bar in downtown Spokane named Crosley's. The bartender, a large fleshy man, had a white dishcloth draped over one shoulder. Lester had written that the man could be trusted. He left a message for Wyatt saying he'd be back at three.

After stopping at a two-bit greasy spoon and choking down a ham sandwich and coffee he killed time walking the neighborhood—it made sense that Wyatt lived near the bar.

On his way back to the bar, he watched a dog trot towards him stopping at a parked Dodge. The dog looked at the front tire. It appraised it with several discriminating sniffs, then lifted his leg to piss on it.

No piss.

He was out of piss from having dispensed it in too many corners, posts and such that he had discovered along the way.

He glanced in under his genitals...He sidled into perfect position, lifted, and failed again.

Lloyd shook his head at the animal's plight and headed to his appointment.

He entered the Nevada Street Bar & Grill a couple minutes after three. He wanted Wyatt to be there waiting. It was less conspicuous this way. Crosley nodded his head to the lone patron at a table in the far back.

A young man sat there guarding a bottle of beer like an ex-con would guard his food in the stir. Young Mister Wyatt had done time.

Lloyd walked to the bar and said, "Crosley, kin you give us two of whatever he's drinking." He walked back to the table with two Olympia beers.

"So you're drinkin' an Ole,' too," Wyatt said as way of greeting. He nodded to a chair so Lloyd sat down across from him.

"Just one, the other's for you."

"Thank you, two's my daytime limit. Don't wanna be groggy for any night work I may acquire."

"Cousin Lester sends his best. I'm Ray."

"Let's drink to Lester—here's hopin' he kin stay out a the stir. He's been prone to get hisself in a fix now an again.

"Ain't we all been. This time I don't aim to go back."

Wyatt studied the man who was about to become his new partner. He was smaller than his reputation. He could see where Russell could be misjudged. "Lester has nothing but nice things to say about you."

Lloyd paused before answering, noting the man's sharp features and pallid face. He had not been out of the stir long."He says you're dependable and can keep your mouth shut. That says enough."

"That's right, I keep the work to myself. Talked to Lester last night. Said to tell you they found the car in the rental garage. The feds paid him a visit cause he was one a the local Fargo resident's on recent parole for just such a job. Said not to worry, they ain't been back since."

"When you talk to him, tell him to be very cool. Stick to stock car racing."

"Yes sir, problem is—there's no money in that. Tried it myself." He scratched at a few sparse whiskers sprouting from his chin.

After sizing each other up, they agreed to meet back here in three days. At the same time and place. Lloyd said that gave him plenty of time to move to the city.

It was the beginning of a profitable partnership. The month of June passed with a slew of successful break-ins, in and around the Spokane area. Lloyd's nest egg was growing while a nervous and concerned Annie grew evermore apprehensive with the frequency of Lloyd's work.

"Honey, don't be so edgy. We're being careful—look, tomorrow night Norm's coming over for supper. Why don't you fix us some of your pork chops and mushroom gravy? We'll have a nice meal watching our new television set."

"The vibes are getting worse, Lloyd. I worry so about you. Your luck is running out. I don't sleep at night when you're out God knows where. We got enough money. Let's take a break, please."

"No," he was emphatic, "We ain't got enough. A couple a more good scores and then we kin go up in the hills somewheres and hole up for a year or two hunting and fishing and getting bored to tears."

"I got a new birth certificate and social security card today, hon. They look like the government printed them. I'm gonna get my driver's license tomorrow."

"Good, I'm happy things are going so good for you."

Lloyd didn't tell her he and Norm had been hauled in the night before for suspicion of breaking and entering of a drug store. They had ditched the tools for the job after an alarm had gone off. They were rid of the burglary tools before they were apprehended

The heist of a late night 'hot spot' on the Fourth of July ended badly when Lloyd had to shoot an over-zealous bouncer who tried to disarm him. They escaped with over $1800 of the full day's take.

Several anxious days followed as the two men waited to see if they had been recognized during the almost failed robbery. News accounts stated that the wounded bouncer was in fair and stable condition but that he failed to recognize his assailants.

Annie watched the television report of the robbery/shooting. She had no doubt it involved Lloyd and Norm. Lloyd was subdued the following day and then unexpectedly took her on a two day fishing trip to Idaho.

She wondered if Lloyd and Norm were laying low for a few days to see if they were among the suspects for the shooting. Her thinking was correct.

They spent the days in idyllic peace. Camping on the edge of the river, they lazily cast their lines into the water and then lay back sipping on a beer and enjoying nature. He heard the beat of wings and looked up to see some ducks rising off the river from the opposite bank.

"I had me a little pet duck when I was a kid."

"A duckling?"

"Huh? Yeah, I guess so. Anyway, Paul had him a golden lab. Well, it was a mutt with some retriever in her. "Well—they became best pals, hanging out together. Where you saw one, the other was right there."

"That's a wonderful childhood memory."

"Well—kinda, but that duck I had got real frustrated. Every time that duck would go down to the pond for a swim—that retriever of Paul's would jump right in and haul my poor duck back out of the water and dump him on the shore."

"That is hilarious," Annie laughed and giggled until tears came pouring out and she had to grab a kerchief to wipe her eyes.

Lloyd smiled at Annie's laughter. *It was a good boyhood memory.*

They returned to their rented house three nights after they had left and life went back to normal. Except for Annie—life would never be normal again.

She knew they were planning something big, and it would come down soon. Lloyd was gone often with Norm who now lived but a block away. They walked back and forth between the two houses often taking off in the Ford for a quick excursion that Annie knew from experience was a casing job.

That night they came home with a brand new blue Cadillac.

56

The Heat

JULY 18, 1954—THE NEW BLUE Caddy backed slowly out of Lloyd and Annie's garage at 7:45 pm, she watched them turn right and go a block before taking a left and heading south.

The 54' Cadillacs were powered by a new, 230 horsepower engine and were according to the copy writers that year, *"the most beautiful motoring creations of all time."*

A definite styling change was in these new models, compared with the more bulbous shapes of 1948 through 1953. Now the general lines were straight and bold.

The distinguishing mark of the 1954 Cadillacs was the front clip with its gull-wing bumpers and "bullet" impact guards or "Dagmars." Identifying the new Caddys was not a difficult task. Something Lloyd and Norm failed to take in account.

Was this the night she loses her man? She felt it was just a matter of time, and—that time was running out. She fretted through the night hardly able to watch the television or even concentrate on the news. She took a bottle of sherry down from the cupboard and drank a couple of glasses which did nothing to ease her angst.

Shortly after midnight lights pulled into the drive, Lloyd got out and opened the garage door. Norm said something that caused both men to laugh as they walked to the house. Annie stood at the screen door waiting in the dark in the humid, stifling air.

She breathed a sigh of relief, *maybe now I can make him slow down for a while. Move away—stay away from the heat, that's what Lloyd preached.* She wasn't speaking of the heat of the Spokane night. She opened the door and stepped aside to let her man in.

"We did good, hon. Another time or two like this, and we'll be on easy street. Get us a couple a glasses, babe, I brought a bottle of sherry for you."

The threesome sat at the kitchen table drinking whiskey and beer and sherry. It was after three when Norm walked home. Lloyd and Annie both were drunk, putting their arms around each other's waists, they stumbled off to bed.

Unknown to Lloyd and Norm, Spokane police were looking for a stolen blue Cadillac. Witnesses had seen it screech out of the Albertson's parking lot right after the strong-armed robbery. Two men wearing stocking masks had burst in just before closing time and had escaped with the day's take.

During routine police work, Raymond Kidd and Norman Wyatt's names came up among a half-dozen suspects. The circle was ever increasingly closing in.

They moved out of their houses on the 20th of July. Moving to Spokane's southeast side, Lloyd drove behind Norm in the stolen Caddy while Annie led the way in the Crown Vic.

A week later they hit a series of places in Coeur d' Alene, Idaho. It was the first time they visited there. It was 4:00 am before they headed west not wanting to press their luck further.

That feed store and grain elevator had a nice haul in its safe. What made you think to try there? You opened that safe like a box of Cracker Jacks."

"Me and Paul done one for over $4,000 in Ohio in '50."

July ended with Spokane in the throes of a heat wave. "Christ, it's hot," Lloyd paced the tiny apartment mopping his brow. "The humidity gotta be 100 per cent."

"I wish you wouldn't take the Cadillac, honey, the cops gotta be looking for it everywhere. Driving all over Idaho and such the other night, it's just a matter of time before you get spotted."

Little did she know—no truer words had been spoken. The state and city police, along with the county sheriff's office had been getting reports of new sightings of the Cadillac in the greater Spokane area.

"Let's go over to the Yankee store and buy another fan," Lloyd said, ignoring Annie's comments. "We'll put one in each window when we go to bed. Plus, the one we got in here, it should be able to move some of this heat around."

As they headed to the store, Annie asked, ""Where's Norm been? I haven't seen him since yesterday."

"Must have gotten lucky with this new dame. A skinny little redhead he met at the Sapphire Club on Beacon Avenue. I ain't seen her, that's just what he toll me."

"He's not the highest prized catch either. His nose is like a hawk's."

"Be nice now, girl. Wyatt's been good to you."

"Yes, he has Lloyd, treats me with respect. Course he knows you'd kick his ass clear to Seattle if he wasn't."

They tied the trunk down for a box containing the biggest portable fan in the store. "It's got three speeds, hon. Did you see when the salesman put it in high? It looked like it would rip the curtains right off the windows."

Monday, the second of August brought more heat. Overheated cars were stalling all over town and the two thieves were putting the final touches to their plan for the following night.

Annie voiced concern about using the stolen Cadillac. "Lloyd, aren't you and Norm pressing your luck with that Caddy? It's sticks out like a sore thumb and the cops from all over the area are looking for it. Why not steal something else to use tonight?"

"This is the last night we're using it. We're gonna dump it out in the country later on tonight. You're worrying too much. We got this job figured out."

"I can't get over this dread that's hanging over me. Let's just get out right now. Head for the Idaho hills. We got enough to live for a long spell."

"Okay. This will be the last one. I owe it to Norm, he needs more cash. I don't back out in the last minute on my pals."

57

Roesauers

OPPORTUNITY, WA—THE TWO MEN SAT fidgeting in the Cadillac...They had donned their stocking masks and were waiting for several shoppers to get their groceries loaded and be on their way. "What's a matter, Lloyd? You look edgy."

Annie's been such a 'Nervous Nellie' lately, she's got me jumpy."

A Washington State license examiner had just pulled into the parking lot to pick up some milk and bread on sale for 89 cents a gallon and 15 cents a loaf. He spotted the stolen vehicle just before exiting the state car. He immediately called the Spokane County Sheriff's office.

In a matter of minutes, two county deputies arrived to investigate. As they approached the Cadillac, the occupants opened fire at the startled deputies. They ducked quickly behind a parked car and yelled out to the men to surrender.

Sirens wailed, the sounds getting louder as reinforcements would soon be arriving.

A man bolted from the passenger door of the vehicle heading for the edge of the parking lot. The deputies opened fired at the fleeing subject, bullets seeking their target.

The bullet with Lloyd's name on it found its victim in the back of his head, and continued until it exited above his right eye. It was over.

Lloyd Reed Russell lay dead on the pavement of the Roesauer's grocery store.

Thursday, August 5, 1954—The Mining Journal

Took Part in Daring Escape From Prison—A bullet in the head has sent Lloyd Reed Russell to the end of his outlaw trail.

Russell, who had been hunted ever since he and six other desperate convicts staged a sensational break from inside the walls of Marquette Prison on May 22 last year reportedly was shot to death Tuesday night by sheriff's deputies in Opportunity, Washington, a suburb of Spokane.

Positively Identified

Fred H. McIntire, special agent in charge of the Detroit division of the FBI informed The Mining Journal of Russell's killing and said the victim had been "positively identified as Lloyd Reed Russell by Undersheriff Carl Fawcett of the Spokane County sheriff's office" who made the identification on the basis of fingerprints.

The prints checked on 28 points, McIntire said.

Spokane officers "feel sure" that the man known in the area as Raymond M. Kidd actually was the 33-year-old Russell.

Russell had been on the FBI"s list of the 10 "most wanted men" for about a year and in recent months had moved near the top of the list.

McIntire said that Kidd and a companion, Norman J. Wyatt, 22, both with Spokane police department records, were wanted in connection with the robbery of an Albertson's Food Center in the Spokane area last July 18. A description of the men and a stolen blue Cadillac they were using had been given Spokane police.

Wearing Stocking Masks

On Tuesday night, McIntire related, a Washington State patrol licensing examiner spotted the car at Roesauer's parking lot in Opportunity. He notified the Spokane County the sheriff's office and two deputies were sent to investigate.

When they approached the car, the two occupants who were wearing stocking masks, started shooting at the deputies. The latter retreated and started returning fire, whereupon Kidd got out of the car and began to run.

Companion Surrenders

He was shot and killed by a bullet that struck him in the back of the head, coming out over the eye, McIntire reported

Wyatt surrendered and is now in the Spokane County jail. He told police he had known Kidd only a year and knew nothing of his past.

"Try less than three months," Annie finished reading the tear-stained account in the Spokane paper. *Why didn't you just surrender, like Norm did?* Annie knew the answer to that only too well.

She had spent the prior evening writing to Lloyd's brother Paul telling him that if he received this letter she was writing that meant his brother was dead. Before dawn she *knew* of his fate. Lloyd was not coming back to her. Her heart told her. She told Paul that at least he had someone else besides his brother who loved him to the end.

Epilogue

MONDAY, AUGUST 19, 1954—THE HEAT wave had broken and the driver of the county hearse worked his windshield wipers as he pulled up to the fresh-dug grave site.

Four county employees removed the casket from within and wasted no time with formalities as they lowered Lloyd Reed Russell into the ground.

One lone mourner wept as her tears mingled with the soft raindrops that fell into the open ground.

The preceding is a work of fiction, based on a series of actual events. All of its principal characters, institutions, and events, are fictional accounts based on newspaper reports during the years 1950 through 1954. Any episodes in which historical figures interact with fictional ones are strictly products of the author's imagination.

I started the research for this novel in the summer of 2002. I wrote Part One based on newspaper accounts of the Russell Brothers break out in 1950 and the subsequent Lloyd Russell-led escape from Marquette Prison in 1953.

Part Two deals with the fictional account of this writer's imagination as to what may have happened to Lloyd Russell after the last sighting during the period in September 1953, to his demise in August of 1954.

I would like to thank the Peter White Library to allow me to scour the micro film account of the Marquette Mining Journal's excellent coverage of the events. Other libraries helping me with my research were in Munising, Lansing, Iron Mountain, and Marion, Ohio.

In chronological order important information was gleaned from these newspapers. The Mansfield News Journal, The Marion Star, The Beaverton Ontario News, The Munising News, The Escanaba Daily Press, The Lansing State Journal, The Detroit News, The Iron Mountain News, The Traverse City Record-Eagle, and The Flint Journal.

DENNIS LEPPANEN was born and raised in Michigan's beautiful Upper Peninsula. He makes his home in Sebring, Florida with his wife Ruth. They make yearly journeys to the UP but try to do so only during periods of bad skiing.

He is the author of WHOO?? and is now hard at work on the next Kell Thomas mystery, RUSH TO GOLD.

Made in the USA
Monee, IL
25 October 2021